AF538280

An Angel and a One-Armed Man

B.D. Lawrence

JVR Publishing, LLC

Copyright © 2022 by JVR Publishing, LLC

All rights reserved.

No portion of this book may be reproduced or transmitted in any form by any means, electronic or mechanical, including photocopying, recording, or by any information storage and retrieval system, without written permission from the publisher or author, except as permitted by U.S. copyright law.

This book is a work of fiction. Names, characters, places, and incidents either are the product of the author's imagination or are used fictitiously, and any resemblance to any actual persons, living or dead, events, or locales is entirely coincidental.

Contents

This book is dedicated to those who work the front lines trying to save girls caught in human trafficking.

Chapter 1

Keyshawn Williams leaned against a red brick wall in the recessed doorway of a former mattress factory watching his women, hands shoved into the pockets of his black cargo shorts.

Even after eleven p.m., waves of heat shimmered on the pavement. He would swear the sidewalks were sweating. But the mid-July temperatures were not high enough to keep partygoers away. They streamed in and out of bars, clubs, and restaurants. And no aberrant weather kept away his girls. Two blocks south of downtown St. Louis, in front of abandoned warehouses and shut-down factories, six-inch spiked heels clicked and high, scratchy voices yelled solicitations to inebriated men returning to their cars. Men who had struck out in their pursuit of love, or at least their satiation of lust.

Streetwalkers were as reliable as postal workers, if not more. Yes sir, his girls would be out in four feet of snow, hail, or a frigging tornado, if that's what it took to turn a trick and make him some green. But for some reason, tonight, the tricks were slow in coming. Maybe it was the heat. Maybe it was the timing, a Thursday night in the middle of the month. Johns didn't have no more money left and hadn't received their next check yet. Maybe it was just an off night. He didn't know.

When the long, black Cadillac limo pulled to the curb across from where Keyshawn stood, a slight grin played across his dark face and he nodded slightly, thinking, this was more like it. Maybe this high roller would want to party with several of his girls. But when clean-shaven King Kong got out of the front passenger seat and motioned to Keyshawn, the wiry pimp's demeanor steeled over. He stood straight and stared at the brother twice his size.

The large stranger had a bit of a drawl. "Come on over, boy. The man here wants to converse with you."

"Who you calling boy? Just because you dress fancy and get to drive that big old car don't give you no right—"

In a deep, commanding voice he said, "The man wants to talk to you."

"Yeah? What man?"

In three strides the large brother closed the distance between them to mere inches. He grinned when Keyshawn removed his right hand from his shorts pocket and started to slip it under his lounge jacket.

"You think you can pull that pea-shooter out and shoot me before I rip your arm off?"

When Keyshawn let go of his compact forty caliber and removed his hand from inside his jacket, the big dude grabbed him around both shoulders and shoved him toward the limo. The back door opened.

"No need to be so rough," came an equally deep but quiet voice from inside the limo. "Sir, if you'd be so kind, I'd like to have a word with you."

Keyshawn bent over and looked in. "And who might you be?"

A large, though nowhere near the size of King Kong, white man reclined at the far side of the limo. He held a half-empty plastic bottle of Dr Pepper and smiled. White teeth glittered through a salt-and-pepper goatee. Keyshawn admired the tailored, gray suit but wasn't fooled by the soft, brown eyes.

The driver shoved Keyshawn in and slammed the door behind him, then got in the front seat.

"Hey, what the—" Keyshawn protested, but stopped when the white man spoke again.

"I'd like a young and pretty girl."

Keyshawn straightened and smoothed his baby blue lounge jacket, one his main squeeze had bought for him saying it went well with his baby blue eyes. She still didn't know they was only colored contacts. He smiled his best salesman smile. "That'd be Angel."

She'd worked for Keyshawn for about six months and was still beautiful. Not worn looking like so many of his girls, even ones younger than her. She'd said she was eighteen. He wasn't sure he'd believed her, but it really didn't matter.

"How much for her?"

The partition between the front and back silently rolled down. The driver faced them, watching intently.

Keyshawn ran his hand over the polished wood grain bar and wondered if any prime liquor was inside the cabinet. He adjusted himself in the smooth black leather seat, getting comfortable. He didn't really care for the strong pine forest smell, though.

"Seventy-five for an hour, my man."

"You don't understand, my man." All pleasantness vanished from his voice. "I don't want her for just an hour."

"Okay. That's cool. I'll give her to you for three hundred for the night. And believe me, that's a bargain."

The rich dude glanced at his driver and shook his head. "He still doesn't get it, does he?"

King Kong also shook his head. "Nope. He doesn't. Shall I explain it to him?"

"Explain what?" Keyshawn switched his gaze between the black dude and the white dude.

"Please do."

The driver smacked Keyshawn in the head with an open hand.

He started to reach for his piece again. King Kong gave a slight shake and rested a nine-millimeter with a six-inch barrel on the partition between them, pointed at Keyshawn's chest.

"The man wants Angel," the driver said. "Not for the night. He wants her, period."

"You suckas crazy or something?"

The driver smacked Keyshawn again. "He's gonna buy Angel from you. Permanently."

"Uh-uh. That ain't happenin'. He can't have her. She's one of my best. Brings in three to five hundred a night." Time to leave. Keyshawn tried the door handle. It didn't open.

"Ten thousand for her," the white dude said.

"You're crazy, man. I ain't selling you Angel."

The white dude slammed him in the face with his elbow—surprisingly fast for an old man.

Keyshawn saw stars and heard a crunch, figuring his cheek bone just cracked again.

"I'll give you ten thousand for Angel. Go get her. Now."

"Screw you, man." Again, he tried to get out. The door still wouldn't open. He yelled, "Let me out of this frigging car. I ain't selling my property."

"I just can't seem to get through to this man."

The driver reached through the partition and grabbed Keyshawn's collar, then pulled him against the seat. He felt cold steel against his cheek. Then King Kong reached inside Keyshawn's jacket and extracted his Smith and Wesson forty-caliber MP Shield and tossed it on the front passenger seat.

"You are one dumb brother. You only have two options. Option one is to sell Angel to us for ten large ones." He stopped.

After several seconds, Keyshawn choked out, "And the second option?"

"Don't sell us Angel." Another long pause. "And we'll take her, anyway. And you get nothing."

Ten minutes later, Keyshawn watched the limo pull away with Angel in the back seat. At least he had a stack of hundred-dollar bills in his pocket. But what would he tell Big Eddie? Certainly nothing about the ten G's. He'd think of something.

Chapter 2

When the fly came within range, George Bruder snatched it from the air, then slammed his hand onto the bar, opening it as he did so.

The bartender—a young, buxom, dark-haired woman—jumped, and nearly dropped the beer mug she was wiping dry. She glared at him. "Really, Lefty. Was that necessary?"

He shrugged, smiled, then turned his attention to the dead fly. He stared at the squashed and twisted bug, one wing bent too far forward, white goo leaking out its back end. Conversations in the crowded joint blended into a deep buzz, like thousands of flies, companions maybe of the deceased on the bar, swarming together, swapping war stories, telling tales of woe, yet excluding him. He was an island in a sea of activity, the waves of life lapping at his shore, repelled by his rocky cliffs.

The man next to Lefty lit a cigar. Great puffs of pasty smoke billowed from the man's fat cheeks and wafted around Lefty's head. He tried to ignore the acrid smell, the burning in his nostrils, but soon his head started to swim, so he swiveled and found himself staring at the buttons on a denim shirt, a shirt which bulged nicely in the appropriate places.

Lefty let his gaze linger a moment, then slowly lifted it, past a slender, pale neck, a small, slightly rounded chin, thin, lipstick-less lips, a wide nose, and finally two deep brown eyes.

"Wanna dance?" the woman asked.

Lefty looked left, then right, then swiveled toward the man next to him, but the smokestack had turned away, so Lefty swiveled back and looked at the woman. She was still there staring at him.

"Me?" He pointed to himself.

She nodded.

He leaned back a little to take in her entire face. Put together, all the components worked quite well. She had short, brown hair, feathered on both sides, parted in the middle. When she smiled, he blushed. When she held out her hand, he instinctively looked at his right shoulder, where the arm would have been, if he still had that one.

He looked at her again and said, "I only have one arm."

"Really? I hadn't noticed. Though I did notice you have two legs."

All he could do was nod and feel like an idiot. Why had he said that?

She raised her thin brows and said, "Well?"

Lefty shrugged and followed the woman to the dance floor. She walked stiffly. Her right knee did not bend. They pushed past other gyrating couples, into the middle of the floor. The music was too loud, the song not all that familiar to him. The joint, called The Roaring Twenties, usually played big-band and old-time swing. But on Thursdays, ladies' night, they played the newer swing and the crowd was always younger, as was this woman who had uncustomarily asked him to dance. He guessed maybe thirty. Maybe even younger. Or not. He never was good at guessing ages. Either way, she was considerably younger than him.

She stopped and turned. "By the way, my right leg, from just above the knee, is a prosthetic."

He grinned. He couldn't help it. He just had to grin. Then, he stuck out his left hand and said, "George Bruder. Though my friends, all two or three of them, call me Lefty."

She arched her brows, then shook her head and grasped his hand. "Eileen Seager. It's a pleasure to meet you. Let's dance."

And they did. Well, at least he moved around on the dance floor. Calling it dancing may have been a stretch. But for three lively songs he moved and watched Eileen Seager dance. Kind of embarrassing that a woman with one artificial leg could dance better than he could, but she was pleasant to watch, and he only had one arm. He wondered, though, what she wanted.

When the music slowed, Lefty reached for Eileen, but she slipped away and walked back toward the bar. He shrugged and followed her, again wondering what she wanted. Certainly not a hooker. Dressed way too conservative for that. No makeup caked on her face. She wore tennis shoes, not high heels, jeans, not a short skirt.

"Can I get you anything, honey?" the bartender asked.

Eileen replied, "Soda. Whatever you have that is dark and not diet."

"Sure. Lefty? Another one?"

He hesitated, then said, "Same."

The bartender stared, blinked, then said, "Really?"

"Yeah, really."

The bartender gave a knowing smile and filled two glasses, setting them on the bar. Lefty put a five on the bar and turned to face Eileen, who was staring at him.

"So, George Bruder, also known as Lefty, do you have any siblings?"

Strange question to start a conversation. But whatever. These days, he couldn't be all that picky when it came to having conversations with attractive women, or anybody, for that matter.

"Yeah, one brother. He lives in Memphis."

"See him much?"

"Once or twice a year."

Eileen nodded. "Are you close?"

"I suppose. Why?"

"I had a sister. She died seven years ago. We were very close."

"Um, I'm sorry?"

"I'm not looking for sympathy. Anyway, I was also close to her daughter, my niece. Angel was eleven when her mother, my sister, died."

She looked out over the dance floor. The place was all varnished oak with a few of the original brick walls exposed. Like much of revitalized downtown, the building had been a warehouse transformed into a nightclub. The ceiling was darker wood. Yellow, tear-drop shaped lights hung down and provided low illumination. Couples embraced, swaying gently to the soft song.

Lefty nodded, not knowing what else to do or what to say. He studied her profile. She had a small mole on her left cheek, just below the cheekbone. From the corner of her eye to almost her temple was a faded scar, a childhood injury maybe. Baby-fine hair covered her cheek, so soft looking he had to will his hand to remain in his lap and not stroke it. He hoped he'd get the chance to feel it.

She turned back toward him and smiled. But it was a tired, sad smile. "For the past seven years, Angel's stepdad raised her." Her eyes grew moist. "I think he abused her. At least over the past two years."

She was getting there. Why she'd asked him to dance. Disappointment crept in on him. Apparently, her reason wasn't his rugged good looks, his still mostly black hair, three-day beard, or his stylish faded jeans and still almost white T-shirt.

"Why do you think that?"

"She stopped calling me. We used to talk at least three times a week. And I stopped by nearly every Saturday morning." A pause. "He was usually so hung over he slept in on Saturdays. Anyway, the last time I stopped by. Scratch that. The second to last time, she was evasive. I could tell something was wrong, but she wouldn't tell me what."

"Maybe she was doing drugs or something. Doesn't sound necessarily like she was being abused."

Eileen's jaw tightened. She clenched and unclenched her hands. "When her stepdad came in the kitchen, awake early for some reason, you should have seen the look of fear she shot him. She started trembling and could only whisper that I should probably leave."

"Oh."

"And when I did leave, she followed me to the front door. I hugged her and she clung to me. Squeezed me so tight I could barely breathe."

Again, she looked out at the dance floor. The music had changed. Something from The Squirrel Nut Zippers was playing. He recognized the tune. Couples, mostly men and women, some women together, cut the rug. When Eileen faced him again, tears clung to the corners of her dark eyes. He resisted the urge to wipe them away.

"The last time...the last time I stopped by, she was gone." She looked down, cleared her throat, sighed deeply. "He...he just shrugged it off, said good riddance. I...I tried to slap him, but he shoved me out the door and slammed it on me. It's been six months."

She took a drink of her soda. "After a lot of prayer and several fruitless attempts to get information from her stepdad, I started looking for her in the system. I tracked her to this city." She reached into her pocket and pulled out a photograph and showed it to Lefty. "Her name is Angel. She was such a sweet child. I want to find her and take her home. To my home, not to that nasty brute's home."

They stared at each other for a moment. Lefty wasn't sure what to think or feel. Used, maybe. Did she already know who, or more importantly, what he was? Or was this one of those moments of serendipity?

"You said you tracked her. How did you do that? You a cop?" He knew she wasn't, or at least wasn't anymore. The leg and all.

"No. I'm a records clerk for the Iowa Highway Patrol. I kept looking for her through the computer and finally got a hit." She took a deep breath. "She...she was arrested a couple weeks ago for prostitution. I couldn't get off until three days ago."

"You've been here three days?"

"Yes."

"And?"

"Nothing. No one's seen her. Or at least no one will admit anything."

Again, she looked out at the dance floor, but Lefty suspected she didn't see anything inside the night club. Finally, she returned her gaze to him. Before she started speaking, she bowed her head. And when she did speak, she spoke so quietly Lefty had to lean closer to hear her. She smelled clean, like a spring day after a heavy rain.

"I was ready to give up, to go home. I prayed to God that if I was supposed to keep looking, He'd lead me to someone else who could help." She raised her head and looked intently at him.

He shifted in his seat.

"This afternoon, a lieutenant at the county police called me. I'd left my number there two days ago. He gave me your name. Said, more than likely, I'd find you here."

Lefty made a mental note to thank Lieutenant Pratt next time he saw him. Although now, he really was feeling used.

"So, the dance, that was just a way to soften me up?"

She shook her head and put her hand on his arm. "No, no. Not just. I mean, I could have just sat down and told you my sob story."

"Then why the dance?"

"I...I wanted to dance with you. I don't know. When I saw you, there was...there was something in you that I liked."

"Feeling sorry for me?"

She jerked her hand back. "Yeah, right. Why would I feel sorry for you?"

"Gee, I don't know. Missing limb, maybe."

She reached across the table and knocked him on the head, then reached down and wrapped her knuckles on her prosthetic. "Hello. Missing limb and all."

"Oh, yeah. I forgot."

Silence between them for a moment. Lefty sucked on his soda, wishing he had ordered the usual, a double Scotch, neat. At least the soda was cheaper. Eileen rested both her hands on the bar and watched him for a few seconds. No wedding ring. In the low light he wasn't completely sure, but looked like there was a lighter band around her ring finger. She swiveled and stared at the people dancing. Lefty examined her a little more. Faded denim shirt, jeans, no jewelry, cheap slip-on sneakers, the kind found in discount department stores.

"You even took your wedding ring off, I see."

"What?"

He grabbed her hand and ran his index finger over the whiter area. "Tan line."

She snatched her hand back. "You jerk."

"What?"

"My husband left me about two years ago. After fifteen years. I only recently took the ring off."

"Oh." Then, trying to salvage himself, he added, "You must have been really young when you got married."

She shook her head and chuckled. "You want to know how old I am, just ask."

"That's not what...what the heck. How old are you?"

"Thirty-seven."

"Really? Ten years younger than me."

"Whoopee do."

He creased his brows. "What do you want from me?"

"Your help finding Angel. I thought that was obvious."

"What did the cops say?"

Eileen shook her head and swallowed hard. "She's an adult. Her eighteenth birthday was that last Saturday I stopped by. Nothing they'll do without evidence of foul play."

Lefty raised his glass and sucked down some more soda, again wishing it was something stronger. "Why me?"

"The lieutenant said you're a bulldog. And he said you know a lot of people who, as he put it, walk in the shadows."

Lefty again reminded himself to give Pratt a big thank you. Maybe one right across the chops.

"I'm too busy right now. Can't take on a case."

Eileen scrunched her face and shook her head. She brought her hands together then up to her chin and looked up. Her lips moved, but no sound. Then she looked at him.

"Too busy doing what?"

"Stuff."

She stood quickly. "You're pathetic, Bruder. You know that."

As he started to speak, she held up her hand.

"Nope, don't say anything. Don't want to hear your lame excuses. Here." She threw a piece of paper and a picture on the table. "In case you change your mind."

He tried to say something, but she turned her back on him. She hesitated and he started to get up, but then she walked off toward the door. He fell back onto his barstool. As he watched her limp away, he felt a stab of pain in his stomach. And when he again looked at the picture of Angel, a beautiful young girl, the pain spread to his entire midsection.

The piece of paper was a key sleeve from the downtown Hilton with a phone number scrawled on it. Six-four-one area code. Iowa, he assumed. He wondered how long a records clerk could afford to stay at the Hilton.

Chapter 3

Angel opened her eyes and stared into the darkness. She was laying on her back in a bed, crisp sheets and a light blanket over her. She felt to the left of her then to the right of her. A twin bed. No one else with her. As she tried to think what had happened the night before and where she was, the shakes overtook her. For several minutes, she trembled uncontrollably. Gooseflesh danced over her entire body, which was still clothed—but not in the same clothes she'd worn last night.

When the trembling finally stopped, she flung the covers off and sat up. Blood rushed from her head and the thin line of light under the door wavered, becoming four or five lines. She fought a wave of nausea. When the nausea passed, she slowly stood.

Before moving toward the door, she took inventory. Gone was the short black jean skirt and the orange tights. In their place a pair of cotton pajamas. Gone were her vest and midriff top, replaced by a long-sleeved cotton pajama top. All her jewelry was gone. Rings, necklaces, bracelets, even her nose stud and eight earrings. Gone.

She tried a step, then another. Okay so far. She approached the door and first tried the doorknob. Locked. She felt around the wall on the right and found a light switch, which she flicked up. Strobe lighting at first, crackling, then bright, fluorescent lights caused her to squeeze her eyes shut. Another wave of nausea broadsided her. She caught the doorknob and stopped herself from falling.

When everything settled, she slowly opened her eyes, blinking rapidly, until she could leave them open. She looked around. The room she was in looked nothing like what she thought she remembered from last night. Brief images of white walls, white sofa, glass tables, zebra-striped chairs and a large man with a goatee offering her a drink. Then nothing more.

In this room, a mattress on an oak wooden frame. A simple nightstand, also oak, just a tabletop with four legs and a second shelf halfway down. Nothing on either shelf except a book. She walked over to the table and examined the book. A Bible. That was it. Nothing else at all in the room. Bare white walls. White, drop-down ceiling with the fluorescent fixture. Plain, wood door. Brass doorknob. And a doggy door?

She knelt by the door and examined what she at first thought was a pet door. A square portion of the door had a small separation running all the way around. She shoved on it, but it did not budge. No visible hinges. Didn't slide right, left, up or down. She scooted back and kicked at it.

"Ouch! Oh, dang, dang, dang."

She pulled her legs back, thinking she had broken her heel. She rubbed the aching heel to ease the pain.

"Hey! Anyone out there? Let me out."

Silence. Eerie silence. Only the faint humming of the fluorescent light. The pain in her foot eased a bit, so she stood gingerly and put weight back on it. She pounded on the door with her fists.

"Hey! Anyone! Hello? Anyone there?"

Still nothing.

"Let me out of here. You can't hold me here. Let me out."

The small door within the door opened. But before Angel could get to the floor to look out, someone shoved in a tray and slammed the little door closed.

"Hey, you. Open the door. Hey!"

Silence.

Angel examined the cardboard tray. A glass of water. A bowl of what looked like oatmeal. An apple. And an oblong pill. She picked up the apple and heaved it at the wall. It broke into several pieces, leaving a wet stain.

The walls were painted plywood, not drywall.

"Let me out," she whimpered. "Please, just let me go."

More silence. She put her head between her knees and cried.

Chapter 4

Lefty opened his eyes and stared into the darkness. Something was wrong. He rolled over and looked at his alarm clock. Six-eighteen. In the morning? He tried to remember the last time he'd awoken so early. Probably when he was still on the force. When he still had a right arm. And where was the headache, the dry throat, the empty feeling in his gut?

He sat up and shivered as the window air-conditioner blasted frigid air over his nearly naked body. Just a pair of boxer shorts. What had happened last night? Oh, yeah. Eileen. He'd danced, talked, and drank...soda? And then had left the night club shortly after she'd stalked out.

The clock now read six-nineteen. What was he going to do up this early? He fell back onto the bed, but he didn't feel at all sleepy. All he could think about was Eileen...and Angel.

"Crap!"

He sat back up, knowing what he'd do after he showered and ate something. He padded off to the bathroom. After a quick shower, he whipped up a three-egg omelet with shredded cheddar cheese. Packaged, of course. Shredding his own cheese was too much of a challenge with one arm. He could do it, but why bother when they sold it already shredded? While his breakfast finished cooking, he stared at a whiskey bottle on the stained vinyl counter. For some inexplicable reason, he felt no compulsion to reach for the bottle.

"What did that woman do to me?"

A slight singed smell reminded him of his eggs. He flipped the omelet onto a plain white plate and sat at his nineteen fifties diner-style table. It was getting a little rickety and some rust played along the edge. The matching chair—there was only one—complained as he scooted in and started on the eggs.

Where would he start? There were so many pimps, and the landscape constantly changed as they moved in and out of St. Louis. He knew three local ones, all working for Big Eddie. Scratch Johnson, Bony Harris, and Keyshawn Williams. That's where he'd start. Good old Keyshawn. Worked his girls out of several hotels, both in the city and the county, and had some walkers on Lemay Boulevard at the edge of South City and St. Louis County. More street walkers closer to downtown. He also ran a strip joint on the East Side. Keyshawn knew most of the players and saw a lot of girls.

When he'd finished eating, he dropped the plate and fork in the sink and picked up his cell phone. Only seven-seventeen, but so what. She'd gotten under his skin, so the least he could do was wake her up.

No such satisfaction. Eileen answered the phone on the second ring, sounding out of breath. "Hello?"

"Ms. Seager?"

"Hey, George." A couple deep breaths. "Whew. Just a minute." More deep breaths. "Didn't really expect you to be up this early."

Ignoring the comment, he asked, "Are you out of breath?"

"Yup. Just got back from running. Went about two miles this morning."

Figured. However, impressive as well, considering her leg situation and all.

"So, what gets you up so early?" she asked.

"I changed my mind."

"About?"

"I'll find your niece."

Silence.

Quietly, she said, "Praise the Lord. Thank you, George. God bless you."

"I assume this was your cell phone I dialed." The area code did not match his, so he figured it wasn't the hotel number. Brilliant detective work, considering the early hour.

"Yup. I'll have it with me at all times. Where are you going to start?"

"I'll call you when I find anything. Talk to you later."

"Okay. I'll be praying for—"

He hung up. If he told her where he was going, he figured she was just the type to show up and get herself in trouble.

Chapter 5

Calvin Rockport savored the flavor of his Eggs Benedict. Serena was the best cook in the state, hands down. Outside his three-season porch, a cardinal flitted from a branch to the bird feeder hung in the silver maple. Through the glass, Rockport could just hear the single cheep the cardinal repeatedly made. He toyed with opening the windows to hear the morning sounds better, but the thermometer hanging off the porch read eighty-three already. The condensation on the windows betrayed the high humidity. He decided air conditioning was more important than hearing the birds.

The door from the family room opened.

Rockport said, "How is she doing?"

"She hasn't taken the Suboxone yet." Sara Hanley was a tall blond-haired woman of twenty-four who had been with Rockport for seven years. The first girl who had stayed with him.

"Did you ask her to?"

"Not yet. I will when she starts showing symptoms." Sara joined him at the glass table.

He continued to stare out at the small grove of trees behind his house. "Did she eat anything?"

"Nope. Didn't touch anything." Sara also gazed out the window. "Oh, other than the apple. Which she flung against the wall."

"Spirited."

"If you say so. Chester won't be happy to have to clean up the mess."

"He's cleaned up worse."

"True. And that still may come to pass."

They sat in silence. Rockport took another bite of his Eggs Benedict. With mouth full, he asked, "Want something?"

"Already ate."

"See that she takes the pill."

"Use force?"

"If necessary. Give her a shot if you have to."

"Okay. Though Methadone isn't as effective. I'll try to get her to take the pill."

She left, and Rockport finished his breakfast. He stayed on the porch for another half-hour, not wanting to take a chance. He hated hearing them scream and struggle. That first pill was so hard to get them to take. If they'd only do so willingly, things would go much easier. Oh well. Chester knew how to handle them without hurting them, and Marsha, their resident nurse, was efficient with a hypodermic, if it came to that.

Finally, he made his way inside and upstairs to his office. Sara was already there, sitting in a red leather armchair.

"Well?" He walked past her to the red leather executive chair behind the kidney-bean shaped mahogany desk.

"Had to give her the needle. Methadone mixed with a sedative. She should be out in about fifteen more minutes. But she still hadn't eaten anything."

Rockport stared at the inert fireplace beyond her. He raised his gaze to the flat screen television mounted on the wall above the fireplace and watched the stock ticker scroll by. "When she gets hungry, she'll eat. They always do. She should wake up in about what, four hours?"

"About that." Sara busied herself on the laptop computer perched on her lap. "She had a driver's license. I'll find out more about her."

"Thank you. Let me know what you discover."

She nodded, folded the lid on the laptop, and left his office. Rockport extracted his cell phone, found the number he wanted in recent calls, and hit the call button.

"Hello?" answered a throaty, deep voice.

"I have another one," said Rockport. "Just brought her in last night. Got the first dose in her. Can you be here tomorrow?"

"Nine okay?"

"Perfect."

He hung up and rotated his chair so he could look out the large plate glass window. The Southern magnolia was in full bloom. The tree, planted when the house had been built twenty years ago, had been his wife's favorite. She'd visited him often in his office during the day, especially in July. He suspected it was mainly to gaze at the tree.

His thoughts drifted to his daughter, when she used to run into his office and in her stocking feet skate on the oak floor, then jump on the gray sofa at the far end until he got too nervous watching, afraid she'd fall right through the sectioned window behind the sofa. When he yelled at her to stop, she'd jump off, run to him, and leap up onto his knee.

He shook the painful memory away, opened a file folder and looked through mug shots of prostitutes.

Chapter 6

"Thirty-seven." Lefty breathed out and let himself down, then pushed up. "Thirty-eight." Breathed out, let down, pushed up, counted, repeat.

When he exhaled "Fifty," he collapsed onto the natty rug covering his faded and scuffed wooden floor. He rolled onto his back. While he stared at the yellowing ceiling, his mind drifted back six years earlier.

A couple weeks after leaving the hospital, after taking the bullet in the shoulder and having his arm amputated, he first tried the one-arm push-ups. It had taken him an hour to be able to do two in a row.

He fast forwarded to last May, to the state arm wrestling championships. He remembered the look of his opponent in the finals as he assessed Lefty's skinny body and only slightly less skinny left arm. Lefty had just smiled at him. And like all the previous opponents had dispatched the man in two seconds flat.

The nationals had been a different story. He'd made it to the semifinals, where he faced off with a man not dissimilar to himself, only instead of missing an arm, he had no legs and had been that way for twenty years. Those twenty years of doing everything with his arms had made him too much for Lefty. The match lasted a full ninety seconds, but he finally succumbed to the double-amputee's incredible arm strength. Lefty took comfort though—his semifinal opponent won their weight division, both with his left and right arms.

Enough ruminating. He swiveled and swung his feet up on the sofa and did a hundred stomach crunches. The next hour consisted of thirty minutes with the cardio-strike bag and fifteen katas. He ended his workout with ten non-stop minutes on the speed bag, ducking and swaying to avoid imaginary strikes from his invisible foe.

When he finished, he rested leaning against his graying laminate kitchen counter, staring at four days' worth of dishes, deciding another day wouldn't matter. Besides, he had a case now, no time for trivialities.

His gazed shifted to his bottle of scotch, Johnny Red, about a quarter left. He took a glass down from the cupboard, grabbed the bottle, unscrewed the top and started to pour, but stopped before any liquid escaped. He sighed, replaced the cap, put both bottle and glass on the counter and went to shower.

What had that woman done to him?

Lefty entered the windowless building on the East Side. He remained just inside the door while his eyes became used to the dark blue lighting. Outside, ninety plus and bright sun. Inside, refrigerator cold with a dense fog of cigarette smoke. Small round tables that looked like they were made of polished lapis lazuli were scattered throughout, each surrounded by two or three high-backed padded chairs. Half the chairs were occupied. At this time of day, all were men, all sitting alone. Social distancing at its best.

In the center, a figure-eight shaped stage with a dark wood floor reflected dark blue and purple from the overhead lights. At the center of each loop on the stage a fire pole rose to the ceiling and a woman clad in a skimpy bikini made mock love to the pole. At several of the tables, a girl gyrated on a man's lap. No social distancing there. Languid music blared through tinny speakers. On the far wall hung two televisions, each framed by light blue neon light. Playing on the screens were more dancing women.

Lefty shivered, not just from the cold but from his disdain. As pathetic as his life had become, it paled compared to the men visiting this fine establishment.

A topless girl with long, straight, black hair greeted him.

"Hey, darling. Can I see you to a table? What will you have?"

He briefly glanced at her bare breasts then looked into her dark, empty eyes. While she looked at him, her gaze seemed to go right through him. And while there was a smile on her face, her words came out flat, emotionless.

He pointed to a corner table.

"Over there will do. I'll take a scotch, neat."

Without a word she turned and sashayed toward the table. He followed and sat in one of the padded chairs. She left to get his drink.

Seconds later, another girl, this time a tanned, short-haired blonde stood close to him.

"How about a table dance?"

He had to tilt his head nearly all the way back to avoid staring at her belly button, which sported a silver ring. She didn't even bother to look at him but stared straight ahead. He noticed small red dots on her arms, especially around the elbow joint. No attempt to hide the needle marks.

"No thanks. Can I ask you something?"

"Sure." She slightly tilted her head, but still did not look him in the eyes.

"Why do you do this?"

Without hesitation, "The money's good."

He started to ask more but decided against it. She shifted her weight from foot to foot. He turned away and she moved to another table.

The brunette returned with his drink. He took a sip and fought the urge to spit it out. Not only was it severely watered down, but it tasted rancid, like vinegar. He put a ten on the table and looked around the gentlemen's club, as it billed itself. However, the patrons looked like anything but gentlemen. Except for the one dude toward the back who wore a gray suit with slicked salt-and-pepper hair and several gold rings on his fingers.

Lefty spotted Keyshawn at the bar talking with the bartender, an older woman. Older relative to the strippers—probably in her thirties.

She handed Keyshawn a stack of bills, from which he peeled off a couple and gave them back to her. He then slipped the rest of the stack into his pocket. Keyshawn turned away from the bartender and went through a door off to the right of the bar. Lefty scooted back in his chair, got up and walked past the bar to the door Keyshawn had disappeared through. Without hesitation, he knocked.

"What?"

He opened the door and walked through, closing it behind him. Keyshawn leaned back with his feet on the top of a cluttered cheap metal desk. He removed the joint from his mouth and blew out a puff of smoke.

"George Bruder. What are you doing here? Looking for a girl? 'Cause this is the only place you'll find one who'd have anything to do with you now."

Lefty said nothing.

"For a price, of course. But for you, I'll give you a discount." Keyshawn brought his other hand from under the desk and pointed a finger gun at Lefty, then made a clicking sound and winked.

Lefty stepped forward until his thighs rested against the desk. Above Keyshawn's head, on the wall behind him, hung a calendar advertising motor oil. A girl in a tiny red bikini leaned seductively on a flame embossed black '57 Plymouth. A fake plant with dusty leaves occupied the left corner of the office. A file cabinet stacked with disarrayed papers occupied the corner on the right. A single vent near the ceiling spewed musty, frigid air.

"As a matter of fact, Keyshawn, I am looking for a girl."

Keyshawn swung his legs down and leaned forward. "Then you come to the right place. What's your pleasure? Tall blonde. Short brunette. Maybe some sweet chocolate?"

Lefty tossed the picture of Angel on the desk. "Her."

During his short stint as a detective, Lefty always felt he had incredible luck, often making decisions on nothing but vague hunches that solved tough cases. He'd had a one in three chance of which pimp to visit first who could have handled Angel, and he knew from the quick glance Keyshawn gave the picture then back at him that he'd come to the right one on his first choice.

"Ain't never seen her."

"Are you sure about that, Keyshawn?"

"She's a hot one. I think I'd remember her." He handed the picture back.

"Think harder, Keyshawn." He rested his hand on the desk and leaned forward. "Think real hard."

The door opened behind Lefty.

"You okay, boss?" asked a deep voice.

"You want us to toss this toothpick?" asked a much higher voice.

Lefty smiled at Keyshawn. "Only two of them?"

He had seen both heavies on his way in. A muscled black man had been sitting at the far end of the bar from the door to Keyshawn's office. And a white guy with crew cut and a four-day shadow had been lurking by the stage.

Keyshawn said, "Three. There's me, sucka."

Still smiling, Lefty said, "Seriously. You really want to try me?" He noticed a darker mark on the pimp's left cheek. "Looks like someone already did a number on you."

Keyshawn swallowed. He eyed his men, then looked back at Lefty. After a pause, he waved his hands, shooing the two men out. "It's okay. I got this."

The door clicked shut.

"You ain't a cop no more, so what's the deal?"

"Private."

"Why should I tell you anything, then?"

Lefty shrugged. "You'd be doing the right thing."

Keyshawn smirked.

"Or, because Big Eddie may not take kindly to you skimming from him."

"What are you talking about? I don't skim from Big Eddie."

"Really?" He told Keyshawn what he'd seen at the bar.

"That wasn't skimming." Keyshawn looked past Lefty, fidgeted in his seat, drummed his fingers on the desk. "I plan to deposit that money later."

"Okay, sure. It doesn't really matter, Keyshawn. 'Cause if I described what I saw to Big Eddie, he'll make his own judgment."

Keyshawn frowned at Lefty for a full minute. Sweat stains widened in the pits of his dark blue dress shirt. Lefty straightened his arm, getting tired of leaning on it. His tricep bulged. The white Cardinal's T-shirt he had on was a size too small, so the sleeve barely reached below his muscular shoulder.

"What you want this girl for?"

"Her name's Angel."

"Yeah, I know. Used to work for me."

Lefty arched his brows. "Used to?"

"Yeah, used to. Till some rich white dude with a giant brother stole her away from me."

"Stole her?"

"Okay, bought her, but only ten G's, man. She was gold."

"When did this transaction take place?"

"Last night."

"Mind explaining?"

Keyshawn went through the events of the night before, telling Lefty about how Angel was taken away in a black limo.

"Who was this guy?"

"I don't know, man. If I knew that you think I'd be sitting around here jawin' with you?"

Lefty pushed away from the desk. "Describe him."

"White. Big. Had a goatee streaked in gray. Brown eyes, I think. Nice hair, slicked back. Brown with some gray in it."

"Why do you think he wanted Angel?"

"I don't think he was lookin' for Angel. He asked for the prettiest, youngest girl I had. That was Angel."

"Youngest? She's eighteen. Do you really expect me to believe that?"

Keyshawn shrugged. "Well, prettiest, anyway. And this dude looked rich, so that's why I suggested her."

"Who do you think he was?"

"Either one of them dudes that makes porn, or maybe a high-end call-girl pimp. Coulda been a pimp from another city. They come through here a lot."

Lefty turned away and paced to the door, then back. "This kind of thing happen often?"

"Not to me. People know better."

Lefty chuckled.

"What you laughing at? It happens, but not to me."

"If you saw him again, would you recognize him?"

Keyshawn smiled. "Oh, yeah."

"Any names used in the transaction?"

Keyshawn thought a moment then said, "Nope. They was careful."

"Big Eddie know about this?"

Keyshawn straightened and looked Lefty in the eyes. "Of course, man. Got the word out looking for this dude. He ain't getting away with this."

Keyshawn was mostly show and no go, but not Big Eddie. He was a force to be reckoned with.

"Thanks." Lefty turned away and opened the door to leave. Over his shoulder he said, "That wasn't so hard, was it?"

"Don't you be talking to Big Eddie 'bout what you think you saw."

Lefty smiled and shook his head. He walked past the two bouncers, giving both a grin and a wink, then reentered the bubbling cauldron of St. Louis in July. He was going to talk to Big Eddie, but he wouldn't mention what he'd seen Keyshawn doing, because he might need the pimp later.

Chapter 7

From the seedy East Side to the lush mansions bordering Forest Park, the location of the 1904 World's Fair. Despite the heat and it being a weekday afternoon, the concrete trail bordering the park streamed with joggers, bikers, and dog walkers. Blankets and towels littered open spaces filled with sun bathers. Pockets of friends played Frisbee.

Lefty pulled his rickety Nissan to the curb of Lindell Avenue. He exited his car and walked the sidewalk opposite side of the park until he came parallel with a three-story, light brown brick home with bright white trim. A walkway led to the front entrance on the far left of the home. The driveway continued past the house to an attached garage that also had a second story. There were no visible guards and no obvious cameras, but Lefty knew that Big Eddie had state-of-the-art surveillance and plenty of firepower lurking on the grounds.

As soon as he'd made it halfway up the walk a large black man in a Hawaiian shirt and khakis opened the front door and stepped out.

"You lost?"

Lefty smiled at him. "You wouldn't hurt a one-armed man, would you?"

The man said nothing. He widened his stance and put his right hand behind his back.

"Keep cool. Just tell Big Eddie that former detective George Bruder needs to see him."

The man said, "You hear that?" But he wasn't talking to Lefty.

"Another hot day, huh?"

The man said nothing. Lefty guessed him to be about six-four, probably weighing in at two-sixty, unless the bulk was all muscle, then possibly three hundred.

"How's Big Eddie doing these days, anyway?" Nothing.

The front door opened again and an even larger black man stepped out. "George Bruder! I am doing wonderful, sir. And how about you?"

Big Eddie wore a linen short-sleeved shirt, untucked, and matching linen pants. His shaved head glistened in the sun. His eyes sparkled and even in the bright afternoon sun, his teeth glowed.

Lefty started back up the walkway. The guard stepped toward him, right hand still behind his back.

"It's okay, Roland. George here's a friend. 'Specially now he ain't no cop." Big Eddie boomed out a laugh.

The guard turned ninety degrees and Lefty closed the gap between him and Big Eddie.

"And don't let this skinny man fool you, Roland. He's quite the fighter. Even with his handicap, so I hear."

Lefty ascended the two front porch steps, stuck out his hand, and lost it inside Big Eddie's massive paw.

"Come in, my friend. Way too hot out here."

Lefty followed Big Eddie into the foyer and did not bother to remove his sunglasses. White everywhere. The walls the ceiling, trim, the patterned marble tile floor. The foyer began a long hallway that ended in a door identical to the one he'd entered. Even the glasswork above and next to the door was a twin to the front entrance. Other than a slight blue tinge and the dark blue etching, the stained glass was white. Halfway down the hall a white crystal chandelier hung from the ceiling. Small gold lampshades covered the six candelabra. Below the chandelier was an ornate wooden table with a fake orchid with, what else, white flowers.

"Let's go in the library."

Lefty chuckled.

"I know," said Big Eddie. "You're thinking, what am I doing with a library." He stopped and turned to face Lefty with a Cheshire Cat grin. "I'm learning to read. What do you think of that?"

"I'm impressed. Good for you."

Big Eddie clapped Lefty's shoulder and nearly knocked him over, then entered the library. Lefty followed.

"What do you think?" Big Eddie waved his arms indicating the room they'd entered.

"It's bright."

More white. Though at least the walls were a light beige with bright white trim. The library, as Big Eddie had called it, was more a family room. To his credit, he did have a long, white of course, cabinet full of books. The cabinet had eight glass doors with bright white muntins. Above the cabinet a modest television, probably sixty inches diagonal, and some shelves with several gold vases and some more books. The room was furnished with a beige sofa, two pale green slipper chairs and two things Lefty thought were footstools, but they sat alone. All these surrounded a table with a glass top and mahogany frame. The floor was oak, mostly covered by an off-white rug.

Lefty said, "And wow, you must have bought out the library, you have so many books." He tried to hide his sarcasm.

Big Eddie, still smiling wide, sat in the middle of the sofa. Lefty chose one of the slipper chairs.

"You are almost right. I bought all of them at the library's last sale. Most of these books were two dollars. Can you believe it?"

"Amazing."

Big Eddie laughed again. "But I'm sure you didn't come here to talk books. Like I told Roland, you ain't no cop no more. So what brings you here?"

"I'm looking for a girl."

"A good-looking man like yourself? Surely you don't need one of my girls."

Big Eddie, the walking, or in this case, sitting enigma. Always full of compliments, friendly, generous, yet would not hesitate to blow someone away who stood between him and something he wanted.

"Thanks, Big Eddie. But I'm trying to find a girl whose gone missing. A girl whose aunt has hired me to find her." He tossed the picture on the glass table between them. "Her name's Angel."

Big Eddie picked up the picture. "She certainly is an angel." He stared at the picture a bit then said, "If she's working for me, there will be a price, but I'll let her go if she wants."

"Very generous of you, Big Eddie, but she's not working for you anymore."

"Explain, please."

Lefty recounted the conversation with Keyshawn, after which Big Eddie pulled out his cell phone and called the pimp. It wasn't that he didn't trust Lefty, but that he didn't trust Keyshawn. After some yelling, threatening, and finally a long sigh, he hung up, and stared past Lefty for a minute or so.

Lefty took the opportunity to admire the rhinoceros picture hanging above the—wait for it—white fireplace. Okay, the mantel was white, surrounding a light brick. The rhino stood in profile on a, what else, white background.

"Funny," Lefty said, "Keyshawn told me he'd told you."

Big Eddie just stared at him for a full minute. "This is not the first time this has happened to me." All joviality gone from the large man. He narrowed his eyes. "I've lost eight girls in the past three years."

Lefty started to say something, but Big Eddie interrupted with, "But this is the first time we've seen the person responsible."

"Who do you think it is?"

"Probably not a local working the hotels or streets. That would be too stupid. It's either someone making porn or someone selling them to other markets."

Lefty couldn't help himself. "You know, these are young girls we're talking about, not pieces of meat."

Instead of getting angry, Big Eddie said, "You'll not hear any excuses from me, George. It's a nasty business. But a profitable one. And we don't kidnap girls, like this man who has stolen my property."

Lefty shook his head and said nothing.

"Hold on one moment, George. I just remembered something." He took out his cell phone again and made a call. "It's Eddie. Remind me, when's the buy? Uh-huh. Where? Uh-huh. Thanks.

Back at ya." He hung up. To Lefty he said, "Sunday night. Down on the river on the East Side. Pitzman Road in Sauget. Used to be an environmental services company. One of the old warehouses. There's a buy. I don't attend these because like I said, I don't do kidnapped girls. My girls come to us looking for extra green."

So they can feed their drug habit one of your pimps probably hooked them on, is what Lefty wanted to say, but restrained himself, as he might need more information from Big Eddie. But he did ask, "And they're free to leave anytime, right?"

Big Eddie just smiled. "If you find Angel, you can return her to her family. But if you find the man who took her, I want his name. Deal?"

Lefty said nothing. Instead he stood, shook Big Eddie's hand again, and left the large, mostly white, house.

Chapter 8

"Well, look who the cat dragged in. If it ain't Lefty Bruder." Sergeant Ronald Donaldson smiled at Lefty as the one-armed former St. Louis County beat cop and detective walked into his former place of employment in Clayton, the so called "second downtown" just west of downtown St. Louis.

"How are you, Ronny?"

"I've been getting on okay."

Donaldson's wife had died about nine months ago of a brain tumor at only fifty-one. Lefty had not attended the funeral and felt terrible about it. But at the time, he'd still been dealing with his own issues, not having yet accepted lack of employment and lack of a limb.

"Hey, I'm really sorry about Joanne. And even more sorry I didn't make the funeral."

"No problem, Lefty. I heard you were having a bit of a rough go at it." He scratched his bald dome, then ran his hand over the gray stubble on the back of his head.

Lefty nodded.

"What brings you here?"

"I need to talk to Lieutenant Pratt. "Hold on a sec." Donaldson picked up his desk phone and punched in a number. "Lieutenant? It's Sergeant Donaldson up front. You have a visitor." He listened a couple seconds, then said, "It's a surprise, sir." Another pause. "I believe a pleasant one, sir." After listening a couple more seconds, he said, "Yes, sir." Then hung up. To Lefty he said, "Have a seat. He'll be right down."

He started to say something else, but at that moment two uniformed officers dragged in a young girl kicking and screaming, trying to get out of their grip. She cursed them and anyone else around. She was maybe seventeen or eighteen, Lefty guessed. She looked a bit like Angel, but had black-dyed hair that just brushed her shoulders. He examined her closely enough that she noticed and said some unpleasant words to him, accusing him of being a pervert and of questionable birth.

Taking a chance of more abuse, Lefty said in as pleasant a voice as he could muster, "What's your name?"

She stopped struggling and stared at him a second. Her blue eyes were bloodshot. She wore a tight, black leather skirt and a black button-down top, mostly buttoned down. A wide white belt wrapped around her slim waist, accentuating the other curves of her body.

"Why, honey, you interested? I should be out in a couple hours."

Playing along, Lefty said, "Maybe. What's your name so I can ask for you later?"

"Miranda."

"You grow up in St. Louis?"

"Yeah? Why does that matter?"

"I like hometown girls."

The officers took advantage of her calmer demeanor and dragged her away. The girl looked over her shoulder and shouted, "Ain't never done a cripple before."

Donaldson said, "Nice. Real good upbringin' there."

Lefty just shrugged. He wondered what had driven her to drugs and the street.

As the girl and the two officers disappeared around a corner, Lieutenant Pratt appeared from the around the same corner. When he saw Lefty, he smiled and shook his head. Without a word, he walked up to Lefty, who stood, and gave him a big hug.

"Detective Bruder, it's great to see you."

Pratt insisted on calling Lefty by his former title, one he knew Lefty had worked so hard to attain, only to have it stripped from him three years later when a forty-four caliber slug tore through his upper arm, shattering the bone and shredding the muscle.

"Good to see you, too, Lieutenant." Anyone who knew him called him Lieutenant or Pratt, because calling him by his first name—Seymour—earned a hard stare or worse. "Sorry it's been so long." He paused, feeling a little embarrassed. "This isn't a social visit."

"Figured as much. You've never been a real sociable person."

"Hey."

Pratt looked at Donaldson. "Am I right, Sergeant Donaldson?"

"Absolutely, sir."

"You're just a suck-up," Lefty said to the sergeant.

Donaldson shrugged.

"Come on up to my office," Pratt said.

Lefty followed the six-four, well-built head of the detectives division around two corners, down concrete block hallways painted a dull yellow, and up two flights of stairs, then into a small but neat office on the backside of the building. One small window looked out over a large grassy circle in front of the ten-story county office building, a much newer building than the police office. Two worn leather armchairs fronted a blonde-colored wooden desk. On the left side of the desk was a triple stack of black, plastic letter trays, one labeled In, one labeled Out, and one labeled Urgent. On the right side of the desk were four framed pictures, both facing away from Lefty. Probably Pratt's wife and three kids.

"How's the family?" asked Lefty.

"Wonderful. Have a seat." He went around the desk and sat heavily in his worn executive chair. "Jamie is graduating this year. Can you believe that?"

Lefty slid into one of the armchairs. What Lefty found hard to believe was that he'd been out of touch so long. Pratt's daughter had been a sophomore in high school when he'd left the force. "Hard to believe, sir."

"Sir? You don't have to call me sir anymore."

"Force of habit, I guess."

"Speaking of guessing, let me guess why you're here. Looking for a girl named Angel Atkins from Ottumwa, Iowa, right?"

"I would say I'm impressed, but I already know you steered her aunt Eileen to me."

Pratt smiled. "Never could pull one over on you, Detective. Yeah, professional courtesy, as Ms. Seager works for the Iowa State Highway Patrol."

Pratt leaned back and interlocked his hands over his nearly non-existent stomach. "Ms. Atkins was busted once for prostitution. She's an adult who left home on her own. Nothing we can really do at this point."

"I know. So, let me tell you what I know about her."

Over the next few minutes, Lefty related the story about Angel being abducted and his conversation with Keyshawn. He left out the talk he had with Big Eddie and information about the buy Sunday night.

When he finished his story, Pratt swiveled and gazed out the window a few seconds, then swiveled back to face Lefty. He smoothed his thick, graying mustache and rubbed his hand over his even thicker nearly all gray hair. "I want to introduce you to someone."

He picked up his phone and punched in two numbers. After a couple seconds he said, "Detective Fischer, it's Pratt. Come to my office, would you?" He hung up. "Fischer is a seasoned detective in our special investigation unit. He works mainly on sex crimes. He may not have specific intel on Ms. Atkins, but he'll be able to give you a lot of info on sex crimes in St. Louis County."

Pratt paused. "What have you been doing, George, with all your time?"

Lefty grunted. "As little as possible."

"Doesn't sound like you." Pratt stood and slipped off his gray suit jacket and draped it over his chair. "And it doesn't sound like it's good for you."

Pratt had called Lefty at least once a week for the first year after he'd been released from the hospital, but he had ignored the calls and not called back. For the next four years, Pratt had called every few months. Lefty always let them go to voicemail.

"I was wallowing in self-pity."

"You look good, like you've kept in shape."

"Over the past nine months I got back into my martial arts training. Home, dojo, bar, home. That's been my routine."

Pratt nodded and scratched his chin. He shifted his weight then said, "How about joining my family and me at church Sunday? The kids would love to see you again."

"Thanks for the offer, Lieutenant, but I think I'll pass."

The door to Pratt's office opened and Pratt said, "Okay, but the offer is always open. And you know Jeannine makes a mean fried chicken."

A slim, shorter man walked in. He was bald on top and close cut on the sides. Clean-shaven, he had dark, deep-set eyes. He wore khakis and a dark green sports coat.

Pratt said, "Detective Fischer, this is George Bruder."

Lefty stood and stuck out his left hand. "People call me Lefty."

Fischer took his hand and said, "Nice to meet you, Lefty. You can call me James."

Pratt said, "And remember that. James, not Jim. He hates Jim as much as I hate my first name."

Fischer gave a thin smile, then asked, "What can I do for you, Lieutenant?"

Pratt gave a quick synopsis of Angel. When he finished, Fischer shook his head and said, "A tragic story repeated over and over in this city." He stared hard at Lefty. "You familiar with the sex trafficking problems we have here?"

"A little. I know most of the players—the pimps, anyway."

"Hard numbers are difficult to obtain. Human trafficking, thus forced prostitution, is on the rise in this country and in our city. St. Louis is in the corridor both east to west and north to south."

"These girls are kidnapped?" asked Lefty.

"Sometimes, but like I said the percentages are hard to come by. And the definition of forced prostitution varies as well. But I think the percentages are growing." Fischer paused.

Lefty nodded, but said nothing, figuring the detective had more to say. He was right.

"Nearly half of all prostitutes come from sexually abused backgrounds. Many are runaways or loners hanging out in the wrong place. Some turn to the profession for financial reasons, however, the primary financial reason is to get money to feed their drug habit."

"They're druggies who have run out of cash?"

"Yes and no. Many are given the drugs by the pimps, free until hooked, then prostitution becomes the way to keep getting them. The pimp or someone working for him finds likely candidates, pretends to be interested in them, may even become their boyfriend. Gets them hooked. Then gets them working. Heroin is the drug of choice these days. Addictive after just one hit. Almost all the girls are addicts."

"And the other group, the ones that are there by choice?"

"Choice is a subjective word." Fischer motioned for Lefty to sit in one of Pratt's armchairs. He took the other. Pratt mumbled something about having something to do and left the office. "Like I mentioned, even the ones doing this by choice are usually slaves to their drug habit, and hooking is an easy way to get drugs."

"Easy?"

"Yeah. Easy. At least that's the rationale these girls use."

"Are they mostly local or from somewhere else?" Lefty asked.

"Both, here. Many runaways, often from smaller towns around Missouri and Illinois, or Iowa, like Angel. They come to the big city thinking there will be more opportunity." He scratched his head. "They can't find a job, or at least one that pays enough.

"Many start in strip clubs. Again, easy money. Sex is optional. But, again, the pimps running those places get the girls addicted. They need to earn more money, so they start hooking on the side. Pretty soon, they're on the street or doing the hotels, too messed up to work in the strip joint."

"And Angel?"

"She's a bit unusual."

"How so?"

"She's eighteen. Most of these girls are fourteen or fifteen when they start hooking."

"What are you guys doing about this?"

Apparently, Lefty's tone came off a bit abrupt as Fischer glared at him. "As much as we can and budget allows. We can bust the girls, but they won't give up their pimp. That would cut off their source of drugs. We can't get them to flip and without their testimony we have nothing on the men behind this form of slavery. They'll never testify they were kidnapped unless we get them before they're addicted. We work with social services, pair them up with the girls. A few success stories, but too few and too far between."

"Sorry, I know you guys do what you can. Used to work here, remember?"

Fischer only nodded.

Lefty then told Fischer what Keyshawn told him about Angel. "So, who do you think this guy was?"

"Four options I can think of." He looked out the window and thought a few seconds. "First, he could be a local rival, but that's doubtful."

"Why?"

"Not that much stealing from each other. And with Keyshawn, you have to contend with Big Eddie. It would take someone pretty powerful to go against him. And we haven't heard of any newbies setting up shop recently."

"And the other options?"

"Out of towner. In to grab some girls to take back to New Orleans, Dallas, Kansas City, Memphis, you name the other big cities around us. They use the Interstate 44 corridor. But again, doesn't sound like it."

Again, he paused, so Lefty asked, "Why not?"

"You said the guy asked for the youngest and prettiest. That sounds more like a porn producer looking for a new girl. But that isn't real big in St. Louis."

"But why would he kidnap her? Wouldn't advertising work better?"

"Could, and probably would. Though we're watching for that, trying to bust these guys for using underage girls."

Sirens sounded outside and faded in the distance. Fire truck. "What's the last option?"

"A rescue."

"Rescue?"

"Yeah. Could be a group that does this routinely. They grab these girls and try to get them rehabilitated. Works for some. If they can find out where they came from, they can often return them home and get them off the drugs. Or it could be a private dick like yourself who was hired to find her."

"That last one doesn't make sense, since I was hired to find her."

"Good point. And again, because he talked to the pimp and asked for a particular type of girl, doesn't match the MO of the rescue groups. They usually just follow girls and talk them into coming with them."

They both sat in silence for a minute. Then Lefty asked, "How do I find these porn guys?"

"Advertising. Craigslist, other places like that. But we'd prefer to do the looking."

Lefty frowned. "Pratt told me there wasn't anything you could do to find Angel."

"That was before you told me she was abducted. If the pimp would come in and testify, we'd have a kidnapping case."

"Feds?"

"Probably not. Too low profile for them. But we'd work it, and we work with the FBI."

"You need Keyshawn, though?"

"Yup. Can't open a case on hearsay."

"I'll see what I can do."

Fischer stood as another siren passed by on the street. "I hope I was helpful."

Lefty also stood. "Very." He extended his left hand and Fischer awkwardly shook it. Lefty smiled. "Hard to get used to, isn't it?"

Fischer colored a little, said nothing, then turned and left Pratt's office. Lefty waited a few seconds and when Pratt didn't return, he also left to go pay another visit to Keyshawn.

Chapter 9

"Hey look, the one-armed toothpick has returned." The thin crew-cut bouncer thought himself a comedian.

Lefty just smiled at him and walked to the bar, where Keyshawn was drying some glasses. "I'm impressed. Doing dishes."

"Are you serious? You're back? Man, what do you want this time?"

The larger, black bouncer approached Lefty on one side and Crew Cut the other.

"Should we toss him, boss?"

Apparently, Keyshawn was at the end of his fuse because he snapped at his employee. "Four of you wouldn't stand a chance against this guy. Just go watch the stage."

Both bouncers looked at their boss a second, but then walked to opposite sides of the stage.

"You want to talk here, or your office?"

"Here is fine."

"If you'll tell the cops what you told me, they'll open a kidnapping case and help find Angel."

"Man, what dope you been smoking? I ain't about to talk to no cops."

"Have a heart, Keyshawn. Let's get this girl back to her family."

Keyshawn set the glass down. "If I talked to the cops—for any reason—Big Eddie would plant me six feet under."

"I'll talk to Big Eddie."

He threw the towel in the corner. "You already talked to Big Eddie and he's already pissed at me. I don't need your help."

"Hey, I didn't tell him about the skimming."

Keyshawn turned away and walked toward his office. Over his shoulder, he said, "We'll take care of this ourselves." He opened his office door and slammed it shut.

Lefty stared at the closed door, debating whether to press the issue, but in the end decided he wouldn't get anywhere. He turned to leave and found himself face-to-face with the black bouncer blocking his way out. Crew Cut watched from the shadows, grinning.

Lefty sighed, then rammed his fist in the man's throat. The bouncer issued a strangled gurgle. Lefty then put his knee in the man's groin. He shoved him aside and just about made the door when he felt a hand on his shoulder. He stepped forward fast, whirled and planted his right foot on Crew Cut's cheek.

Not waiting to see the effect, he moved in and slugged the bouncer in the solar plexus, brought his arm back and elbowed the man in the temple. He went down hard. Lefty walked out into the humid late afternoon feeling like he had accomplished little that day but feeling surprisingly satisfied.

Chapter 10

"Is this the only place you know?" Eileen Seager joined Lefty at the bar of The Roaring Twenties, where they'd first met. "Can't we go somewhere a little classier for dinner, like say Steak 'n Shake?"

"What's wrong with this place?"

"First of all, I don't drink. Second, it's loud."

"Fine." He pushed back and tossed a five on the bar. "Steak 'n Shake it is. There's one right down the street."

They walked out of the bar and headed to the iconic St. Louis restaurant. He walked fast on purpose, to ease his stinging pride. But Eileen kept up. The restaurant was only two blocks, but by the time they reached it his black T-shirt clung to his back. When they entered, the blast of frigid air caused him to shiver.

"Two," Eileen said to the hostess, an older lady in black pants, white shirt, and a red bow tie.

She led them to a booth in the back next to a window. The booth had black and red vinyl benches. Eileen and Lefty sat opposite each other. Lefty rested his arm on the metal-framed, white linoleum table.

As soon as the hostess left, Eileen said, "Well? Did you find Angel?"

Lefty glanced over the menu and decided on a Chicago dog. He could feel Eileen's stare, but to her credit she picked up her own menu and looked it over. He put his down. "I found the pimp she used to work for."

"Used to? She's not on the street anymore?"

The hope in her voice pierced his heart. "I don't know where she is."

"What did the pimp say? Is she still alive?"

A teenage girl approached wearing a red Polo shirt, black pants, and black apron. She asked them if they were ready to order. Lefty ordered his Chicago dog and an iced tea. Eileen ordered a double steak burger and a chocolate shake.

When the waitress left, Eileen repeated, "Is she alive?"

"As far as I know." He told her about the abduction.

"Who was this guy?"

"Detective Fischer believes he may have been after someone for a porn flick."

"Who's Detective Fischer?"

"Works on sex crimes for the St. Louis County police department."

"What does he mean?"

"He means this guy is making a movie and wanted someone young and pretty. I don't know for sure. That's my next angle, look into the St. Louis porn scene."

"Oh, Lord. My poor girl." She reached across the table and grabbed Lefty's wrist. "Please, George, find her. Please. I...I don't want her exploited like that, splashed all over the internet."

"I will."

The waitress brought their iced tea and chocolate shake and deposited them on the table.

"How was your day?" Lefty asked after the waitress left.

"Okay. I walked around downtown and the Arch grounds." She unsleeved her straw and then folded the wrapper over and over until it was a tiny square. Then she unfolded it and started over.

"Did you go up in the Arch?"

"No. I'm not a fan of tight spaces or heights."

"Gotcha."

Eileen set the straw wrapper down, then stared at the table as she sipped her shake. Several strands of her hair escaped her ponytail and brushed the glass. Her knuckles around the glass were white. She blinked rapidly.

"I'm sorry I didn't make more progress today."

She looked up, her eyes sad, watery.

"We'll find her, Eileen. We'll find her." Trying to lighten the mood, he added, "But the day wasn't a total wash I got to kick some butt."

"Oh, yeah?" She straightened in her seat. "Are you some kind of tough guy?" She attempted a smile.

"Actually, I used to be. Had quite the reputation around town. It was a bad reputation, at least until I became a cop. I used to fight at the old Kiel Opera House downtown on Market Street. It's now called the Stifel Theatre. Does plays and stuff. The fights have moved mostly to the casinos."

"Boxing?"

"Martial arts."

"Really, you're into martial arts? What kind? I used to do tae kwon do until I lost my leg. Now I do Tai Chi."

"I've done quite a few. I started with mano mano."

"Never heard of it." She sat back, seemed to relax a little.

"It's a Filipino style. Means 'hand-to-hand'."

"Where did you learn that style?"

"The Philippines, obviously." He smiled.

"Obviously. So you lived in the Philippines?"

"My dad was in the Navy. When I was eight he was transferred to Manila. Lived there for five years. I used to get beat up all the time by the locals. As you can see, I'm not that big." He smiled. "My dad enrolled me in a martial arts class."

The waitress brought their food. He was hungry; no lunch that day. So he took a big bite. After swallowing he continued his story. "For five years, I studied mano mano along with Sikaran, which is a kicking style, and Dumog, which is grappling." He shrugged. "I gave that one up. Kind of hard to grapple with one arm."

"Yeah, I know what you mean. Kind of hard to kick with one leg." She smiled, and he felt warmth wash over him.

He continued. "I was both a quick and motivated study then, so I got pretty good."

Eileen ate slowly, listening to him, nodding.

He didn't particularly like talking about himself, but it was distracting her, so he kept going. "When I was thirteen, we moved to Okinawa. There I studied under a brilliant grand master and learned karate, incorporating the Sanchin kata. When I reached eighteen, I left the island and moved to St. Louis, where I had other family. I've studied tae kwon do some and aikido."

She raised her eyebrows.

"The style used by Steven Segal," he said.

"Ah. What made you become a cop?"

"A fighter named Pat Miletich. He did a swing through St. Louis the year before becoming the UFC champion in 1998. He's an Iowa boy, born in Davenport, I think. Anyway, I was good. He was great. Beat me to a pulp. That's when I learned I wasn't going to be a professional."

"But why a cop?"

"The only legal profession I could think where I still might get to beat people up." He grinned. "Hey, I was only twenty-three." He took another big bite of his hot dog, chewed a bit, then spit out the stem of a pepperoncini. After washing the bite down with his iced tea, he said, "Funny thing is, as a cop, I never really beat anyone up. But I have to admit, I felt more alive today than I have in three years, so I want to thank you for insisting I take this case."

She furrowed her eyebrows and asked, "Isn't that what you do? Being a private detective and all?"

"Yeah, that's what I do. But mostly I either spy on people's spouses or I investigate potential insurance fraud, which means spying on people claiming to be hurt. Today was as close to real detective work as I've done in some time. And as bad as it probably sounds, it felt great to beat those two goons up." She said nothing, just watched him, so he added, "I don't normally pick on people, you know, use my skills against them. I don't know, it just invigorated me today."

"Glad I could help. God has a reason for everything."

"Yeah, well, I don't know much about religious stuff, but like I said, thanks for finding me."

They ate in silence for a few minutes.

Eileen asked, "How'd you lose your arm?"

He sighed and looked away, waiting for the usual apology, her telling him he didn't need to talk about it if it was too painful. But then he remembered her own handicap and knew no apology would come. He looked back at her.

"Well? What happened?"

He chuckled.

"What's so funny?"

"Usually, I can look pained or sad when asked that and people back off, but I guess you're not going to do that, are you?"

"No, I'm not." She stuck her leg out. "You can ask me about my leg when you've told me how you lost your arm."

Again, he sighed. "I had been a detective for just over three years. Coming into my own, you know. Really getting into it, getting pretty good."

She nodded.

"We were working a vigilante case. The guy was killing pimps but shot an innocent man one night. That escalated the case. It was a prostitute's father the guy shot. In front of her."

"That's terrible. Did he do anything to her?"

"No. And she wouldn't talk to us, but I had a friend." Lefty paused because his friend, Holly Day, had been murdered shortly after that case. "A friend who was also in the business. Anyway, she got this girl to talk, and we were able to find out why he was killing pimps. That helped us track him down."

Eileen nodded. "That's good."

"We visited his apartment building in South St. Louis. As we were heading up the stairs, he comes running out of his third-floor apartment. Knocked me aside. Pushed my partner down a flight. I chased him. At the first-floor landing I stopped to look for him.."

He paused and breathed deeply. A phantom sensation seized him. An incredible urge to itch his right arm. He hadn't had one of those for some time.

"Go ahead, George. Believe me, it's better to talk about it."

"Maybe for you."

She patted his arm. "Take your time."

He drank a slug of tea. "Anyway, he was waiting for us below. He had this cannon. A forty-four magnum with a nine-inch barrel. Hard to miss with that thing. The slug tore into my shoulder. It shattered the bone and shredded the tendons, so they said. I lost my balance and started to fall. It was only one flight, but still. I reached out and grabbed the railing. Unfortunately, that was with my right arm. It came off. I fell. Landed on my feet. Somehow got my gun out and took a shot. Then I lost consciousness."

He paused. Eileen said nothing, only waited for him to continue.

"They tried to save it, but just couldn't."

"Wow. That's tough."

"I've adapted."

"Did you have someone to help you through this?"

"For a while. I was married. But my wife left after about six months. I guess she just couldn't cope with my deformity."

"You sure it was the deformity?"

"What's that mean?"

"I guess it's my turn," Eileen said. "Remember I told you my husband left me after fifteen years of marriage?" He nodded. "How long had you been married?"

"Eight years."

Eileen looked out the window. A young couple with three kids climbed out of a minivan. "When my husband left me, I thought he left because he couldn't cope with me being an invalid, just like you think. It took me several months, but I finally realized, it wasn't that he couldn't cope with my handicap, he couldn't cope with me. With what I had become."

She looked at him. He looked down and studied his placemat.

"I'd become a bitter, withdrawn person. I'm the one that drove him away. And maybe that's what you did with your wife." She paused and sipped her milkshake. He only stared, sensing she wasn't through, unsure how to cope with her frankness, which felt like a sword going through his gut. "If I'd have stayed the same inside," she continued, "I could have lost all four limbs and my husband would have stuck with me." She shoved her plate aside. "Unfortunately, I figured this out too late. But then, God is in control, and sometimes what we perceive as a major setback, God uses for our growth."

"What's that mean?"

"When my husband left I plunged to the lowest point in my life. I started drinking. Withdrew from everyone. But then God put a friend into my life I would never have had otherwise."

Lefty sipped his tea and stared at her, longing for a shot of something stronger. Someone dropped a dish in the back.

Eileen continued. "I got sick as a dog one night and tried to call my doctor to ask for some antibiotics. This lady answered. Thinking I had reached the doctor's emergency service, I told her what I needed. She told me I had dialed the wrong number. For whatever reason, I broke down and started sobbing." She stirred her straw in her soda and again looked out the window. "Most people probably would have hung up on me. She didn't. And two hours later, I had told her everything. I told her about the cancer in my leg, about losing my leg, about my husband leaving, my drinking, having thoughts of suicide, everything. She listened until I stopped talking. Then she asked me if she could tell me her story."

The waitress walked up to the table and started clearing the dishes.

"Anything else I can get you?" she asked.

"No thanks," Lefty answered. "Just the check."

"Be right back." She left.

Lefty asked Eileen, "What was her story?"

"She had been in a car accident that left her a paraplegic. Her husband lasted about a year before he left her. At her lowest point, she wheeled into a church, where she found Jesus."

"And did He heal her?"

"In a way, yes. And He healed me the same way."

"You're still missing a leg."

"But I have peace and I know where I'm going when I die. And I know all the trials of this life will be nothing compared to the glory of Heaven. What about you, George?"

"What about me?" He fidgeted with his napkin.

"Wouldn't you like peace?"

"Sure. But I don't think religion is what's going to give me peace."

"I'm not talking about religion," Eileen said.

She started to say more, but the waitress reappeared and deposited the check on the table. Lefty reached into his pocket and took out his wallet, balancing it open on the table. Before he could extract a twenty, Eileen snatched the check.

"I'll take care of it. You'll probably charge me for it, anyway." She smiled at him.

He shrugged, closing his wallet and putting it back in his jeans pocket. "I guess this isn't a date, then."

She shook her head. "I'm flattered, but right now the focus needs to be on finding Angel."

"And after that?"

She smiled again, and again he felt a warmth flow through him.

"We'll see. What's your plan now?"

"Like I said, look into the porn scene and also check out this other tip I got." He told her about the buy that Big Eddie had mentioned.

"Be careful," she said.

He shrugged. They both sat in silence for a few minutes. He looked at her, but when she looked at him, he diverted his eyes out the window.

"I should let you get home," she said. "So, you can get an early start."

"Sure."

They sat for another minute in silence, then Eileen pushed back from the table.

"I'll go take care of the check." She walked to the cashier.

He felt a stab of guilt watching her limp away. Lefty lingered at the table. The last question Eileen asked echoed in his brain. Wouldn't he like peace? For so long, martial arts allowed him to achieve a centered peace. But since losing his arm that had not been sufficient. But then he thought, if there is a God, why would He take limbs from decent people? And Eileen was certainly a decent person.

"You going to spend the night here?" Eileen asked. She laid a hand on his shoulder and he thought he could stay there like that for quite some time and be perfectly happy.

"I suppose not." He stood and followed her out the door.

In the parking lot they faced each other in awkward silence. Finally, she said, "Let me know what you find tomorrow."

"I will." Some more awkward silence. "Well, goodnight."

"Goodnight, George." She turned away.

He watched her walk to her car. After unlocking her door, she looked over her shoulder and smiled at him. He smiled back but didn't move until she backed out and drove away. He glanced at his watch. Eight-fifteen. What was he going to do with the rest of his night? On the way to his car, he decided a couple hours at The Roaring Twenties would have to suffice, absent Eileen.

As he drove to the bar, his thoughts bounced back and forth between Eileen and finding her niece.

Chapter 11

Angel yelled in her sleep and startled herself awake. She reached for the rumpled sheet and blanket, kicked down to her feet, as she shivered so hard her teeth chattered. The sheet underneath her was soaked, adding to the chill. Her racing heart thumped in her temples, each beat like someone banging a kettledrum in her ears. She finally managed to grab the blanket and pull it over her, pulling her legs up to her chin. After a minute or so, her shivering subsided enough to yell out.

"Hello! Anyone there? I need water."

Dark in her room. Was it the same day or the next? When was it that Godzilla had held her down and that chick gave her a shot? It had knocked her out, but for how long? What had they given her?

"Hey, I need a drink." She paused. Then louder. "And I need to pee!"

Angel heard low voices from outside her room. She listened intently.

"I'm coming in. Please stay in your bed," said a female voice.

Angel said nothing. Someone unlocked the door, which opened slowly. A wedge of light widened across the room until the door was halfway open. Angel sat up and brought her knees up to her chin and wrapped her arms around them. The overhead lights switched on. Angel squinted and put one arm over her eyes.

"My name is Sara. How are you feeling?"

Angel slowly removed her arm from her eyes, opened them and saw a tall, blonde chick, not the one who had given her a shot. She held a plastic cup with water in one hand and what Angel thought was an opaque white, plastic pitcher in the other. Sara put the pitcher in the corner then handed Angel the cup of water, which she took and gulped down.

"Why am I here?" Angel demanded.

"We're here to help you," the blond chick replied. She smiled. White, straight teeth. She was wearing a pair of tan cargo shorts, a light yellow pullover top, and Adidas brand tennis shoes with dark anklet socks.

"This some kind of porn thing or something? Getting me off the juice to put me in your sick film?"

The woman named Sara shook her head. "Do you need more water?"

"Sure."

Sara backed out and closed the door. Unfortunately, Angel heard the lock turn. In less than a minute, the lock turned again, the door opened, and the blond woman returned with another cup of water. Angel finally figured out that the pitcher wasn't a pitcher. Oh joy, she had to pee in a plastic bottle.

She stretched, rotated, and slipped her legs off the bed until her feet touched the floor. She didn't reach for the cup of water. Sara approached a little closer and extended the cup. Angel started shivering again, wrapping her arms around herself. Sara moved a little closer, paused, then she moved even closer.

Angel stopped shivering and took the cup of water from Sara. For a few seconds, she just looked at the cup. She sprang off the bed and flung the water at Sara, hitting her in the face. Angel tried to shove Sara aside, but Sara managed to grab her arm. With her free hand, Angel scratched Sara's face. The tall blonde shrieked and let go of Angel, who bolted out the door and ran into a brick wall. At least that's what it felt like.

Large, beefy arms encircled her. She felt herself lifted from the floor and carried back into the room.

"You okay, Sara?"

Angel could not see anything with her face crushed against the large man's chest, but she heard Sara's reply.

"I'll be fine. Put her on the bed. I think we can skip any more medication."

She felt herself deposited on the bed. Above her hovered the same giant of a black man that had held her down before so a different chick could give her a shot. She considered trying to run again, but his glare and scowl convinced her otherwise. Instead, she yelled, “I want to leave!”

The two others left the room without saying a word. They closed the door and locked it. At least they left the light on. Must be daytime, then, she reasoned. The doggie door opened and one of them slid in a tray with some kind of sandwich, another apple, and some more water. Angel rolled onto her side, then got up and retrieved the tray.

“I'm not making some dirty movie for you morons. Just let me go.” Silence.

She placed the tray on the nightstand, grabbed the sandwich, and bit into it. Tuna. Actually pretty good. Some sweet relish mixed in. She was famished. In no time, she devoured the sandwich and the apple.

“What about dessert? Do I get a cookie or something?” No reply. And no cookie.

Another bout of shivering hit her, so she curled back up into a ball and waited for it to subside. She'd heard about these guys who make the worst of the porn flicks. They grab girls off the street, clean them up so they're presentable, then promise more drugs if they do the movie. Well, she wasn't doing no freaking movie. And that's when the craving hit.

Half an hour later, her resolve wasn't so strong.

Chapter 12

Sara stared in the mirror and dabbed the scratch with a tissue soaked in peroxide. Her last tetanus shot had been two years ago, so she should be okay there. When the burning started, she winced and watched the little bubbles drive out germs. The scratch didn't appear to be deep enough to need stiches, but it was deep enough she decided to put on a Band-Aid. Once patched up, she walked upstairs to the second level and straight into Rockport's office.

"What happened to you?" Rockport asked.

"The new girl scratched me."

"Her name's Angel."

"Yeah, sure. Right now, I have a hard time calling her that."

Rockport chuckled.

"I'm glad you find this funny." She touched the Band-Aid on her check. "She got me good. Chester had to pull her off me."

"I remember a young girl a few years back who first tried to seduce me, then kicked me in the shin and punched me in the nose."

Sara sighed then collapsed into a leather armchair.

"Her, Chester, that's the one." Rockport pointed at a thin blond with high cheekbones, long legs, and full lips. She wore white, short shorts, fishnet stockings and a black crop top and black, three-inch heels. "Pull over."

Chester pulled the limo to the curb. Rockport pushed a button and the back-passenger side window descended. The girl, who had seen them, immediately walked to the limo.

"Hey, baby, looking for some fun?"

Rockport pushed the door open and the girl climbed in the back seat, then scooted as close to Rockport as she could. She placed one hand on the inside of his thigh and the other behind his neck. He pushed both hands away.

To Chester he said, "Drive." Then, to the girl who looked so uncannily like his daughter, he said, "What's your name?"

"Pleasure."

"Your real name?"

She frowned. "Hey, I want my money up front. You're creeping me out." She looked around, then out the window. "Where are we going?"

"Somewhere safe." Rockport pulled a wallet from his sports jacket's inside pocket and handed her a hundred-dollar bill. "Will that suffice?"

Her seductive smile returned. "Sure. Now, what can I do for you? Nothing too kinky, though."

"Tell me your real name."

Her frown returned, but she said, "Sara. Sara Hanley." Then she affected a strong Southern accent and said, "I'm from Birmingham. Nice to meet you, suh. What's your name?" She smiled big and stuck out her hand.

"Calvin Rockport. Nice to meet you, Sara."

Accent gone, she demanded, "Where are we going?"

"My place. You'll like it. It's in Huntleigh Woods"

"Wow. And what are we going to do there?"

"Be patient. You'll find out."

"Like I said, nothing too kinky. I'm not into that stuff."

"Don't worry, nothing like that."

They rode in silence for the next fifteen minutes. He kept glancing at her, his heart aching. He wanted to reach out and pull her to him and tell her everything was going to be okay, that they'd get by without her mother, his wife.

On Highway 40, traffic streamed by. The intermittent flashes of headlights strobed the inside of the limo. With each flash, Rockport saw another brief flash in his mind, his daughter barely dressed, some nameless tattooed man's hands all over her.

Chester pulled into Rockport's estate in the same neighborhood as one of the Busch sons lived.

"Whoa. This is yours?" asked Sara.

Rockport nodded. Chester opened the door, and Rockport stepped out of the limo. He started to go around to the other side to open her door, when Chester whispered in his ear "What are we going to do with her?"

"Keep her."

"But..."

Rockport nudged past his protesting companion and opened Sara's door.

She slipped out and stood in the driveway staring at the two-story brick house built in a chalet style. Two lions on pedestals framed the front stoop. A light shone through the large porthole window centered on the second floor. She leaned her head back, then side to side.

Rockport just watched her, saying nothing.

"You got a pool?" she asked.

"Yes, I do."

"Let's go skinny dipping." She skipped up the front steps and waited for Rockport.

Chester went ahead and opened the door. She practically ran inside. Rockport followed. Inside, she gaped, head tilted back at the chandelier above her.

"Look at all that glass."

"Crystal, my dear. It's crystal."

"Whoa." She twirled, taking in the massive foyer. The wood floor glistened in the light of the chandelier. Left was the formal dining room. In front of her the carpeted staircase made two turns to the second floor.

"This way." Rockport headed right through an archway, into the sitting room. Sara flew past him.

"Whoa? So...clean." She darted to the middle of the sitting room and did another twirl. "This place is huge. I love the zebra stripes." She sat in one of the zebra-striped chairs with brown leather cushions. She bounced up and down a couple times.

Rockport sat in one of the two white sofas, perpendicular to each other and the chairs. In the middle of the room were three glass tables. On two of them sat crystal bowls. On the bigger one were three crystal candles and a light blue tinted crystal statue of what looked like a tree in winter.

Rockport asked, "Can I get you a soda or something?"

She cocked one eyebrow at him and frowned. "Seriously? A soda? Got anything stronger?"

He almost answered no as he didn't keep liquor in the house, but then remembered his plan. Instead he said, "Let me look."

He walked to a cabinet at the far end of the living room and opened it, retrieving a syringe, a spoon, a rubber tourniquet, and a small jar with crystal powder, hoping he guessed right. His friend at the St. Louis County Police department had told him heroin was back in vogue and the prostitutes' drug of choice these days. He deposited the paraphernalia on the larger glass table. Sara was leaning back with her feet on the table tossing a yellow pillow up and catching it.

"Well, well, look at this. A Franklin and some brown sugar." She switched to her heavy Southern accent again. "Aren't you accommodating to little ole me." She swung her legs down and batted her eyes at him, then patted the cushion next to her. "I'm sure you could squeeze in with me."

Instead, he sat back on the sofa, then picked up the spoon and scooped some of the powder onto it, then fished a lighter from his jacket pocket. She carefully took the spoon from him.

"I'll hold it."

He flicked the lighter on and held it under the spoon. As soon as the powder was liquefied, she handed him the spoon. Like an experienced nurse, she wrapped the tourniquet around her upper arm, then palpitated her vein in the crock of her elbow. She then picked up the syringe and sucked up most of the liquid.

"How pure?" she asked.

"Pretty good." He wanted her to shoot it all.

And she did. Then she collapsed back onto the couch to wait for the effect. "Now, don't you be taking advantage of little ole me." She winked at him and lifted up her top to expose her breasts in a lacy black bra.

He watched her face. She smiled. Her eyes grew heavy. Then she frowned and tried to sit up but could not. A few seconds later, her eyes shut tight and she breathed heavy, unconscious. Rockport pulled his cell phone from his inside jacket pocket and texted Chester.

A minute later Chester entered the sitting room and the two of them picked up Sara and took her upstairs to a small room right above the sitting room. They put Sara on a twin bed. Rockport removed her heels then gently put a light blanket on her. Chester left the room, but Rockport stayed and just stared at her face for several minutes.

He whispered, "I'm so sorry, Carolyn, that I wasn't there for you. I'm so sorry."

He left the room and closed the door.

Rockport stood outside the locked door.

From behind the door, Sara tentatively said, "Hey, is anyone out there? Hello. Open the door, will ya?"

Rockport wrapped his hand around the doorknob. He must have made enough noise to alert her.

"Hey. Let me out of here."

Rockport felt the doorknob vibrate in his hand.

"I know you're out there. Open the door."

He opened the door and entered the small, windowless room. Sara backed away toward the twin bed. She bumped into the nightstand.

"What did you give me last night? That wasn't brown sugar."

"It was a sedative."

"What do you want with me?" She leaned to the side a bit, looking beyond him, gauging her chances of running, he figured.

"I want to help you."

"Help me? By knocking me out and locking me up?"

"I'm sorry about that. You need to stay in here a few days."

Her eyes widened. "What?"

"For your own good, you'll need to stay in here. We'll bring you food and water."

"Look, buddy, I don't know what you're into—"

"And we'll have a doctor here to help you with the withdrawal."

She charged him and tried to dodge around him. He grabbed her arm. She wrenched it free, but he got his other hand around her and wrapped her in a bear hug.

"Let me go! Help! Help me!"

They had not taken her shoes from her, a mistake Rockport would only make that once. She kicked back and down, driving her three-inch heel into his shin.

The pain shot through him. He lost his grip on her and she wriggled free, then turned around and slugged him in the nose. For an instant, he only saw bright white. Almost immediately, he tasted blood. His vision cleared enough to watch Sara turn away from him and run directly into a wall, a wall made of flesh standing six feet five, weighing over three hundred pounds.

Chester bear hugged Sara and pushed her back into the room. As he drew even with Rockport, he released one beefy arm and shoved the older man out the door. He then pushed Sara to the bed and quicker than anyone would believe, darted out of the room and closed the door.

Seconds later, the door shook violently as Sara must have launched herself at it. She screamed. "Let me out, you sons of bitches. You can't keep me here. Let me out!"

Chester led Rockport down the hall to the bathroom and attended to his nose, which was still bleeding.

"Spirited, isn't she?" Rockport chuckled, wincing at the pain, both in his ankle and on his face.

"What are we going to do with her?" Chester asked.

"Keep her in there until she goes through withdrawal. Then we'll try to reason with her, explain to her what we're trying to do."

"And if she doesn't want any part of it?"

"We'll cross that bridge when we get there."

They never reached that bridge.

Rockport smiled at Sara.

"What are you smiling at?"

"Do you remember that first day?"

"Yeah, I remember. However, most of those first couple months are pretty hazy."

"Withdrawal is tough."

He gazed out the window. A catbird perched in the magnolia tree. Several new blooms had opened overnight. At least something liked the heat. "Especially since I didn't really know what to say or do with you." He sipped his orange juice. "Not only did you have to go through all the physical stuff but you were scared and had no one to talk to. It would—"

"Enough already. I'll talk to her when she wakes up. I have to do the initial interview, anyway." Sara pushed up out of her chair.

"You have such compassion, Sara." He grinned at her.

"I hate you, Rockport."

He chuckled. "I doubt that very much. I think you love me more than you'd ever admit."

As she left his study, she said over her shoulder, "Sometimes I wonder why."

He chuckled again, then sighed deeply and gazed back out the window, feeling the ghost of his daughter sitting on his lap, hearing her laugh and seeing her point at a cardinal or a blue jay in the magnolia tree. Another deep sigh, then he pulled himself out of his painful memories and focused on his computer screen.

Chapter 13

The only thing hotter than a St. Louis July afternoon was enjoying that same afternoon standing in the middle of a blacktop road with dust from the gravel shoulder blowing all around. Heat shimmered over the road. Lefty leaned on his white 2005 Nissan Sentra and surveyed the landscape. About fifty yards east were two warehouses made of sheet metal on the other side of concrete road barriers. One warehouse was perpendicular to both the road he stood on and the road on the other side of the warehouse. The other warehouse was parallel to the roads, that one close to one hundred feet long. He knew from studying online maps that another warehouse paralleled that one behind it. A diesel truck rumbled down the road from the north and turned into the fertilizer plant behind him. Beyond the fertilizer plant the Mississippi River flowed wide and dirty. He also knew from studying the satellite images that the only access road to the warehouses was that road on the other side of them. One way in, one way out for vehicles, making security easier. He wondered if they'd have guards on the backside, watching the road he stood on. He hoped not.

A small plane gained altitude over the warehouse. What was called the St. Louis Downtown Airport was about two and a half miles farther east. Another convenience, he figured. The airport catered only to private and charter planes.

Behind him, at the fertilizer plant, a train clanked and screeched as it jockeyed the next hopper car into position. Noisy place, even on a Saturday, but he assumed come Sunday night, the place would be deserted.

He debated whether to leave his car and walk the fifty yards of long, brown grass to the concrete barriers or to drive the quarter mile on the blacktop road, then back the quarter mile of the gravel road that fronted the warehouses in order to check out the other side for doors. In this weather, easy debate. He climbed back in his car, pulled a U-turn, and head to the gravel access road. It wasn't so much laziness, it was more the safety of being in the car so he could leave quickly, if needed.

On the gravel access road, the first parking lot he passed—fronting a series of smaller buildings, also metal—was half full. The next parking lot was empty except for rows of abandoned semi-trailers. When he arrived at the warehouse perpendicular to the road, he figured that would be where the sale would be held. Just left of the building's middle was a section built out that was large enough to house offices. It had a double door with heavily tinted glass. On both sides of this area were large overhead doors with loading docks.

He pulled forward until he was even with the end of the warehouse and was pleased to see a door—and even more pleased that there was no reinforcement plate around the doorknob. Getting in would not be technically difficult, depending on the guard arrangement.

He pulled a little farther forward. Several waste containers lined the back of the building, but he didn't see any doors. No one was around that he could see. One car was in the parking lot of the waste treatment plant to his left.

Leaving the car running, he got out and walked between the warehouses, confirming no doors on the backside of the one of interest. He reached the edge of the concrete. A grass strip, then a mostly dirt ditch led down to two sets of railroad tracks, another grass strip, a gravel road, then the cement barriers he'd seen earlier. Nothing he wouldn't be able to cross Sunday night, but also no real cover between the blacktop road and the buildings, other than the cement barriers. Sweat ran down his back as the sun beat on him. He returned to his car.

As he was climbing into the Sentra, he glanced back up the road in the direction he'd come and noticed a large black car a couple hundred yards from him. It was too far to see the license plate. He got in his own car and pulled the door shut and watched the black car in his rearview mirror. The black car started to move slowly toward him. He moved forward. A ten-foot chain link fence guarded the entrance to the waste treatment plant, and as he moved farther forward, the distance between the road and the fence lessened. The black car stopped even with the warehouse he'd been looking at.

What he really wanted to do was circle around and return on the same road he was on behind the black car, but that wasn't possible from where he was. He'd already passed the one crossroad, now behind the black car. The only option he had was to swing around and drive toward the black car.

At the end of the road, he came to a parking lot that seemed to be a graveyard for hopper cars and semi-trailer trucks. Maybe the buildings belonged to the fertilizer plant across the railroad tracks, but he had no way of knowing. No signs. His only clue was the truck loading station. He had plenty of room to turn around in the parking lot, which he did. Now facing north, back toward the black car, he noticed it was parallel to the gap between the warehouses, where he'd looked for back doors.

He sat a minute and watched. No movement from the black car. He started moving forward. The black car turned right on the road between the buildings and backed out, pointing itself the same way Lefty moved. He slammed the accelerator down, moving fast toward the black car. He closed the gap to maybe two hundred feet.

The black car, a limousine, started widening the gap, spewing gravel dust behind it. The limo skipped the first right turn, then angled right at the next road.

Lefty reached the same road and did the same.

The limo, now looking no bigger than a Matchbox, continued widening the gap. At Illinois Route 3, the limo turned right, going south, toward Cahokia and eventually, Lefty assumed, Interstate 255.

Lefty slowed down. No way he was catching whoever that was. He turned right on Route 3 but stayed within the speed limit on the way home.

He had managed to memorize the first three characters of the license plate before gravel dust obscured it. He'd have his good buddy Lieutenant Pratt run him a list.

Chapter 14

"Is the car still behind us?" Rockport asked through the open partition in the limo.

"Nope. I don't see it," answered Chester.

"Turn left on Queeny. While we're here, might as well check on the plane."

Chester made a fast turn onto Queeny Avenue, curved to the right onto Falling Springs Drive, then made another hard left onto Curtis Steinberg Drive.

"Any sign of that other car?" asked Rockport.

"Nope."

The limo reached the entrance to the St. Louis Downtown Airport, and Chester turned in. They passed several large, open hangars and curved around the north side of the airport until they reached a series of small hangars.

"Pull into our hangar, Chester. Let's wait a little while to make sure whoever that was clears out."

"Sure."

"In the meantime, I'll try to find out who it was." He pulled his cell phone from his jacket pocket and found his St. Louis County police contact in his contact list. Detective Lisa Warren of the St. Louis County Special Investigations unit answered the phone.

"It's Rockport."

"Calvin, how are you today? Staying out of trouble?"

"Define trouble."

"Never mind. I don't want to know."

Rockport chuckled. "And how are you, today, Lisa?"

"Peachy. Actually, we just brought in a sleazebag that was distributing child pornography, so all in all, not a bad day so far. Sucks working on Saturday, but crime seems to never take a weekend. What's up?"

"I need a license plate number run and any information you have on the owner."

"Fire away."

Rockport told Detective Warren the number he'd seen on the small car when it had gotten close enough to read. "It was some type of Nissan, I believe."

"I'll get back to you in five to ten."

"Thanks, Lisa, I really appreciate it."

"Glad to help, Calvin. Stay out of trouble."

"You know that's not happening."

She laughed and hung up.

Rockport climbed out of the limo and started walking around his Cessna Citation M2. Chester also got out and positioned himself at the hangar entrance, surveying the road. Rockport pretended to inspect his jet, but his mind wandered back to when he'd first met Detective Lisa Warren.

"What do you mean, you can't do anything?" Calvin Rockport squared off with the burly St. Louis County detective in the lobby of the main station in Clayton. Slightly behind and to the right stood a woman detective. Rockport knew neither one of their names.

"Sir, I understand your frustration and your pain. But your daughter is eighteen."

"So what! She's missing." Rockport's face grew hot. He clenched and unclenched his fists.

"Sir, without evidence of foul play, we can't go looking for adults that have decided to disappear."

"She didn't decide anything, you idiot." Rockport stepped closer, so close their chests were millimeters apart.

The taller detective did not back away until the woman beside him, probably ten years his senior, spoke. "Detective Johnson, I'll take this. Please, go back upstairs."

Johnson frowned, glanced over his shoulder and saw that the senior detective behind him meant what she said. He relaxed his pose and backed up a couple steps, then turned and walked briskly to the elevator.

The woman detective watched until the elevator doors had closed, then turned to Rockport. "I'm Detective Lisa Warren, Mr. Rockport. Please, let's go into a conference room and talk."

They moved to a conference room off to their left. The windows looked out onto a small park where several people sat eating their lunches that noon on a Wednesday in late spring.

"Please, have a seat." She waved her hand, sort of like a game show hostess.

Detective Warren was tall, about five-ten, Rockport figured. She had straight brown hair, full lips, brown, piercing eyes, and a full figure. Her demeanor was gentle, but Rockport sensed strength beneath the calmness. She wore a light gray pantsuit and powder blue shirt. No jewelry that he could see. He pulled out a high-backed chair and sat.

She moved around the table and sat opposite him. "Do you have a recent photo of your daughter?"

"I thought you couldn't do anything because she's an adult." He felt bad about the heavy sarcasm and bitter tone, but just couldn't help it.

"What Detective Johnson said is officially true. But I have a personal reason for working sex crimes, so I want to help." She held his gaze for a few seconds. "So do you have a picture?"

Rockport pulled out his wallet, extracted a high school senior picture of Carolyn, and gave it to the detective. "And may I ask what that reason is?"

She paused, looked at the picture, then swallowed audibly and visibly. "My older sister was abducted her junior year of high school and forced into prostitution." She stared hard at Rockport. "She died of a heroin overdose at age twenty-three."

"I'm very sorry."

"Don't be. Just understand that I know what you're going through."

He nodded. "So, what you're doing is unofficial?"

"Yes, sir. But believe me, I'll give it all that I can."

"I do believe you. And if you need anything, let me know."

He stood and walked to the window. A bicyclist in tight, black cycle pants zipped by. Several other people strolled along the sidewalk. Everyone seemed content, happy because of the nice weather, oblivious to his problems. "I may not have been the father I should have been. I certainly wasn't the husband I should have been. But, one thing I did, and do very well, Detective." He faced her. "I make money. And I make important friends. So, again, if you need anything, let me know."

She nodded, stood, and stuck out her hand. He shook it.

"Let me read over the report you filed, then let's get together tomorrow night for dinner. I'm sure I'll have a lot of questions about your daughter."

"It's a date."

Thus began four years of collaboration between Calvin Rockport and Detective Lisa Warren. A collaboration that did not end when they found Rockport's daughter dead from a heroin overdose.

"Boss man, your phone is ringing," Chester said loudly over his shoulder.

"Huh?" Then Rockport felt the vibration and heard the siren, his ring tone for Detective Lisa Warren. He answered. "Yes, Lisa, what did you find?"

Instead of answering his question, Detective Warren asked her own. "What did you do, Calvin, that would have a private detective looking into you?"

"What do you mean?"

"The plate you gave me belongs to one George Bruder. Used to be a man in blue. Worked for us. Made detective, then three years later went out on disability."

"What happened to him?"

"Lost his arm as a result of a shooting."

"And now he's private?"

"Has a license, anyway," Detective Warren said.

"Hmm."

Rockport thought for a few seconds. Detective Warren remained silent. The roar of twin turbos filtered into the hangar as a plane taxied out toward the runway. "Can you do something else for me?"

"Probably."

He chuckled. "When I get back, I'll email you a list of our current residents. Can you tell me if any of them have showed up on a missing person's report?"

"That I can do."

Chapter 15

As Sara descended one of the semi-circular staircases in Rockport's house, Rockport and Chester entered the front door. She reached the foyer and Rockport passed her, ascending the spiral staircase on the other side. She followed him, getting her steps in at least. He headed toward his study. Once there, Rockport immediately sat at his desk and began punching at the keyboard of his computer. She watched for a little while, as always amused at his hunt-and-peck technique, though amazed, as usual, at how proficient he was using only the index finger of each hand to type.

When she had enough entertainment for one day, she said, "I'm going to check on Angel. Where were you?"

"Scoping out an auction site."

"Antiques or girls?"

"What do you think?"

"It's fifty-fifty with you. Everything in this house was made around the time of Louis XIV, so I'm not sure."

"You're a funny girl. Not antiques."

"When?"

"Tomorrow night."

"Well, be careful. Those aren't exactly your typical socialites."

"Thanks for the advice."

Sara winked. "Anytime, old man." She started to leave.

"And by the way, the taste in furniture was my wife's. I just never replaced it."

"At least the living room is somewhat modern."

Sara walked down to the basement and approached the one locked room. The doors were open on the two others, currently vacant, but after tomorrow, Sara figured, one more would be occupied. She put her ear to the door and listened. Not a sound. She knocked softly.

"It's your house, come on in," Angel said.

"Are you going to behave?" Sara asked.

"Are you going to stick me with anything?"

"I haven't stuck you yet."

"Don't be funny. You know what I mean."

"It's just me. No needles."

"Then I suppose I'll behave. I'm sure Godzilla is with you anyway."

Sara opened the door, slipped in, and closed the door behind her. "Actually, it's just me. And if you've forgotten, I'm Sara."

Angel was sitting on the bed, leaning against the wall, feet out straight. Sara sat at the foot of the bed.

"How are you feeling?"

"Crappy."

"It'll be that way for a few days."

Angel said nothing for a minute, just stared at Sara. She narrowed her eyes and scrunched her brows. Then she asked, "How long you keeping me here?"

"That depends."

"On what? And why are you keeping me here?"

Sara moved further up the bed and smiled at Angel. "Please believe me, we're here to help you."

"Yeah, right. By locking me up and sticking me with needles full of God knows what." Her eyes blazed. She squeezed her fists closed, taking a handful of sheet in each.

"Not only does God know, but I know and I'll tell you." Sara smiled. Angel continued to frown. "The pill you didn't take is Suboxone. The shot was methadone. I'd really prefer you take the pill. Less side effects and not addictive. Both are to help you through your withdrawal."

"I don't want help through withdrawal. I want a fix."

"And that's why you're locked up."

Angel crossed her arms and brought her knees up to her chin. Her demeanor deflated. She no longer looked like the streetwise hooker she thought she was, but a lost little child.

"I just want to go home."

"Really? Is that really where you want to go?"

Angel slowly shook her head. "No, I can't go there."

"Why not?"

"I just can't." She dipped her head and squeezed herself into an even tighter ball. Sara reached out and stroked her hair.

"Right now, this is the safest place for you."

Angel looked up, her eyes glistening. "And where is here? Where am I?"

"You're in a big house in Huntleigh Woods."

"I...I don't know where that is. I've only been here a few months. This still St. Louis?"

"Yup. Real nice neighborhood."

Angel put her head down again and rocked slightly back and forth.

Sara again stroked her hair. "If it means anything, I know exactly what you're going through."

"Yeah, right. Did you have to run away from home then have sex with sweaty, disgusting men for money?"

"Yup."

Angel looked up, her eyes wide. "Really?"

"I was a hooker just like you."

"You from some little cow town, too? Coming here to the big city to get away from a bad scene? Thinking it can't be that hard to live on your own?"

Sara hesitated, deciding if she wanted this conversation to go where it was going. But Rockport had told her if she wanted to get close to someone, she had to make herself vulnerable, she had to open herself up. What the heck, she thought. Why not? "Not quite. I lived in a big city and was in a lot of bad scenes."

"Where are you from?"

"Born and raised in Chicago. Didn't come here until I was sold."

"Sold? You were sold?" Angel uncrossed her arms and straightened. "I thought slavery was outlawed."

"May be illegal, hon, but it still goes on."

"I don't understand."

"Like I said, I was a prostitute. I spent six years on the streets."

"Wow, you don't look that old."

She laughed. "I first started hooking when I was fourteen."

"Oh. Why?"

"Like you, I was strung out. Had to get the money to pay for my habit. And I'd gotten used to having a little money."

"You have a rich family?"

"Hardly. I was abandoned by my mother when I was two. Apparently, I was a terrible two-year-old. And a terrible three-year-old and four-year-old. I was a terrible child, period. I was bounced from foster home to foster home. Never stayed anywhere for more than six months. The families just couldn't deal with me."

"You're very pretty."

Sara wondered where that came from. "Thanks. And I learned to use my looks and body real early."

"Oh? What do you mean?"

Sara again hesitated. Did she really want to go this far? But Angel stared at her, not even blinking. She had the girl's full attention. Sara sucked in a deep breath. "When I was twelve, I seduced the man living next door. He was married, had three kids. After we did it, I threatened to tell his wife and maybe even the cops unless he gave me money. He paid me quite a bit before I was shuffled off to another foster home." Sara looked up at the ceiling, then back at Angel.

"And?"

"Finally, when I was fourteen, the father at my last foster home tried to abuse me. That's when I hit the streets. Once there, some slick-talking dude got me hooked on meth, then got me hooking for him. I graduated to heroin not long after."

Angel hung her head.

Sara touched Angel's arm. "Something I said hit home, didn't it? Sounded familiar?"

Angel nodded and again drew her legs up and buried her face in her knees. Sara waited a few minutes, but Angel offered nothing else.

Sara said, "Four years ago, my pimp in Chicago sold me to Big Eddie. You hear of him?"

Angel shook her head, still not looking at Sara.

"Who's your pimp?" Sara asked.

Angel mumbled something.

Sara stroked her hair again. "I didn't hear you, hon. Who'd you say?"

Finally, Angel looked up. "Keyshawn."

"Ah. Keyshawn Williams?"

Angel nodded.

"He's a worm."

"You know Keyshawn?" Angel asked.

"I know most of the players in this town, hon."

"Who was your pimp?"

"Big Eddie himself."

"Who's he?"

"Keyshawn's boss. Big Eddie runs three pimps and owns a lot of the girls in this town."

Angel put her head down again, rocked a bit then peeked at Sara. "They're going to hurt me when they get me back, aren't they?"

"Who's going to hurt you?"

"Keyshawn."

"They won't get you back, not if you stay here until you're clean."

Angel sat back again, her eyes blazing. "Then what? Where am I supposed to go?"

Sara squeezed Angel's leg. "One step at a time, hon. Let's get you clean first."

"But what if they find me?"

Sara smiled. "You've seen Chester, haven't you?"

"You mean Godzilla?"

"That's the one."

"Yeah, I suppose, but still..." She dipped her head and studied her hands for a bit, then looked hard at Sara. "How did you get clean?"

"Stayed here."

"How long you been here?"

"Four years."

"Why?"

"Nowhere else to go, I guess. And I want to help others. Figure I owe that much."

"Why?"

Sara took a deep breath. This was always the hard part for her. "Jesus Christ paid a debt for me. He saved my rotten, filthy soul. I figure the least I can do is try to help other girls like you."

"Jesus? You mean church stuff?"

"Sort of. It's not just about religion—"

Angel groaned and leaned forward, clutching her stomach. "Ohhhh. I think I'm going to puke."

Sara shot off the bed, grabbed the plastic waste can in the corner, and brought it over to Angel, just as she spewed out oatmeal and pieces of apple. At least she'd eaten her breakfast. After several dry heaves, she curled up in a ball on her bed. Sara stayed about ten minutes, stroking her hair, rubbing her back with one hand. With the other, she sent a text to Marsha, one of the other girls, telling her to get a pill and hypo ready.

When Marsha appeared, Sara leaned over Angel and said softly into her ear, "You want the pill or do we have to stick you again?"

Angel mumbled, "I'll take the pill." Then added softly, "Just make it go away."

Sara helped Angel get her head up enough. Marsha handed her a Suboxone pill and a paper cup with water. Angel swallowed the pill and handed back the half-full cup, then curled into a ball, groaning softly. Sara stayed with Angel for a few minutes, stroking her hair until the young woman faded into a restless sleep.

Chapter 16

Rockport looked up from his computer screen when Sara walked into his study. Every time he saw the long, lean, stunningly gorgeous young assistant his heart both ached and swelled. Ached with longing for his own daughter, so much like Sara in looks, though nothing like her in demeanor and personality. His heart swelled with pride, not in himself, but in his God, who gave him the patience and perseverance to never give up on Sara even though there had been many times he wanted to just let her go and never see her again.

Sara collapsed into a leather armchair and let out a long sigh.

Rockport remarked, "Spent some time with Angel, did you?"

Sara nodded. "I think she trusts me now."

Rockport nodded.

Sara added, "You know, something you told me actually worked."

"And why do you sound so surprised?"

"'Cause half the crap you say is B.S." Sara smiled, though, when she said that.

"And what nugget of truth did you put into action?"

"I pretty much gave Angel my life story."

"Oh, that poor girl."

"Funny, old man. Real funny." They both laughed. "She had a bad cramp, but on the bright side, she took the Suboxone on her own. I didn't get a lot out of her other than she doesn't want to return where she came from. My guess is there's abuse there. And she worked for Keyshawn."

"That I knew. Who her pimp was. He was there when we grabbed her."

"Calvin! Why did you do that? Now he knows your face."

"He knows Chester's fist even better."

Sara chuckled. "Still, it makes me nervous that Keyshawn saw you."

Rockport waved her off. His cell phone rang. He glanced at the caller ID. "I need to take this. You can stay if you want."

Sara shook her head, pushed up, and left the room.

He pushed the green answer button. "Lisa, what did you find out?"

"That's what I like about you, Calvin. You just love small talk."

"I'm sorry, Lisa. How have you been for the last hour?"

"Very funny. None of your girls show up on any missing persons reports. But you know two of them are eighteen or older, so there could have been inquiries, but they wouldn't necessarily be in the system."

"Thanks for checking."

"I did find one thing interesting."

"Oh?"

"Angel Atkins has an aunt who works for the Iowa Highway Patrol. I called them to talk to her, see if I could get her to reveal anything, and found out she took a leave of absence. I then did a check and found some credit card charges here in St. Louis. She's in town, Calvin. You might want to touch base with her."

"Not until we understand the relationship. I don't want to put Angel back into the situation that drove her away."

"Understood, but she may be the one who hired Bruder. And I did a little more checking on him. If he can pull his face out of a bottle, he's a bulldog."

"You have had a busy hour, haven't you?"

"And that's just the stuff I did for you, not to mention my real job."

Calvin chuckled. "Thanks, Lisa. This is real helpful."

"Be careful, Calvin. I can't really protect you if others find out."

"I understand." He hung up.

Chapter 17

"Are you sure?" Lefty asked.

He and Eileen faced each other in the parking lot of Dawson's Sports Bar and Grill, where she'd met him for dinner to get caught up. A couple steps beyond a dive, Dawson's did have wonderful hamburgers. Cheap, too.

"Yes. I'll be fine. Call me tomorrow night when you get home. I don't care how late it is."

A hefty man wearing a neon yellow T-shirt stumbled out of Dawson's and shouted over his shoulder, "And tell that other guy he can kiss my butt too." He then staggered toward the other end of the full parking lot.

"It's really no trouble, and with that limo today, there may be people who know we're looking for Angel who don't want her found."

"I appreciate your offer, George, but I'm driving straight to the hotel."

While his offer to see Eileen to her hotel room included not-so-honorable motives, he was concerned about the new unknown player.

She turned to leave. "Goodnight, George."

"Goodnight." He watched her until she got in her car, an older Impala, backed out and left the parking lot. By his amazing powers of deduction, he deduced the car was not a rental and she'd driven to St. Louis from Iowa.

He then proceeded to the opposite side of the parking lot, the same side as the loud drunk. Just before he climbed into his

Nissan, he noticed a flash of orange light from a dark Mustang parked across the street in the lot of a bank. He stared several seconds trying to see inside the Mustang. Maybe it had been a reflection of a passing car, a cigarette, or something else.

He got in and drove out of the lot. South on Lindbergh to Tesson Ferry Road, then Interstate 270. Just before entering the interstate, he checked his rearview mirror and noticed a dark Mustang behind him. He'd never lose the tail on the highway with his heap of junk, so at the last second he veered right and stayed on Tesson Ferry.

The Mustang followed.

Lefty drove a couple blocks, did a hard right turn, accelerated, then another fast turn into an alley between stores. The Mustang followed. Just before reaching the end of the alley, he stopped his car and jumped out. The black Mustang with no front license plate stopped, idled a few seconds then backed up fast, weaving slightly. When it reached the other end of the alley, it backed out into the street, burned some rubber and took off west.

Lefty was pretty sure he'd seen two men in the car, one white and the other black. His uneasy feeling about Eileen increased. He just might have to pay a visit to Keyshawn and his goons and set them straight.

But tonight, he had Pratt's list of license plates to look over.

Chapter 18

When Angel woke that morning, she thought it was Sunday. The first thing she noticed was the clothes on the dresser. They had not been there when she'd gone to sleep. Black slacks and a cream-colored pullover top. They fit well. The neckline was too high for her tastes, but they were clean and beat the pajamas she'd been wearing for several days.

As soon as she'd dressed, Sara entered. "Good morning."

"Morning," Angel replied.

"You clean up quite nicely."

"Kinda plain."

Sara laughed then gestured to Angel to follow her. Angel followed without hesitation because it was the first time she'd been allowed to leave the room since she'd arrived. On the way down the hall Angel noticed two other rooms like hers, the doors open, unoccupied.

Sara led Angel up a set of stairs. Then she held Angel by the arm and led her through a hallway, then through the kitchen and into an open room.

Angel glanced left and saw a foyer and the front door. A rose-tinted chandelier hung from the high ceiling. A dining table was pushed against the far wall next to a black framed glass cabinet holding crystal goblets and decanters. Near the wall to her right was a podium and behind it stood Godzilla, who Angel remembered was named Chester.

The big dude wore a black suit, maroon pinstriped shirt, white tie and white shoes. He looked like the movie version of a pimp.

His head was bent, and his hands were clasped together, his lips moving rapidly. Eight other girls, all dressed in black slacks and cream-colored pullover tops, sat in white padded dining chairs with circular backs arranged in three rows of four facing Chester. A chorus of babble echoed through the rearranged dining room.

"What's this?" Angel asked.

"One of the freebie services this fine accommodation offers," Sara replied. Angel arched her eyebrows, so Sara added, "Church. Every Sunday morning before breakfast."

"Church?" Angel didn't try to hide the distaste in her voice.

"It's a requirement, hon. I take it you didn't go to church at home."

"I don't even know where a church is at home."

"I know the feeling. I felt the same way the first time I attended a church service with Mr. Rockport."

"What changed?" Angel tried to back out of the room, calculating her chances of getting to the front door.

But Sara held her arm firmly. "Saved by the blood of Jesus, hon. I promise, it won't hurt."

Angel stopped pulling against Sara as Chester had looked up and smiled at them. Sara led her to two empty chairs in the second row.

Angel asked, "Who are these girls?"

"Residents. Like you."

"You kidnapped them, too?"

"Kidnapping is a bit harsh."

"True, though."

Sara shrugged. "It's a matter of perspective. Go ahead, ask them if they're here against their will."

Angel sat in an empty chair next to a striking African American girl who looked like she was in her twenties. She had long, straight black hair, bright, round eyes, and full lips. Sitting she was about the same height as Angel, but she noticed the girl's legs extended way under the chair in front of her.

"Hi, I'm Angel."

The black girl turned and smiled, then glanced at Sara, who still stood, towering above Angel. Bad enough when Angel was standing, as Sara was a good four or five inches taller.

"I'm Amanda," the black girl said. She stuck her hand out and Angel grasped it. Her grip was light, her hands clammy.

When Angel released Amanda's hand, she softly asked, "Can I ask you something?"

"Sure."

Angel leaned into Amanda and whispered in her ear, "Are you here against your will?"

Amanda hesitated, and Angel didn't miss the glance up to Sara, who nodded. There's no way she had heard what Angel said, but maybe she'd guessed.

"I'm here 'cause I need to be," Amanda replied.

In her normal voice, Angel followed up with, "But can you leave whenever you want?"

This time with no hesitation and no glance at Sara, Amanda replied, "I could, but I'd be right back where I came from. And that ain't good."

Sara sat next to Angel. "Amanda has been with us for almost a year."

"Are you from St. Louis?" Angel asked.

"Sort of. I growed up in East St. Louis, just across the river in Illinois."

"I know the place." She added, "That's where Keyshawn works."

"You knows Keyshawn?" Amanda's eyes widened and she frowned.

Angel nodded. "He was my pimp."

"Mine, too. He's a mean, dirty son-of-a—"

"Careful, Amanda," Sara interrupted.

Amanda looked down and muttered, "Sorry. I just gets so angry when I think of...well you know."

Sara reached around Angel and rubbed Amanda's shoulder. "I get it, girl. I get it."

Amanda looked up at Angel and said with conviction, almost fervor in her voice, "If you here, then you needs to be here."

Angel nodded. "Can I ask you something else?"

"Sure, anything."

"How old are you?"

Sara whispered, "Tell the truth, hon, not what you told the customers."

Amanda smiled. "I always told the men I was seventeen."

"Why, cause they liked them young?" asked Angel.

"No, cause they felt less guilty. I'm only fifteen."

Angel just stared.

After a few seconds, Amanda said, "I been on the street since I was twelve."

"Whoa." Angel turned her attention to Chester when he spoke.

"Good morning ladies, and to you, too, Mr. Rockport," Chester said in a booming, well-enunciated voice.

Angel glanced over her right shoulder and saw the older man who had brought her here, sitting in a chair in the back row, next to a very young girl with long red hair and a face full of freckles. Angel envied the girl's freckles and her cute face. The girl wore the same black slacks and cream top. Angel searched her for any signs of fear but saw none. She smiled and said something to the older man. He nodded and patted the girl's knee, then looked at Angel and smiled and nodded to her. Angel turned away and re-focused on Chester, wondering if things were as Sara had explained them.

The large man said, "Ladies. And I use that term sincerely, though some of you may not feel like ladies." He paused and scanned the small group.

Angel looked down at her hands folded in her lap. She then looked over at Amanda, who stared intently at Chester. Angel found it hard to believe Godzilla was a preacher.

"Many of you are sitting there asking yourself why you are here."

That's me, thought Angel. You got that right, big boy.

"Asking yourself why you need to hear what this big, bald man has to say. Thinking you got it all together." He stretched out the word all. "Thinking you are on the road to recovery. You can beat what's inside you all by yourself." He raised a meaty arm and pointed to each one of the ten girls, even to Mr. Rockport, Angel noticed. Then he lowered his arm and shook his head. "That is just what the devil wants you to think. That is what the evil one is whispering in your ear. Because the deceiver knows you are weak. But he also knows how desperately you want to be normal."

Angel thought she was normal. What was this dude implying?

"And even worse than that, the evil one knows you're about to hear God's Word. And if you have God's Word in you, there is nothing the devil can do to you." He pounded his hand on the podium. "Nothing. For with God's Word, you can put on the armor of God to protect you from the evil one. Stand, therefore, having fastened on the belt of truth, and having put on the breastplate of righteousness, and as shoes for your feet, having put on the readiness given by the gospel of peace. In all circumstances"—again, stretching out all—"take up the shield of faith, with which you can extinguish all the flaming darts of the evil one, and take the helmet of salvation. Do you ladies have the helmet of salvation? If not, you need to pray to the Lord and accept his gift of grace." Again, he paused and looked each person in the eye.

Angel glanced down and stared at her hands.

"Take the helmet of salvation, and the sword of the Spirit, which is the Word of God. The Word of God is your only weapon, ladies. You must wield it with faith and submission to the Lord." Chester came out from behind the podium. In a softer voice, he said, "You all are fighting your own demons, as am I. Many of you are battling addiction."

He stared directly at Angel. This time she held his stare, though it took every ounce of courage she had.

Chester smiled then looked away, looked behind Angel. "You are fighting distrust because a person close to you betrayed you."

Though he'd looked away, Angel still felt like he was addressing her. She shivered, though the room was warm.

"You are fighting doubt and hopelessness. You see no way out of your life. These are your personal, metaphoric demons. But the devil, he is not a metaphor. He is a real being that wants nothing but to kill and destroy and to steal your soul."

He turned away from them and returned to the podium. When he did that, the young redhead sitting with Mr. Rockport stood and grabbed a pile of books from a bookshelf against the wall opposite the entry Angel had come through. Another girl, a blond like Angel but with a Dutch-boy haircut—Marsha, Angel thought her name was, the one who had stuck her several times with needles—joined her and grabbed a handful of books as well.

Chester remained quiet while the girls handed a book to each person.

The redhead handed Angel hers. "My name's Britany. I'm glad you're here."

Angel said nothing but took the book, which turned out to be a Bible.

Britany and Marsha returned to their seats.

Chester said, "Now, ladies, it's time to put God's Word in your minds and hearts. Turn with me please to the book of Ephesians, chapter two."

Angel just stared at her Bible. She had no idea what Godzilla had just asked her to do. What was Ephesians? She rifled through the pages a bit, at least to look like she was trying. Amanda leaned over and took the book from her.

"Here, let me help you." She opened Angel's Bible and showed her the table of contents. "Each book in the Bible has a name. See, this is Ephesians." She showed Angel the entry, then turned to the page indicated in the table of contents. "And each book is divided into chapters." She flipped a page and came to one that had a big 2 in the middle of the page. "There you go."

Angel muttered thanks and stared at the words.

For the next thirty minutes or so, Chester alternately preached and read from the Bible. Angel tried to follow along, or at least look like she was following along. Several times she looked around her. The room they were in had two wide, arched entrances, neither with doors. The one she and Sara had come in and one directly behind her, leading to the front foyer. Between her and the foyer were Mr. Rockport and Britany, and of course Sara sat right next to her. Angel caught Sara staring at her once when she was looking around. She flashed her guardian a quick, guilty smile then pretended to read her Bible.

Finally, Godzilla asked the girls to bow their heads in prayer. Most of what Chester had said Angel really had not heard and what she had heard she ignored. She was no one's slave. She did what she did because she had to. Angel bowed her head but did not close her eyes. As soon as Chester started praying, she looked up. Everyone had their heads down, even Chester and Sara.

This was her chance. She stood as quietly as possible, eased past Sara and then bolted toward the foyer.

"Angel!" Sara screamed from behind her.

She didn't stop. She reached the front doors and pushed down on the handle. It wouldn't budge. Neither would the other one. She turned to run toward the back of the house, hoping the back door wasn't locked, wherever that was, but collided with a solid mass and grunted. Massive arms in a black suit wrapped around her and she was lifted six inches off the ground.

How could Godzilla move so fast? She started hitting and kicking.

"Please stop kicking me," Chester said.

It wasn't the low, menacing growl of Chester's voice that stopped her, but the use of please.

He lowered her back onto her feet, wrapped a massive paw around her arm, and led her past the sitting girls, through the arched entrance, through the kitchen, and back down the stairs, into her cell, as that's what she thought of it, and gently deposited her on her bed.

Then the storm really let loose.

Chapter 19

Sara followed behind Chester. She clenched and unclenched her hands. Clenched. Unclenched. Clenched. Unclenched. Her footfalls were in time to her hands, vibrating the floor with each step. She breathed hard, felt her nostrils flaring. In her tunnel vision all she saw was Angel's blonde hair past Chester's left shoulder. Down the stairs, each step jolting her entire body, but she didn't notice. Finally, they reached Angel's room.

Chester sat her down. Why didn't he throw her down? He left the room.

For a few seconds she just stood in the middle of Angel's room and breathed hard. She stared at Angel, who defiantly stared back. She knew she should walk away, but Sara just couldn't.

Finally, she erupted. "Why did you do that? I trusted you. I...I trusted you and you betrayed me. You ran. You...you...you."

Angel replied just as loudly, "You have no right to keep me here. I want to leave."

"Why, so you can shoot up?"

"What if I do? What's it to you?"

They stared at each other a few seconds longer then Sara yelled, "Marsha said you weren't ready. Chester said the same. Even Rockport said to wait until next week. But no, I said you should have some freedom. You should get out of your room. It would be good for you. And what did you do?"

"I want to go home."

"No, you don't. You want to go crawling back to Keyshawn."

"I want to go home."

"You want to get high."

"I want to—" Angel clutched her gut, moaned and curled up into a ball.

"What's the matter, little angel?" Sara's tone became mocking. Then in a voice like a mother talking to a baby—except edged with venom—she asked, "Do you want a needle? And what needle do you want? Something to put you to sleep or maybe some heroin!" She leaned close to Angel and screamed, "What do you really want, Angel? Huh? What do you want?"

"Sara!"

The whip crack of her name from Rockport cut through the red fog of her vision. She straightened so quickly her back cracked.

"Sara, come with me, please." Not loud, but stern. No nonsense. "Marsha, prepare a sedative for Angel, please."

Sara gave Angel one last glare, then turned military style and marched off with Rockport to his study, where she fell into the armchair and buried her face in her hands. No tears. Just fury. Hurt. A feeling of betrayal.

She heard Rockport move, felt his breath on her hands.

From close, he softly said, "Mandy wasn't your fault."

Then the tears gushed and through her mind played another day in Rockport's study about seven months ago.

She could tell by the fallen look on his face the news wasn't good. Rockport pocketed his iPhone and took both Sara's hands in his, like they were about to dance. "That was Detective Warren. They found Mandy." He swallowed hard.

She started to tremble. Her lip quivered. She prepared to scream.

"I'm sorry, Sara. She's dead."

No scream, just a low moan, "Nooo." She collapsed against Rockport.

He hugged her tight and whispered, "It was an overdose."

Again, "No."

Then the anger broadsided her, and she pushed away from Rockport.

"No! She wouldn't have done that. She was...she was done. Over with it. I know she was."

"It's possible she didn't inject herself. But the cops didn't find any evidence suggesting someone forced it on her."

"They must have. She wouldn't have gotten high on her own."

"She was an addict, Sara. It's always a possibility."

"No. She was done. I know she was."

As quickly as it had come, the anger dissipated, replaced by exhaustion. She collapsed into the armchair and stared straight ahead, seeing nothing but Mandy's long, blond hair, her bright blue eyes and huge smile two days ago when Sara told her she had free rein of the house.

"She was ready. I was so sure of it. I was so sure of it."

"Go ahead, say it," Sara said through her hands. "Tell me you were right. Angel wasn't ready. Go ahead. I know you hate me anyway. Go ahead."

She lifted her head from her hands and glared at Rockport, then screamed, "Go ahead. Tell me! Tell me how stupid I was. It was too early. Tell me. Tell me. Tell me."

Like a rag doll she folded back into the chair and started sobbing. "Everyone hates me. I'm so stupid. Why do you keep me here? Why?"

Her voice faded away and all she could do was bawl. Finally, that too dried up and she just sat there waiting for Rockport to kick her out.

Instead, she felt his hands gently lift her head. She clenched her eyes shut, fearing the expression he'd have.

"Sara, please open your eyes."

Reluctantly, she did.

"Mandy wasn't your fault. And Angel is fine. She's still here. She'll get better, but only if you keep working with her."

Sara shook her head.

"You're the best, Sara. I couldn't do this without you. What you're doing here is awesome, and these girls all owe you a lot. And they all love you, just like I do."

She leaned her head on his shoulder and cried softly while he stroked her hair. Her self-loathing finally abated, replaced by anger at herself. He had told her that if she invested in them like she needed to, that there would be times she'd get hurt, maybe hurt badly. Could she continue to do this? Could she pour herself out into these girls?

Rockport said, "Just remember, for every Mandy, there's ten others like Jillian, Ashley, Karen. Remember them?"

She nodded against his shoulder.

"And don't forget the most important part."

"What's that?" Sara asked.

"Mandy accepted Christ, so you'll see her again someday."

Sara nodded again and decided she could go on. She could do this. And she would.

After all the rest of the residents finished their lunch, Sara went downstairs with a tray of food for Angel. She knocked on the door to Angel's room.

"Go away."

Sara opened the door.

"What do you want? Just leave me alone."

Sara set the tray with the chicken salad sandwich, banana, and baby carrots on the nightstand and sat on the bed near Angel's feet. For a short time she studied Angel, who glared at her. Sara said, "There was this girl named Mandy." She swallowed hard. Wow, this was going to be difficult. But she pressed on. "Anyway, I'm really sorry I yelled at you. I shouldn't have."

"Who's Mandy?" Angel pouted and glared.

"She was a young girl I had gotten really close to. She was younger than you, sixteen. Very pretty. I was like a big sister to her."

"Yeah, so what? Why are you telling me this?"

"About seven months ago, I convinced Rockport she was ready to have free rein of the house." Sara hesitated, looked at the ceiling, took a deep breath. "She bolted. Ran."

"Good for her. I'd do the same."

"Angel, listen." Sara squeezed the younger girl's ankle, but Angel yanked her foot away. "Please, Angel."

"What are you, a lesbo or something? What do you want from me?"

"I want to help you." She kept eye contact with Angel despite the intense anger burning in the younger girl's glare. "About Mandy."

"She took off, yeah you said that. Good for her."

"They found her dead, Angel. From an overdose."

Angel looked away, then back at Sara, her expression defiant. "Yeah, well that's not me. I know how much I can handle."

"You're an addict, Angel. And that's not a life you want to live. Do you really want to keep selling your body to get your next fix? Do you really want to have sex with guys you don't know, who could have AIDS, herpes, or God knows what else?"

"It pays the bills."

"Fine." Sara shook her head and stood. "You need to be here. One day you'll understand that. Until you do, no privileges."

Sara left Angel's room, closed the door, and made sure it was locked. Halfway up the stairs she heard the tray hit the door. Sara shrugged. She had other work to do.

Chapter 20

From behind the concrete barrier, Lefty watched the parade of luxury cars pull up to the previously abandoned warehouse, the place he'd checked out the day before. Illumination from inside the warehouse office cast just enough light for Lefty to monitor the activity. His starting position had been directly parallel to the front entrance. But when the first car pulled in, its headlights shone directly on the spot he hid and on him. Now, he was positioned at about a thirty-degree angle.

Dressed in all black, he'd be nearly invisible. The downside—he was roasting in the long-sleeved shirt, black polyester pants, and black stocking hat. He'd put a thin coat of eye black all over his face, as well.

As each car pulled in front of the office entrance, a suited man opened one of the car doors, generally the back passenger side. In every case a man stepped out. About half-and-half between white and black. Each wearing a suit. The car would then pull forward, make a left and drive south between the railroad track and the warehouses. At the end of the warehouses it would make another left, parking in the lot behind the two parallel warehouses.

Parked along the gravel road was a semi-trailer and its connected cab. The trailer doors were open, but as far as he could see, the trailer was empty. The cab was still running and a driver sat inside, smoking a cigarette.

Just as his knees started to ache, the line of cars ceased. Two large men in suits positioned themselves on each side of the closed glass doors. Lefty figured walking up to them and asking sweetly to enter was out of the question, especially since he'd left his suit at home. He waited a few more minutes, then crept along the concrete barrier until he was parallel to the back of the occupied building. The day before he'd spotted only one possible entry point other than the front door. As he'd hoped, the back door proved unguarded. But he waited anyway. Sure enough, a few minutes later, another large man in a suit walked by, head swiveling as he surveyed the area. The man wore earbuds and spoke softly.

When the guard reached the end of the long warehouse, he turned left. Still, Lefty waited, listening to his heartbeat. A plane from the small airport east flew over, loud enough, Lefty figured, to hide crunching on the gravel.

He rolled over the concrete barrier and landed in a crouch on the other side. Not the most graceful move, but not bad for a one-armed man. He waited. Watched. Listened. It was hard to see between the warehouses to the other side. Was the guard heading back toward the entrance or had he stopped to talk with the drivers waiting in the limos?

A few more seconds elapsed.

Was that footsteps? He waited. Then, clearly, he heard walking nearly perpendicular to himself on the other side of the warehouse. Sweat dripped into his eyes, down his face. But he dared not move to wipe it away.

The footsteps faded.

Lefty sprinted as quietly as he could to the back door.

He reached the regulation-sized door and put his ear on the cool metal surface and listened, trying to determine if one of the armed heavys waited just inside. He wanted to enter without a scene to observe the proceedings. That afternoon, he'd wracked his brain trying to figure out a plan to get Angel out if he saw her. After running through a half-dozen, lame-brained ideas, he'd settled on calling the cops. He patted his pocket to make sure his cell phone was still there.

A moment of dread washed over him as he tried to remember if he'd silenced it. But he didn't have any friends anyway, so who'd be calling him? Eileen might. But he was pretty sure he'd put it on vibrate.

All he heard from inside was faint sounds of amplified talking. He lightly knocked on the door and stepped to the side, flattening himself against the outer wall. After a couple minutes, he repeated the maneuver. No one opened the door. He tried the door handle. Locked, as he figured. But no reinforcement plate and no visible deadbolt.

Footsteps to his left. The guard doing another circle. He pushed off the door and sprinted to the other side of a dumpster about ten feet away, behind which he crouched and waited.

The footsteps came parallel to him and stopped. He held his breath.

One step, then two, then three toward him. The guard stopped again.

A kettle drum pounded in Lefty's ears. His shirt stuck to his back. He let his breath out slowly and silently.

Some scraping, then the footsteps receded. Lefty waited until he could no longer hear them. Then he returned to the door.

From his back pocket, he retrieved a thin piece of aluminum the size of a credit card. He worked the metal into the space between door and frame, then maneuvered it between strike plate and the latch. Using a technique he'd practiced for hours over the past couple years, he hooked his thumb over the door handle, while still holding the metal card, and eased the door open. The metal card fell to the ground. To him the clatter sounded like clanging cymbals at the end of a rock song.

He froze and listened. Waited. Hopefully, the guard was all the way at the end, but what about those at the front door. After an excruciating minute, he relaxed. He decided to retrieve the aluminum card on the way out, provided he came that way. If not, well, that's why he used a piece of metal and not a credit card.

He slipped inside and eased the door shut. Offices to his left and right. Straight ahead, a hallway leading to a door flanked by a large plate glass window. Through the window he saw a stage lit by floodlights. Darkness cloaked the rest of the warehouse.

Every so often a light blinked on, briefly illuminating a man in a booth, arm raised. A voice over the sound system announced a number and a dollar amount. The light extinguished. On the stage, a blond haired, naked woman stood, head bent, swaying to an internal beat. On either side of her, straddling the edge between shadow and spotlight, stood two large, suited men.

Lefty moved to the door and watched through the window. A parade of girls were showcased on stage, bid on by corrupt men with nothing better to do with their money. Brunettes, blonds, the occasional redhead. Whites, blacks, Latinos, Asians. Some tattooed. Many looked like they came straight from high school and a few from middle school. All naked. All drugged. All passive. None looking enough like Angel to execute his brilliant plan.

If there was no Angel, he wasn't going to call and burn his contact with Big Eddie. With cell phone in hand, on video mode, he filmed the girl on stage then tried to catch the men making their bids. Several times he filmed a skinny white man to the side of the stage.

A light winked on, revealing a moderate-set man wearing a dark suit, pale blue shirt, and dark blue striped tie. He had a trimmed black goatee and gray-flecked, perfectly combed hair. He held up a card that looked like it had numbers on it that Lefty could not quite read. This man had been the final bid on three other girls. They had been the youngest looking ones.

Lefty felt ill, wanting simultaneously to vomit and put a bullet in the sick deviant's head. He wasn't carrying, though, so that would be difficult. At least he had caught him on video several times, though it was always for only a couple seconds and with it being so dark, he had no clue how well the videos would turn out. He thought he'd heard the announcer say this was the final item for bid.

He actually said, "item for bid." More nausea.

The girl on stage could not have been more than thirteen. A tiny wisp of a girl. Red hair. Unlike the rest, she tried to leave the stage. The two goons to either side slid their hands under her arms and held her fast. She struggled briefly, then collapsed to her knees.

Lefty kept his phone pointed at the man bidding because for some reason this time the light stayed on longer than usual.

Maybe the auctioneer—what sick snake would take this gig?—could not read the numbers either.

Chapter 21

Even though he knew Sara would hit the roof with three girls, let alone four, Rockport had to win this last one. If he didn't, he might do something that could jeopardize his entire operation. There was no way he was letting any of the lizards in that room take this young girl. The poor child was terrified.

The announcer finished his monologue and opened the bidding at twenty-five thousand. Rockport watched several others bid her up to sixty-two thousand. It was time to end it. He took out a notecard and wrote $100,000 on it, pushed his button and held up the card. He kept his hand on the button for several seconds, during which the place was silent. Seemed the cat even had the auctioneer's tongue.

Finally, loudly, exuberantly, the auctioneer said, "One hundred thousand dollars from number twenty-seven. Do I hear one-o-five?"

No other lights came on. The auctioneer repeated the one-o-five two more times, then, "Going once, going twice, sold to number twenty-seven. Thank you, gentlemen, that will be it for tonight. Please pay our cashier for your merchandise. Cash only. Collect your merchandise out back."

Rockport wanted to shoot the man. He pulled his cell phone from his pocket. "We're done," he told Chester. He picked up his briefcase, which held two hundred and fifty thousand in cash, and left the small booth made from a temporary partition. Within two hours, after the last participant left, this would once again be an empty warehouse with no trace that anyone had been there that night.

As he waited to settle on the four girls he'd purchased, he noticed a shorter man, about his age, with slick black hair, a bushy mustache and pock-marked face. He wore a four-thousand-dollar Armani suit. Beside him was a large, unpleasant looking Hispanic man whose eyes darted around the room, never alighting more than a second on any one place. Both men stood with backs close to the warehouse wall. Rockport assumed this was a supplier waiting to collect his cash.

He looked around trying to determine how many bodyguards this guy had. All he saw were other buyers and some suited men helping the buyers move the girls to their cars. He assumed those guys were muscle hired by the organizer but couldn't be sure.

He did some quick calculations. Taking out his one hundred thousand, the other twenty or so girls had gone for an average of about fifty thousand. In total, the supplier would be transporting somewhere around a million dollars. A lot of cash.

Rockport paid. Two of the muscle each took two of the girls and started toward the back door. All of the girls wore off-white gowns that barely reached their knees. However, again, the youngest one, the one he'd bought last, tried to pull away. A third muscle grabbed both her arms and pulled them back. She squealed.

"Hey," Rockport shouted. "Be careful with her. You damage her, you pay for her."

The man let up some, especially after the organizer, a wiry, bald man in his forties, glared at him.

The men led the girls outside the warehouse where Chester had pulled up in the limo. Both Chester and Lewis, a man Rockport sometimes employed for this type of work, someone Chester vouched for, stepped out.

Chester said to Rockport when he came alongside him, "Four?"

"Yup."

"Ooo, Mr. Rockport," Chester said in a fake southern black woman accent, "Ms. Sara is gonna keel you."

"Everyone's a comedian. I'll sit in front with you."

Lewis helped the girls into the back. When he came to the youngest, she again tried to run. Lewis bear hugged her and held her steady. One of the muscle from the building came over and started to grab her.

"Back off," Rockport yelled. "We'll take care of her."

Chester moved between Rockport and the thug, who he towered over. The guy backed away.

Rockport approached Lewis and the girl. He smiled and leaned down so his face was close to hers. "It's okay. We're not going to hurt you. Let's get you away from here."

She stared at him a few seconds then relaxed.

Lewis helped her into the back of the car. Not much of a feat for someone who weighed over two-fifty to place a girl who weighed around eighty pounds in the back seat. The little red-haired girl—who could not be more than thirteen—curled into the corner. The other three girls slouched and stared straight ahead, their eyes blank, resigned.

Chester said, "Hey, man, keep your hands to yourself, or I'll tell your mama.."

Lewis looked over his shoulder and grinned at Chester. He was as large as Chester, and he sported a full afro, like someone out of the early seventies. All he lacked was leather pants and a polyester print shirt. Both he and Chester dressed the occasion, dark suits concealing shoulder holsters, white shirts, and dark ties.

Chester and Rockport got in the car. Lewis joined the girls in the back.

"Don't leave, yet," Rockport said. "Drive back toward the parking lot, but then go behind the warehouse."

"What's up, boss?"

"Just an idea."

Chester sighed, shook his head, but complied.

When he'd stopped the car, Rockport asked, "You have your MAC-10 in the trunk?"

"Two of them." He stared at Rockport then narrowed his eyes. "Why?"

"Pop the trunk." Rockport got out of the car, lifted the trunk lid, and took out both MAC-10s, then returned to the driver side.

Chester rolled down his window. "Have Lewis get out, then lock the doors from the inside and join me."

Chester told Lewis to get out, raised the Plexiglas partition between the front and back then locked the doors in the back, a special modification to the limo Rockport had installed. Chester got out and joined Rockport and Lewis.

"What are you two carrying?" Rockport asked.

"Not sure I like this, boss," Chester answered.

"What are you carrying?"

"My usual. Glock nine."

Rockport looked at Lewis.

"Colt 1911. A forty-five," Lewis said.

Rockport handed the MAC-10 to Chester, ignoring the scowl on the big man's face. "Come with me.

They walked to the corner of the building. Rockport motioned for Chester and Lewis to stop. He whispered, "Stay out of sight." Rockport watched the remaining buyers load their girls into their vehicles and drive out the only road.

Chapter 22

Lefty exited the same way he came in. He flattened himself against the wall and waited. Voices came from the front of the building. He eased to his right, keeping his back against the wall, until he reached the opposite corner. It was all hands on deck at the front of the building. Everyone was finalizing their business. No more bodyguard patrols.

Lefty sprinted to the concrete barrier, then did a roll over it. He waited a minute or so. A barge horn sounded behind him on the river. No other sounds close by. He ran the best he could while keeping below the barrier until he reached that same spot he'd started at earlier. Then he turned on the video recorder on his phone, hoping he had enough memory left, and pointed it at the action.

Big cars, one by one, usually limos, pulled to the front door. In most cases, one girl was shoved into the back seat, usually accompanied by a heavy in a suit. Occasionally, the buyer himself climbed in back, but most of the time, the buyer got in the front. In a few of the cars, two girls were shoved in.

After about seven cars, a black limo pulled up and the man he'd videoed purchasing four of the girls exited the building. Two large, black dudes climbed from the limo. One of them joined the older white man. The other helped the girls into the car, until the last one, the young, tiny red head.

She tried to run, but was bear-hugged by the man helping her in. Another man approached from the building and tried to grab her. Lefty heard the buyer yell at him to back off, which the guy did. Lefty watched the buyer approach the girl, lean close to her, and say something to her. Whatever it was worked as she relaxed, and the black dude helped her into the car. They all climbed in. But instead of heading out the road as all others had, this limo turned right, back toward the parking lot.

Lefty ducked back behind the concrete barrier and sprinted toward the back of the building. He turned off the video recorder on his phone and pocketed it. When he got to where he thought was the end of the warehouse, he peeked over the barrier, but immediately hunched back down, hoping his sight would clear quickly from the headlights that had blinded him and hoping no one had seen him.

The headlights winked out. He heard the drone of the finely tuned engine. For a minute or so, nothing else. He feared the worst. Whoever was in the car had seen him and they were plotting what to do about it.

Car doors opened and closed quietly. Lefty made ready to sprint across the field behind him. Then he heard the shuffle of footsteps on the gravel moving toward him. Just as he was about to take off, the footsteps stopped. He heard what he thought was a trunk slamming. Great, they were getting guns.

For a few seconds, silence, then more footsteps, but this time away from him, followed by quiet conversation. He could not make out the words, but shortly after he heard another car door, followed by still another. Three men were now out of the car. More quiet conversation. Lefty could not catch any of the words.

Three sets of footsteps headed away from him, then stopped. His thighs started to burn. He ventured a peek over the barrier. The three men were at the far corner of the building. One was looking around the corner, the other two leaning against the wall. No one spoke.

Lefty ducked, controlled his breathing, willed himself to ignore the burning in his thighs and waited. And waited.

Finally, he heard shuffling moving away from him. He ventured another peek.

All three had disappeared around the building.

He stood, wobbling a minute while his legs adjusted. After a quick glance at the limo, he climbed over the barrier and sprinted to the near corner of the building, where he plastered himself to the wall. No one emerged from the limo with guns blasting. He quietly approached the far corner of the building, staying as close to the wall as he could.

Before getting to the corner, he slipped his cell phone out and took a quick picture of the front of the limo, hoping the license would show up in the dim light.

His heart skipped several beats when a muffled pounding came from the car. He waited. The pounding ceased. The girls inside. Should he let them out? Tell them to run to his car and wait?

He crept toward the limo. But when he tried the back door it was locked. Same with the front. Okay, that plan didn't work. He moved back to the wall and continued to the corner of the building.

He reached the corner and hesitated a few seconds. While waiting, he turned on the video recorder. When he finally peeked around, the three men were rapidly approaching two other men, one who was holding open the door of a Lincoln, the other about to get in. This man, whom Lefty had not seen until that moment, hesitated, then straightened. He had a pock-marked face and shiny black hair.

The three men from the limo trained their guns on the two at the car. When the guy with the afro drew parallel to the guy holding the door, he slammed the butt of his handgun into the guy's head. The door holder collapsed.

The owner of the car jumped back a couple steps, but the big bald guy rapidly closed the distance and kicked out, catching the man in the groin.

When he doubled over, the big man hit him in the back of the neck with the butt of his submachine gun. The Lincoln owner crumpled to the ground.

The older of the three, the buyer Lefty had watched, reached inside the Lincoln and drew out a briefcase. Then all three turned and jogged back to the corner of the building.

Lefty ducked back and sprinted to the barrier, diving over it, rolling as he landed, and settled on his back, staring up at the few stars able to twinkle through the St. Louis city light. He stayed still, trying to breath quietly while his heart hammered.

About fifteen seconds later he heard car doors open then slam shut, and then the limo sped away.

As soon as he could no longer hear the car, he jumped up and trotted across the field back to his car. He would never catch the limo, so didn't bother trying.

Chapter 23

"That didn't go so bad," Rockport said.

"They both saw our faces." Chester scowled, an expression that had never left him since they had exited the limo.

"If they remember them after those knocks on the head, I'll be surprised."

Chester turned left onto Monsanto Avenue, the first paved road. When they reached the crossroad by the fertilizer plant, Rockport glanced out the driver's side window. He saw car lights in the distance, about parallel to the warehouse they'd just left, he figured.

"Go straight," he commanded. "Pull into the parking lot of the fertilizer plant and turn around, then douse the lights."

"Alright." Chester complied. "Now what?"

"We wait a bit."

In about two minutes a car drove past.

"Didn't that car look familiar?" Rockport asked.

"Yeah, like the one we saw out here yesterday. That private dick."

"Exactly." After a few more minutes, Rockport said, "Okay, let's head home."

Chester pulled back onto the road, turned left, and headed toward the interstate.

Rockport glanced over his shoulder to make sure the partition was closed. It was. "Can we trust Lewis with this?"

"Completely."

Rockport stared out the windshield.

Chester added, "There's only one person he fears more than me and that's his mama. And I'm not sure that's the right order. Besides, I think you know, he came to Christ in prison a few years ago. He's a changed man." They drove awhile. "And if that ain't enough, you've been good to him. He's not about to bite the hand that feeds him." He glanced at Rockport. "And he digs this sort of thing. I'm sure this was the most fun he's had in some time."

Chapter 24

Jackson McCormitt opened his eyes and stared at a chunk of gravel. Then he remembered what had happened. Despite the ringing in his ears and the wooziness he got up. He kicked his bodyguard in the stomach, not hard, but enough to make him groan.

"Get up. I told you we shouldn't have let Rory leave with the truck until we were on the road." He cursed, then marched toward the open door into the warehouse. Sullivan had better still be there or he'd hunt him down and beat him to a pulp.

Behind McCormitt his bodyguard grunted. McCormitt heard footsteps, and the bodyguard caught up to him. The big man said nothing, having worked with McCormitt long enough to know that at times like these it was best to remain silent and obey orders.

McCormitt spotted Sullivan, the organizer, overseeing several of his men as they packed up the electronic equipment. How long had he been out? He glanced at his watch. Only ten minutes. Good.

When he approached Sullivan, the wiry, weasel of a man glanced at him, then said, "What'd you do, fall down in the parking lot?"

McCormitt glanced down and saw gray dust all over his black suit. He brushed it off and said, in a not very pleasant voice, "I want the names and pictures of every one of the buyers."

"Why?"

McCormitt nodded at his bodyguard. The six-six, crew-cut ex-Army ranger took out his Glock and put it against the head of Sullivan.

"Because one of them just ripped me off."

Sullivan didn't even turn. Instead he shouted at one of his men, "O'Hara, keep the computer up and running. Get me a thumb drive." He casually stared at McCormitt. "Have your gorilla put his gun away and follow me."

Again, McCormitt nodded to his bodyguard, who holstered his handgun, and he followed Sullivan into a small enclosure containing several computers on fold up tables. The chairs had already been moved out.

Sullivan leaned over one of the computers, typed a few keys, moved the mouse around, and brought up a picture of a man. "Scroll through them and tell me which one attacked you."

McCormitt did just that and when he landed on a picture of a man with salt-and-pepper hair and goatee, he stopped. "That's him."

Sullivan hit print, then inserted the thumb drive that one of his men handed to him. McCormitt watched while the organizer copied the picture to the thumb drive. When he finished, he took it out and handed it to McCormitt.

"Compliments of the house. I even copied the guy's bio on the drive. Happy hunting." He pushed through McCormitt and his bodyguard. "Now beat it. I have to get us out of here quickly. Maybe this guy will drop a dime to the cops as well."

"I'll be in town awhile," McCormitt said.

"Good for you. Any complaints, take it up with Big Eddie." Then under his breath, he said, just loud enough for McCormitt to hear, "If you dare."

Chapter 25

Sara's head dipped forward, her eyes slowly closing, the book in her hand slipping from her grip. But then her head snapped back up as she heard a car door. Finally, they'd returned. She had both rooms ready, just in case Rockport brought two girls. She laid the Ted Dekker novel aside, left the living room, and waited in the foyer.

Chester was the first through the door. Following him, a tall, leggy, blond with short hair, head down. Then came a redhead, shorter, with startling green eyes, who refused to hold Sara's gaze. She could not have been more than sixteen. And then another girl. Another girl? What was Rockport thinking? Three girls? This one a brunette, long hair, also no older than sixteen. Finally, a fourth girl walked through.

"You've got to be kidding," Sara muttered under her breath. "What are we going to do with four more girls?" She watched this last girl.

The three girls before had all been looking down at their feet, shuffling, stoic expressions, like patients in a psych ward. But not this one. A medium height, very thin red-haired girl, very young, she looked all around her with a defiant glare. She walked stiffly, reluctantly. Lewis followed close by her, every now and then nudging her forward. Rockport completed the parade. He closed the door and smiled at Sara, who scowled.

"Take them to the living room," Rockport said.

Chester and Lewis led the girls into the room Sara had just exited.

"Four," is how Sara greeted Rockport. "Are you serious? What are we going to do with four of them?"

"We'll get by."

"We only have two rooms open downstairs. All but one room is full upstairs. And Angel is obviously not ready to move upstairs. Calvin, we're busting at the seams." She felt hot. Her voice rose in volume. "We can't handle all these girls. Who's going to—"

"Come here, Sara."

Rockport walked past her to the living room entrance. Sara joined him.

"Look in there. What do you see?"

"Four girls," she said petulantly. "Two of whom we don't have room for."

"Key word being girls." He stared at Sara, his gaze intense. "Look at that young redhead. She's the last one I purchased. I knew it would be a strain, having already bought three of them. But look at her."

Sara looked. The girl continued her darting looks. Her hands trembled. She reminded Sara of a small bird caught in a corner, a cat just feet from her, watching, waiting to pounce. She didn't look streetwise, she didn't look strung out.

Rockport walked through the entryway. Sara started to follow, but he held his hand up and motioned for her to stay. He approached the youngest girl. She backed away from him, so he stopped.

"We're not going to hurt you. How old are you?"

For a minute she said nothing but continued her frenetic glances around the room. Finally, her gaze alighted on Sara, who smiled at her, trying to ease her fear. The young girl then shifted her gaze to Rockport and defiantly said, "I'l be thirteen next month."

Oh, my Lord. Sara's heart melted. A lump blocked her throat and her eyes burned. She wiped a tear from the corner of her left eye.

"Chester, get the girls some water," Rockport said.

He rejoined Sara. "She's twelve, Sara."

"I heard."

"What would you have done if you'd been at the sale? Would you have let those animals have her?"

Sara studied her shoes—black flats—and shook her head.

"I didn't think so." He laid a hand on her shoulder. She looked up at him and he said, "Let's try this. Double up the older redhead and the brunette. Put the blonde in the other room. And let's put the young one with Angel."

"With Angel? Why?"

"Just a hunch, but I think it might shock Angel out of her defiance. Or maybe bring out the nurturing in her."

Sara nodded.

Rockport added, "Have Chester check the basement. I think there are some air mattresses we can use."

Sara nodded again then walked into the room with the girls. She wanted to try and talk with them. The oldest was maybe seventeen. God, what a sick world. What a sick world.

"Hey, girls. My name's Sara. Welcome to our home. Please, have a seat." She waved her hand.

Obediently, the three older girls sat, never looking at her, the tall blond in one of the zebra armchairs, the brunette and older redhead on the white love seat. The twelve-year-old remained motionless other than her eyes, which darted everywhere.

Sara approached her, but she backed away until she bumped into the wall. Fine she could stand. Sara sat in the other zebra armchair. She smiled at all the girls.

The two on the couch both had bloodshot eyes with dark circles underneath them. They all wore off-white featureless gowns. They were barefoot and, Sara suspected, naked underneath the gowns. She thought about asking the men to leave, but one look at the young redhead by the bookcase changed her mind. That girl would bolt first chance she got.

"My name is Sara." She turned to the brunette. She had pudgy cheeks, a small turned up nose and dark eyes. "What's your name?"

The brunette looked up at Sara, though not meeting her gaze. "Chelsey."

"That's a pretty name."

Chelsey nodded then returned to studying her hands in her lap.

"And yours?" Sara turned to the older redhead, who was also studying her lap. She trembled and one of her legs vibrated up and down.

Freckles dotted the high cheekbones on either side of her wide nose. When she looked up, those amazing green eyes were vacant. She looked right through Sara. "I'm Natasha." She spoke with a heavy accent. Russian, Sara figured. Natasha bowed her head again and started rocking.

"Nice to meet you, Natasha."

The girl didn't say anything more.

Sara looked over at the blond, who watched her, a smug look on her gorgeous face. Statuesque. Narrow eyes, flawless nose, full lips. None of the girls wore makeup, and this one didn't need any. She had smooth, creamy skin, not a blemish anywhere, high forehead and hair that glowed in the incandescent light.

"And what's your name?"

"Sarah. With an H."

"Well, nice to meet you Sarah with an H. I'm Sara without an H. How old are you, hon?"

"Seventeen," she answered proudly, like she'd earned some badge of honor. She met and kept Sara's gaze. This one must have been a call girl, a higher end prostitute, certainly not a streetwalker nor someone who worked the cheaper hotels. "Can I ask you something?" She had a southern accent.

"Sure, hon."

"You our new bottom bitch? And that old man, he our new pimp? I ain't never had a pimp so old before."

Sara stifled a laugh but smiled. She'd have to share that comment with Rockport. "No, hon. He's not a pimp, though I do work for that old man. He bought you to set you free."

"Set us free? Free from what?"

The young girl against the wall shouted out, "Then let us go. Why are you holding us here?"

Sara ignored the youngster a moment and answered Sarah. "From slavery, dear."

"I ain't no slave. I make good money doing what I do."

"Oh? You were just sold."

Sarah with an H looked around, a confused look on her face then said, "When can I get a fix?"

"What's your drug of choice, hon?"

"The big H." Again, that proud tone of voice, like she'd accomplished something major.

"Soon, hon. Where are you from?"

"Houston."

"Why won't you answer me?" the twelve-year old asked.

Sara turned her gaze to her. "What's your name?"

"Emily. I want to go."

"Go where, Emily? Do you even know where you are?"

This gave Emily pause. She stared at Sara then slumped against the wall and shook her head.

"Do you want to go home?"

Again, Emily shook her head, then eased to the floor and started crying.

Sara turned back to the two girls on the couch. "Where are you girls from, Chelsey, Natasha?"

In unison, they quietly said, "Houston."

Sara turned back to Sarah. "How did you get here?"

"Truck."

"What do you mean?"

"We was all shoved in the back of a big semi. Long ride. Threw us around all over the place. If we had to pee, we had to do it in the corner of the truck."

"You're in St. Louis. Did you know that?"

She shook her head. "They didn't tell us nothing. Just threw us in the truck. It was gross. Pee sloshing all over the place every time we turned or stopped or went." She paused and Sara just smiled at her, hoping she'd go on. And she did. "When we got here, we were taken off the truck, thrown in showers then made to wait in a room. We was naked. They took our clothes. Do you have some clothes we could put on?" She started to shake. "And maybe that fix now."

Sara got up. "Yes, hon. We'll get you what you need."

She walked to the living room entrance. Calvin and Chester joined her. Marsha walked in holding four syringes. Sara glanced at Emily, still curled in a ball against the bookcase. She wasn't displaying the same symptoms as the rest, but she decided the sedative was still a good idea. She waved Marsha in.

"Just a sedative for the youngest one sitting on the floor. Nothing else. I'm not sure she's on anything."

Sara left the living room.

Chester said, "Did he tell you what else we did?"

Sara saw the glare Rockport shot Chester, so she knew something had gone down she wasn't going to like. But she and Chester had an understanding. They both told each other everything that went on in that house. Both had grown up in tough situations and both wanted to know what was going on at all times. Neither one liked surprises.

"Calvin, what did you do?"

"What is it with you two?" Rockport asked.

"Don't avoid the question. What did you do?"

In answer he pointed to the two briefcases sitting just inside the door. She had noticed him carrying both of them when he walked in. She thought he'd left with only one.

"What's in that other briefcase?" she asked.

"Money."

"Whose money?"

Chester piped in. "Ain't our money."

"Calvin? What did you do?"

"Hit the SOBs where it counts."

From the living room, they heard a high-pitched, extended, "No."

Emily, Sara figured, not wanting the shot. So she wasn't on heroin. She hoped Lewis would be gentle with her. Marsha wouldn't need much room or time. Her injection technique was sniper precise.

Rockport started to turn away, but Sara stopped him. "Whose money and how did you get it?"

"One of the sellers and we took it."

"Calvin, how could you?" She put her clenched fists on her hips and glared at him.

"The opportunity presented itself and we took advantage of it. There's a million or more in there."

"We don't need money."

"That's not the point." Now Rockport's voice rose. "We struck yet another blow against these predators."

"But you've put us in danger. These guys won't just pack up and leave. They'll come looking for us." She felt her face growing hot. Her breathing came fast.

"They don't know who I am."

"But what if they find us?"

"They won't."

She tried to calm herself by practicing some breathing techniques and praying to God. In a softer, controlled voice she said, "This isn't just your operation, you know. It's mine. It's Chester's. And there's the girls. What would happen to them?"

"They won't find us."

"They'd be right back where we found them, if not worse."

"As far as they know, I'm Jack Martinson from Toledo."

"I hope you're right." She shut her eyes, breathed in deep, opened her eyes and asked, "So what happened?"

"Chester can tell you. I'm going to bed." He walked away from them to the front door, grabbed both briefcases and headed up the staircase. Sara watched him until he disappeared around the first turn then looked at Chester, who just shrugged.

"So, what happened?" she asked.

"Lewis had fun."

When Chester finished telling her how the operation went down, Sara asked him to get some air mattresses from the basement.

She went back into the living room. All four girls were groggy, nearly out. Lewis waved to her and smiled. She waved back, but just could not bring herself to smile with the boulder in the pit of her stomach.

"Chester will be right back. Then, please bring them downstairs."

Lewis nodded.

"Carefully."

Again, Lewis nodded. "Always, ma'am. Always."

Over the next thirty minutes, they blew up air mattresses, and settled three of the girls, leaving Emily until last. Sara gently opened Angel's door and peeked in. Angel was sleeping, turned toward the wall on her side.

Sara opened the door wide and Chester slipped the air mattress on the floor. There was barely enough room between the nightstand and the far wall. She put a sheet over the mattress.

Lewis, who cradled Emily, gently laid her down.

Sara covered the young girl with a light blanket.

They left the room and Sara quietly closed and locked the door. She let out a huge breath and wondered what the next day was going to bring.

Chapter 26

"Twice in three days," Sergeant Donaldson said. "You having an affair with Pratt?"

"You're funny, Ron." Lefty leaned on the Sergeant's desk. "Actually, I'm here to see Detective James Fischer. Do you know if he's around?"

"Let me check."

Donaldson picked up his phone and punched in a couple numbers. After a pause he said, "Detective Fischer? Yeah, hello, this is Sergeant Donaldson up front. Lefty Bruder is here to see you." A pause. "Yes, sir. George Bruder." Another pause. "Uh-huh. Will do, Detective." He put the phone down. "He'll be right down. Have a seat."

When Lefty sat in one of the barely padded, metal chairs, Donaldson asked, "Why you talking with a sex crimes detective, if I may ask?"

"You may. I'm looking for a girl."

"Strange way to find a date."

"Always the cut up. It's a job. I'm doing some PI work."

In a low, television-announcer voice, Donaldson said, "Lefty Bruder, gumshoe. Join us tonight as the one-armed PI puts his life on the line." He laughed.

"You do realize I could kick your butt any time."

Donaldson stood up and stroked his substantial belly. "You think?"

Lefty just smiled and Donaldson sat back down. Five minutes later, Detective Fischer opened the door to the waiting room and motioned Lefty to join him. After Lefty entered the detectives' area, the slim, short detective put out his right hand to shake hands, quickly realized his mistake then put out his left hand, never breaking eye contact with Lefty, who shook hands with the detective.

"What can I do for you, Mr. Bruder?"

"Lefty, please. That's what my friends call me."

The detective arched his brows as if to say, we're friends, are we?

Lefty said, "I want to show you something. Do you have an office we could go into?"

"Sure." Fischer turned and walked briskly into the hall.

Lefty followed him up two flights of stairs, down another stark hallway to a small office. In it a desk with nothing on top other than a couple pictures. To the side, another smaller desk held a computer monitor, keyboard, and mouse. Two three-shelf bookshelves, full of what appeared to be psychology and sociology books, flanked a five-drawer filing cabinet. On the wall to the left hung a picture of a group of racing cyclists with a trite saying about teamwork underneath. The right wall sported only a couple nail holes. A small window let in the brutal summer sun. One chair, similar to the spartan ones in the lobby, completed the décor.

Fischer motioned to the one chair, went behind his desk and sat in the well-worn imitation leather office chair. "What have you got, Mr. Bruder?"

Lefty extracted his cell phone from his pocket and pulled up the video from the night before. He tapped the play icon and set the phone on Fischer's desk.

The detective leaned over and watched in silence. The voice of the auctioneer rang out. When the video ended there was silence. For about thirty seconds, Fischer stayed bent over the phone, fingers of his right hand drumming his desk, pinky to index, pinky to index, over and over. A car horn sounded. A squeal of tires. Finally, the detective looked up, his thin brows scrunched, equally thin lips pursed.

"You knew about this, I assume. It's not something you just stumbled onto."

"Yeah, I knew about it. From Big Eddie."

"You two friends?" Still hunched over, still drumming his fingers.

"Nothing that formal."

"Why didn't you alert this department beforehand? We could have raided it. Made a lot of arrests. Liberated these girls."

Lefty doubted they would have liberated anyone. The girls would be back on the street in a matter of hours looking for their next fix. "I'm looking for Angel Atkins. She might have been there. By the time I figured out she wasn't, it was too late to call you guys. Besides, I wasn't about to betray Big Eddie. I may still need him."

Fischer frowned. "What do you want from me?"

"Names."

"Of?"

"People in the video."

"The buyers?"

"Yup."

"Why don't you ask Big Eddie?"

Lefty smiled and didn't bother to answer that one. He snatched his phone off the desk, found the second video, and started it. Very little sound came from this one. Fischer watched in silence.

When the video of the snatch and grab ended, Fischer said, "Interesting. Don't know those guys, though."

"Which guys?"

"Any of them. The perps or the victims."

Victims? That's a laugh. Lefty asked, "What about any of the others from the first video?"

"Just a minute." Fischer picked up the phone. After a pause, he said, "It's Fischer. Fine, sir. How are you doing? Uh-huh." Another pause. "I have Mr. Bruder in my office, and he has an interesting video." Another pause. "Okay, sir." He put the phone down. "Pratt is on his way down. We'll wait for him." He turned away from Lefty and started punching keys on his keyboard. Lefty tried to see what was on the monitor, but it had one of those security screens.

After a few minutes, there was a knock at the detective's door, and Pratt walked in. "George. How's the case going?"

Lefty stood. Pratt put out his left hand without hesitation and they shook.

"Slowly, Lieutenant."

"Detective Fischer said you have an interesting video. Can I see it?"

Lefty played both videos for Pratt, who watched in silence. When the second video completed, Pratt looked at Fischer, who still frowned. "Relax, Detective. There's no way George would have alerted us of this beforehand. He'd compromise his source and possibly lose his target."

That's why Lefty had always liked Pratt. He just plain got things. He had a deep intuition and an immediate grasp of situations.

"Yeah, that's what he said, sir."

Pratt turned to Lefty. "What are you looking for, George?"

"Names."

Pratt glanced at his watch. "Would love to stay and chat but got a meeting with the captain." On his way out, he said, "Detective, give him the names you can." He then paused at the door, looking over his shoulder at Lefty. "George, I don't think I need to tell you this, but stay within the law. Otherwise, I won't be able to help you."

"Will do, Lieutenant."

Pratt turned to face Lefty full on. "And I know you said you didn't want to come to church, but how about lunch with the family next Sunday, after church?"

"Should work. I'll let you know. Depends on how things are going."

Pratt looked at Fischer. "Detective, be cooperative. Maybe George can save one of these girls."

"Yes, sir."

Pratt left, closing the door behind him.

"Mr. Bruder, come around here," said Fischer.

Lefty went around to the other side of the detective's desk and stood right behind him so he could see the computer screen.

"This one is from Chicago." The screen showed an African American outside a restaurant on a busy street. Lefty didn't recognize the area, so must have been somewhere in the guy's hometown. Underneath the picture was the guy's name, last known address, and other vital statistics. "Name is William Washington. A cousin of Big Eddie's or something. Some relation."

"Can you print that?"

In the reflection of the monitor Lefty saw Fischer frown, but he moved his mouse and a few seconds later the ink jet printer whirred to life. The detective navigated to a list and clicked another entry. Up came a picture of a bald white guy, mid-forties, mustache, deep-set eyes. "Meet Fenton Ashbury from Des Moines. Comes here often. We've never been able to pin anything on him."

Before Lefty even asked, Fischer printed the page.

"Don't you recognize anyone that's local?"

"Yup. One of them." He did some more mouse work and up came a picture of a scrawny white man with a long, sharp face, squinty eyes and feral grin showing bad dental work. "This would be the organizer. Mr. Russell 'Stick' Sullivan. Called 'Stick' for obvious reasons. Works for Big Eddie and anyone else who will pay him a buck or two. He's the consummate middleman. Makes the deals. Moves the merchandise, but nothing sticks to him. The guy's like Teflon." Fischer twisted in his chair and Lefty had to move back. "We could have had him last night if someone would have called us." He glared at Lefty.

"Can I get that print out?"

Fischer stared at Lefty. "What are you going to do with Angel if you find her?"

"Return her to her aunt."

"What if she doesn't want to go? She's an adult, you know."

Lefty shrugged. "My job is to find her, not rehabilitate her. All I know is if I don't find her, there's little chance for her."

Fischer nodded. "You got that right."

He turned back to the computer screen and printed the information sheet on Sullivan. When he handed it to Lefty, he kept his grip on the page a few seconds. "Remember what Lieutenant Pratt said. Do anything beyond the law and you're on your own."

Lefty smiled. "I'm a one-armed man. What do you think I can do, Detective?"

Fischer shook his head and released the page. Lefty exited his office.

Lefty pushed open the door of the strip joint managed by Keyshawn Williams. The pimp was at the bar.

Keyshawn shook his head. "Man, today ain't a good day. Go away."

"Nice to see you, too, Keyshawn. I just want to show you a picture and ask you one question."

"Make it quick, man. I got things to do."

Lefty scanned the place. He saw neither of Keyshawn's bouncers. Only one patron occupied a blue-topped table. Eleven a.m. and already some scumbag was ogling a short blonde in a G-string wrapping herself around a pole.

Lefty held up a finger. "One minute."

He turned back around and exited the joint. As he suspected, a black Mustang was just pulling into the parking lot. Tweedle-dumb and tweedle-dumber. Lefty went back into the strip joint.

"I ain't got all day, stumpy. What do you want?"

Lefty ignored the jab. At the bar, he pulled out his cell phone and brought up the video. He played it until it came to the sophisticated man with the beard who had bought the most girls and, with his goons, had jumped the pocked-marked guy. Every time he saw the guy, he thought of the original ad about the most interesting man in the world. Only this guy looked a little younger. He held the cell phone for Keyshawn to see.

"Well?" Lefty asked.

"Yeah, that's him. The dude that ripped me off and took Angel."

Lefty fast forwarded the video and stopped at the snatch and grab. He showed Keyshawn the screen again.

"And that's the brother that punched me." Keyshawn pointed at the biggest of the two African Americans with the older white guy.

"And you don't know who they are?"

"Man, you dense or something? If I knew who they was, I wouldn't be here talkin' with you. And they wouldn't be here, period."

The music changed from the drippy ballad to a more upbeat seventies disco tune with four notes that repeated constantly. The door opened. Lefty glanced that way and saw the two bouncers enter. He pushed away from the bar and walked quickly toward them. The black guy managed to slip back outside, but Lefty trapped the taller, skinnier white guy against the wall. He held up his hands in defense.

"Give me your keys," Lefty demanded.

"What?"

Lefty planted his right foot in the man's stomach.

He grunted and leaned forward, clutching his stomach.

Lefty grabbed the man's right ear and twisted hard. "Your keys. Give me your keys."

"Aaaaah." The man reached into his pocket and extracted a key ring with about twenty keys on it. Lefty took it.

"Let him go, stumpy," Keyshawn said, close by.

Lefty let go of the man's ear and turned around. Keyshawn had a nine millimeter pointed at Lefty's head. Only problem for the pimp was he was only a couple feet away.

Lefty smiled. "Since you've been helpful, I'll forget you pulled that gun on me and leave now." He stepped forward, then around Keyshawn and walked to the door. Before leaving, he said, "You ever draw a weapon on me again, Keyshawn, I'll rip your balls off and shove them down your throat." He opened the door. "And tell your goons to stop following me."

Outside, he saw the other guy sitting in the mustang. Lefty jangled the keys and smiled at him. The guy opened his car door and started to get out, but when Lefty frowned, the guy changed his mind and stayed put.

Lefty got in his own car and drove away. While driving over the Eads Bridge, he flipped the keys out the window and into the Mississippi river.

Chapter 27

Angel rolled over, opened her eyes, and wondered when her little cousin had come to visit. Her next thought was she hoped her filthy stepfather hadn't laid his hands on her, too. Then, she remembered she had left there some time ago

A spasm seized her. She curled into a fetal position, gritted her teeth and tried not to make any noise, not wanting to wake the young girl. Who was she? Not her cousin, Angel realized. In between blinding stabs of stomach pain, she remembered where she was. She closed her eyes and rolled up even tighter, letting out a low, long groan.

When the pain eased, she opened her eyes.

The young girl was standing right over her. "Are you okay?"

Angel unfurled and nodded. She swung her legs over the bed and tentatively sat up. At least no dizziness. "I would be okay if they'd only give me some smack."

"You want someone to hit you?"

Angel squinted at the young girl. She judged her to be slightly shorter than herself. Much thinner. Pointed nose, wide, blue eyes and carrot-red, shoulder-length hair. Freckles dotted both cheekbones. She had dimples even though she didn't smile. Her look of concern seemed so genuine it warmed Angel.

"Smack is heroin. A drug."

"Yeah, I know heroin is a drug. Jeez, I'm not a child."

Attitude as well. "Who are you?"

The girl hesitated. "Who are you?"

Angel smiled. Maybe this poor thing had had an even harder time than she had. "I'm Angel, and I've been kidnapped and stuck in here."

"Really? Me, too. I mean I've been kidnapped as well and then sold and then put in here."

"Sold?"

The girl sat next to Angel on the bed. She clasped her hands together in her lap. She wore something similar to a hospital gown, only it had no opening. Plain white, it went to her knees.

"Last night. It was awful. I was dragged onto this stage. The lights were so bright. I couldn't see anything. Some man kept saying numbers. Then I was dragged backstage and thrown back in the cage with the other girls."

"Wow. Sounds awful."

"It was."

"Then what happened?"

"Some guys stuck me in a limo with some other girls and I ended up here. What about you?"

"Dude picked me up in a limo. I thought he was a John. Drugged me and stuck me in here."

"Why did you think his name was John?"

Angel laughed. "You're so cute. You ain't a whore, are you?"

Her severe look of indignation made Angel laugh even more. "No. Why would you say that?"

"Cause everyone here is. What's your name?"

"Emily."

"Emily, how did you get to the sale?"

"Some guys grabbed me."

A sudden pain broadsided Angel. She wrapped her arms around herself and bent over. This time her groan was loud. "Oh, crap. That was bad."

"What's wrong with you?"

Through clenched teeth, Angel answered, "Withdrawal."

"From what?"

"Smack. Like I said." The pain eased. "Now tell me about these dudes grabbing you."

Emily launched into a long tale about how she had been walking back from a friend's house and two guys in a long, dark car had pulled over and asked her for directions. When she came over to the curb to answer them, someone got out of the back of the car and grabbed her. He put something over her mouth and she had blacked out. When she woke up, she was in a huge truck with a bunch of other girls. She told Angel about the long trip. About how they had to pee in the back of the semi-trailer. They got no food. No water. Then, many hours later, she was herded out of the truck into a warehouse and shoved into a cage until she was sold.

When she finished her story, Angel asked, "Have you even had sex before?"

"Not really."

Angel raised her brows. "What do you mean?"

"Well, Tommy Anderson felt me up once."

Angel smiled though she felt like crying. If only she could say the same.

Emily asked, "Where am I?"

"St. Louis."

Emily said nothing for some time then finally asked, "Why?"

"Why are any of us here?"

Chapter 28

Sara knocked on Angel's door but didn't bother waiting for an answer. She opened it. Chester followed her into the room. He carried a twin mattress with him the way most people carried a book. He put it down in the corner. Emily jumped to her feet off of Angel's bed. Sara smiled. That was a good sign.

"Good morning, Angel, Emily. Sleep well?"

"Peachy," Angel replied.

Emily said nothing.

Sara looked at the youngster. "You doing okay, hon?" Still nothing. Emily just stared at her, arms crossed, solid stance, eyes narrowed. "We're not going to hurt you." Sara glanced at Angel, who had a sly smile on her face. "Angel, something you want to say?"

Angel shook her head, the smile staying put.

"Fine." Sara turned back to Emily. "We got some better clothes for you, hon. Follow Chester and he'll take you to a dressing room."

The young girl brushed by Sara and followed Chester saying nothing. When they'd left, Sara closed the door and joined Angel on the bed.

"Getting a bit crowded in here," Angel said.

"You know what you need to do to get out of here."

"Why won't you just let me go home?"

"You want to go home?"

"Fine, why don't you just let me go."

"You'll have that option soon."

"If I don't die first."

"Dying here is lot more unlikely than dying out there if you left now." Sara stared at Angel for a few seconds. And Angel held her gaze. Another good sign. "What do you think Keyshawn will do to you if he finds you?"

Angel didn't answer. She pulled her knees up to her chin and frowned. "That girl you put with me, she ain't like me."

"Of course not," Sara said, "she's twelve and you're eighteen."

"Naw, not that. She ain't an addict."

"Ohhhh. You're admitting you're an addict?"

"I use drugs."

"Angel, you're an addict. You don't just use drugs. You have to use drugs. That's why you allow men to debase you, to abuse you. That's why you sell your body for sex. You have to get that next fix."

"Emily, she ain't like me."

Sara decided to stop the assault. Angel smiled at her. Again, seemed like progress. Sara suspected Angel agreed she was an addict, but she wasn't about to give Sara the satisfaction of being right. Not yet, anyway.

"Heck, she ain't even had sex yet."

"What?"

Angel smiled again. A self-satisfied grin that she had one up on Sara. Again, not a bad sign. Showing she cared some, had some respect.

"That's right," Angel said. "She's a virgin. Got felt up by Tommy something or other, but that's it."

"How can that be? What's she doing here?"

Angel relayed the story Emily had told her.

"Good Lord," Sara said.

"Obviously, He ain't good all the time."

Sara hesitated, and decided not to pounce on Angel again. She breathed in deeply and counted to five. "Actually, God is good all the time. It's people that aren't good."

"Whatever."

Sara glanced at the ceiling. "Do you believe in God?"

Angel hugged her knees closer and rocked. "I don't know. I used to. But now, I ain't so sure." She rocked a little faster.

Sara stroked Angel's shoulder. Surprisingly, Angel didn't flinch away. "Talk to me, Angel. Tell me what happened."

Angel continued rocking. "You wouldn't understand."

Sara chuckled. "Really?"

"Oh, yeah, I guess you might."

More rocking. Sara said nothing. She heard footsteps upstairs, distant talking, girls going about their day, free to roam the premises, because they could be trusted. They wanted to be there. Knew how valuable this place was.

"Tell me, Angel. What turned you off of God?"

Angel stopped rocking and looked at Sara, her eyes stinging with tears, lips quivering. She whispered, "My stepfather."

"He abused you?"

Angel nodded, looked down, her hands doing laps around each other. She mumbled, "Over and over."

Sara pulled Angel close and wrapped her arms around her. Angel sunk into her and wept, her body shaking.

After several minutes, when the sobs subsided, Angel pushed away, then glared defiantly at Sara.

"Why would a God who supposedly loves everyone let my stepdad do to me what he did?"

Sara had some deep theological answer she could have given about how God allows man free will and Satan rules the earth at this present time, but that's not what Angel needed to hear. "I don't know, hon. I'm an ex-prostitute, not a theologian. Maybe we can ask Chester."

"Sure." Angel buried her head in her knees.

"And you know," Sara continued, "we may not know until we get to heaven. The important thing is to trust Christ, so when the time comes, when you're in heaven, you can ask Him why He allowed that to happen." Angel collapsed against Sara, who again wrapped her arms around the teenager and held her. "Just remember, hon, God brought you here. He put you where you were when Mr. Rockport picked you up, and he brought you here to start healing."

Angel said nothing. Instead, she wrapped her arms around Sara and squeezed tight and went into another round of sobs. Sara stayed with Angel until she pulled away, laid down, and went to sleep. No sedative necessary.

Chapter 29

Calvin Rockport leaned back in his leather office chair and stared at his deceased wife's favorite tree, the magnificent, thirty-year old magnolia with dark green leaves. The tree had already been ten years old when they'd planted it. He remembered with fondness the mock argument he'd had with his wife over the cost of moving a ten-year old tree. Of course, he was going to do it, he always did anything she wanted. Now, he'd give his entire fortune to have back either his wife or daughter. Double his fortune or more if he could have them both back. Ironic, he thought. Maybe if he'd spent less time amassing his fortune, he'd at least still have his daughter.

A knock at his office door.

"Come in." He swiveled to face the door.

Sara and Chester entered.

"Good morning," Rockport said. "How are the new girls doing?"

Chester said, "Settling in like they always do at first. Keeping Marsha busy as well."

"I'll bet."

Rockport looked at Sara. Her face was blank. Was she still angry? "And the youngest one?"

Sara said nothing, so Chester answered. "She's insisting on leaving. No shots necessary, 'cause she's not a user."

"Family?"

Sara finally piped in. "She doesn't want to go home. Doesn't know where she wants to go, just away."

"Suggestions?"

Sara sighed then slumped into one of the armchairs. "If she insists on leaving, all we can do is call family services. I hate that option, but what choice do we have? She's not a hooker, not a drug addict, and so young."

"How did she and Angel get along?"

Sara nodded. "She got to Angel."

"Told you."

"Don't even start, buster. You're still in my doghouse."

Rockport chuckled. "And how is Angel this morning?" Sara told him about her conversation with Angel. "Real progress, then. That's great. Do you think we can delay Emily long enough to wait until Angel wakes up, then put them back together?" Sara nodded. "So, big guy," Rockport addressed Chester, "feel like being a babysitter?"

"I be delighted, sir," Chester said in a mock Southern black accent. He shook his head and started to leave the office.

Before he could leave, though, Rockport said, "About last night, that other car, what do you think?"

Chester turned back. "Not a cop. Only one person I could see. Keyshawn's muscle always come in pairs. Probably not one of Big Eddie's guys. They travel in much nicer vehicles. A private eye, maybe. Looking for one of the girls?"

"My thinking as well. Could have been the same car we saw before. Probably George Bruder?"

Chester nodded. "Could be."

"Thanks Chester. I'll make some calls." Chester started to leave again. Rockport added, "Maybe Emily likes checkers." Chester raised his hand, left the office, and closed the door behind him.

Rockport looked at Sara. She looked absolutely exhausted. "I would have thought you'd be energized after your breakthrough."

She smiled weakly. "It's not Angel. It's Emily. She's twelve, Calvin. They grabbed a twelve-year old. What would have happened to that poor thing had you not bought her?"

Rockport nodded and said nothing for a minute. "Let's get to work." Sara moved over to the other desk with her computer on it. Rockport asked, "Let's go with Chester's theory. So, other than the girls we brought in last night and Angel, where are we with the other girls?"

"All of them have had contact with someone outside."

"Must be Angel, then, he's looking for. What else do we know about her?"

"Not much. But let me do some digging." Sara clicked away on her computer.

Rockport picked up his cell phone, considered calling Detective Warren, but as he started to punch in the number, memories flooded into his consciousness and he gave into them.

Rockport cradled the phone between cheek and shoulder. Outside his office window, snow casually fell. Most of the dark green magnolia leaves wore a frozen white blanket. He'd taken to working from his home office, too keyed up and too depressed at the same time to stay in his company's office.

In his ear a private detective he'd hired, the fifth one, told him he'd run into a dead end in Chicago. The gravelly voiced detective told Rockport his daughter had been seen on the streets, but not for at least two months. Rockport prayed to God she was not living on the streets now, as Chicago was even colder than St. Louis.

"I'll keep digging, sir."

"You do that." Rockport hung up and almost immediately, a knock came at his door and his butler told him he had two visitors. "Show them in."

The door opened and his senior vice president of sales walked in with another man, one he presumed was a sales guy, considering the well-pressed dark blue suit, bright yellow tie and powder-blue shirt. The man's eyes darted from side to side. He would not make eye contact with Rockport.

"Paul, what brings you out here?" Rockport stood and walked around to the corner of his desk where he stuck out his hand and shook Paul Kasper's hand. The tall, thin man had straight, blond hair, a smooth shaved face, and bright blue eyes.

"A personal matter, Calvin. This is Richard Perkins, one of our field sales reps. One of our best, I might add."

Rockport put out his hand again. Perkins shook hands. His grip was firm, but his hand felt clammy. He made only brief eye contact with Rockport. He had black, short hair, spiked with gel. "You seem nervous, Mr. Perkins. What's the matter?"

Perkins looked at Kasper, who nodded.

Kasper said, "He has something to tell you, Calvin. It's a little embarrassing for him. I've assured him he's safe, that we won't fire him for his, um, indiscretions."

"Indiscretions?" Rockport raised his eyebrows. "The good Lord knows I've had enough of those myself." He smiled at the sales rep, then walked back around his desk. "Sit down, Mr. Perkins. Tell me what's on your mind." Rockport sat in his executive chair and leaned forward, arms resting on his desk. Perkins and Kasper both sat in the armchairs directly facing Rockport's desk, Perkins to the right, Kasper to the left. The sales rep studied his hands.

After fifteen seconds of silence, Kasper said, "Go ahead, Richard. Tell him what you told me."

"It's...it's about your, your daughter, sir."

"What about my daughter?" Perkins winced and Rockport regretted his harsh, quick inquiry. Softer, he repeated, "What about my daughter, Mr. Perkins?"

"I, um, I met her at the holiday part last year. She's quite, um, quite attractive. Not someone I'd soon forget, sir." He looked down and rubbed his hands together. Rockport resisted the urge to prod him on. "I mean, sir, if I saw her again, I'd be pretty certain it was her. You know, I even, you know, talked with her some."

Rockport's patience wore thin. "Fine. You've met my daughter. You spoke with her. Come to the point, please."

Perkins heaved a huge sigh then blurted out, "When I'm on the road, I watch porn on my laptop at night. I try not to, but I can't help it. I...I don't want my wife to know, sir, please. And I don't want to lose my job. I know it's against company policy, but no one else—"

Rockport waved his hand. "Get to the point, Perkins."

"Yes, sir." More hand rubbing. "Can I show you something, sir?"

"Sure."

Perkins came around to Rockport's side of the desk. "Excuse me. I need to use your computer." Rockport rolled his chair aside and Perkins bent over the desk. He launched a web browser then typed in a web address. Several pictures of naked women came up with arrows in the middle. Videos, Rockport realized. He looked away, waiting. Perkins did some more clicking. "Okay, sir. This is it." He'd opened a single video. He started playing it.

Rockport forced himself to watch, appalled by what he was seeing. A woman was performing oral sex on a man. He could only see the back of the woman. She was thin, had slightly longer than shoulder-length blond hair. This view lasted for about a minute then the camera panned to the right, coming around to show the woman's face.

All sound ceased. Rockport's peripheral vision collapsed. He saw nothing but the woman. A woman who had his daughter Carolyn's face. Her eyes were dead. Her smile was forced. Her cheeks were sallow. There was a tattoo on her right shoulder of a dragon-like bird. He stared until the camera again panned to the back of the woman.

The spell ended and Rockport fell back in his chair. He buried his face in his hands, fighting the tears, fighting the scream that wanted to jettison from him. His stomach knotted, his throat threatened to close. With sheer will, he composed himself. When he removed his hands from his face, he noticed Perkins had returned to his seat.

The sales rep asked, "It's her, isn't it, sir?"

Rockport could only nod.

Perkins took a piece of paper and a pen from the desk and scratched some words on it. "Here's the web address and the name of the site. Maybe this will help you find her, sir. And again, I'm so sorry for my, um, my problem."

Rockport couldn't talk. He was afraid if he did, he'd explode. Instead he waved his hand. Kasper took the cue and stood, leading Perkins out of the office.

Several hours later, Rockport closed the web browser. He'd not been able to even turn and face it until then. He picked up his cell phone and called the private detective he'd spoken with earlier. When the man answered, Rockport explained the situation and gave him the particulars about the website. He told the PI he wanted the name of the person who had made the film.

"Calvin." Silence for several seconds. "Calvin!" Rockport felt himself vibrate, then heard, "Calvin, are you still on this planet?" He mentally shook himself and returned to the present where Sara was shoving him in the shoulder.

"Sorry. Just some bad memories."

"I was able to find out more about Angel."

"Great. What did you find?"

Sara stared at him. "You okay?" He nodded. "Angel's father died when Angel was one. Her mother remarried when Angel was seven. Then her mother died when Angel was eleven. Looks like her stepfather had custody of her until she turned eighteen. That appears to be when she left home."

"Any police reports?"

"No, not in Iowa. Arrested once here for prostitution."

"For abuse, I meant."

"Yeah, I know what you meant. No, none." She paused. "But not surprising. Girls usually keep quiet, either out of embarrassment or fear."

"The aunt, Eileen Seager?"

"I tried calling again. No answer. Did find something interesting, though. She works for the Iowa Highway Patrol as a records clerk."

Rockport rested his elbows on his desk and strummed his fingers together. Outside a mockingbird went through its repertoire, including a hawk's scream. His wife had always found it fascinating when a mockingbird did that. "Yeah, I knew that. You think she's here? You think she's who hired George Bruder?"

"Could be. I couldn't find a cell phone, but those numbers are hard to get. Should we contact Bruder?"

"Not yet. We need to know more about the relationship with her aunt."

Sara nodded.

Rockport added, "See if you can find out anything about her aunt from Angel. Would she be a safe harbor?"

Again, Sara nodded then pushed back from her desk. "I'll see if she's awake. Maybe I'll do a group session with Angel and Emily together. Maybe they'll talk about their families."

"Worth a try."

Sara left and Rockport punched in some numbers on his cell phone. After several rings a voice from the past answered, a rough, gravelly voice, even more grizzled since the last time Rockport had spoken to him.

"Mr. Rockport. What can I do for you, sir?"

Still impeccably polite, just like he'd been years ago.

"I have another job for you. I need some information on a man named John Stiltson in Ottumwa, Iowa. He's the stepfather of Angel Atkins. I need to know as much about the relationship between stepfather and stepdaughter that you can find out."

"Absolutely, sir. I appreciate you sending the work my way."

"And don't worry about discretion. Angel is safe. Be as heavy handed as you need to be to find out the truth."

"Yes, sir."

They hung up, but Rockport knew this private detective would never be as heavy-handed with someone as he and Chester had been years back when the PI had given him the name of the man who filmed his daughter.

They sat in the car outside the ten-story apartment building on the outskirts of downtown Chicago, on the north side. The sun warmed the car, giving the illusion of a nice day. Outside, though, the wind blew and the temperature struggled to breach zero. It hadn't taken the private detective Rockport had hired long to find the man who made the film featuring his daughter. Rockport had never been able to bring himself to watch any more of that video. But his imagination did quite a number on him.

Since talking with Perkins, Rockport had barely slept. When he closed his eyes, a movie played in his head, his daughter doing all kinds of unspeakable acts with faceless men. With his nerves frayed, both from lack of sleep and anticipation of learning more information, he knew he wasn't thinking straight. He knew there was no reason for him to be here, that it should be Chester and some of his friends, not him and Chester. But, there was no way he could keep himself away from this. He trusted Chester implicitly, but still, maybe he'd miss something or not ask the right question.

"You ready, boss man?" Chester asked.

Was he ready? He didn't have the experience with this type of thing. He didn't have street sense. He really shouldn't be here at all, but sure, he was ready. Rockport nodded.

"Let's go." Chester opened the car door. "Ain't getting any earlier. Pretty sure he's still in there. No reason for him to slip out the back."

They had seen the man the PI had identified walk through the glass front doors of the apartment complex thirty minutes earlier. The PI had told them the guy, who looked to be in his mid-twenties, had a place on the fourth floor, third window from the left. They'd watched that window and had seen a light come on. No one else had entered or left the building in that thirty-minute span. It was a Wednesday morning, eleven-fifteen. Most people were probably at work.

The PI had told them he did his filming at a small warehouse about four miles from there, on the shores of Lake Michigan. Chester had suggested talking to him there, but Rockport could not bring himself to visit the place his daughter had been filmed. Besides, he wanted to talk to this guy in private.

Rockport pulled out the five by seven photo of Carolyn, one printed from the video she'd been in. It showed only her face. The PI had printed it for him. He returned it to his inside coat pocket.

Chester got out. Rockport followed, pulling his long wool coat tighter around him. Chester wore a black turtleneck sweater and jeans, no coat. They shuffled quickly to the door, trying to avoid icy patches on the sidewalk. The outside door of the apartment complex was open, but the inside door was locked. Three stacked rows of mailboxes took up most of the wall to the right. The majority had names typed on a sticker. All of them had a button to buzz the apartment. They located the one belonging to Daniel Osborne, the name the PI had given them. Chester punched the button and held it down a few seconds.

"Yeah, who is it?" asked a nasally voice.

"I'm here for the audition," Chester said. He had called Osborne a few days earlier, posing as someone interested in getting into movies. Osborne had set up the appointment. Rockport had been surprised he'd set it for the apartment, but when they'd last spoken to the PI, he'd said this apartment was his office, where he did auditions, not where he lived. Chester had convinced Rockport it would be easier to pose as someone wanting an audition rather than trying to visit him where he lived. Besides, the PI had said Osborne had two roommates, which could complicate things.

They heard a loud buzz, then the nasally voice said, "Room 408."

Rockport grabbed the door. Chester went through, followed by Rockport. They took a slow elevator that smelled faintly of urine to the fourth floor. The hallway was dim. Naked forty-watt bulbs lined the ceiling every twenty feet or so, only half of them actually working.

At 408, Chester knocked. Rockport stood off to the side so he wouldn't be seen right away.

The door opened.

"You Maurice?" asked the nasally voiced Osborne.

"Yeah. You alone?"

"Um, yes, but why?"

Chester shoved the man back and in one fluid motion pulled a nine millimeter from under his sweater. Rockport followed them through the door.

"What are you doing?" Osborne's voice went up two octaves. "There's no money here."

Chester shoved him again and knocked him into a ragged gray couch. Osborne fell over the back, rolled, and crashed into a laminated coffee table that had Hustler magazines on it. The table scooted forward on the scratched wooden floor. Osborne fell between the table and couch. Chester moved quickly around the couch. He grabbed Osborne by his collar and planted him on the couch, shoving the gun in his face. Rockport also went around the couch, stood off to Chester's left, out of reach of Osborne.

"What do you want?" Osborne asked. "I got nothing of value."

Osborne probably weighed no more than one-forty and was around five-ten. He held up his bony arms—both had dark red spots up and down the insides, along with some bruising. He had shoulder-length greasy brown hair. Several days' stubble decorated his gaunt face. His brown eyes were wide and shifted continually between Rockport and Chester.

Rockport reached inside his coat to pull out the picture. Osborne flinched and again held up his arms. "Don't shoot me, man."

Chester kicked his legs. "Shut up. Ain't no one going to shoot you as long as you cooperate."

"Cooperate with what? I didn't do anything."

Rockport gave Chester the picture who showed it to Osborne. "You did a movie with this girl. What do you know about her?"

"I...I don't know that girl. Never seen her before."

Chester smashed the top of the nine millimeter across Osborne's face. A nasty gash opened in the thin man's cheek. "Wrong approach, little man. We know you made the video."

Rockport started to tremble. He clenched and unclenched his hands, wanting desperately to shove Chester aside and pummel this man to within an inch of his life. But he stayed put, breathing hard, audibly.

"Let's try this again," Chester said. "When was the last time you saw her?"

Osborne hesitated, the wheels turning in his brain. He rubbed his cheek, examined the blood on his fingers. "I filmed her about a month ago. I remember 'cause she's real pretty. That's the last I saw of her, though."

The dam broke.

Rockport screamed "Liar!" and launched himself at Osborne. He grabbed the man's throat and started banging his head back and forth against the sofa. The backing was hard enough that Osborne's head made a dull thump each time it hit.

"Where is my daughter?"

Thump, thump.

"Tell me where she is."

Thump, thump.

"Where's my daughter?"

Thump, thump.

Chester pulled Rockport back and whispered in his ear. "Let me handle this."

Osborne looked woozy. His head bobbed, eyes out of focus. He rubbed the back of his head. "I'm really sorry, man. I am. But I don't know nothing."

Chester reached down and grabbed Osborne by the front of his shirt, picking him up and bringing him to eye level. "I suggest you think real hard and tell us anything you know about her."

Osborne shook his head. "I don't know nothing."

Chester threw him over the couch. He pocketed his nine millimeter, then went around the couch and grabbed Osborne, again lifting him up to eye level. "Last chance. What do you know about her?"

Again, Osborne shook his head and started to say something, but shut his mouth as Chester picked him up further. "Alright, alright. I'll tell what I know."

Chester dragged Osborne around the couch and threw him back on it. Osborne spent the next fifteen minutes telling them about how Carolyn had come to him, strung out on heroin, but tired of turning tricks to earn the bread to buy her drugs. She had heard of him and that he paid good money to do movies. She worked with him for about a month and made three videos. He paid her after each one. One day about a month ago, he was setting up for the fourth with her, but she never showed up. He hadn't seen her since.

"You sure that's it?" Chester asked.

"I swear man, that's it."

"Let's go, boss." Chester started toward the door. But before he could reach it, Rockport again launched himself at Osborne, again grabbed his throat, and again started banging the man's head against the back of the couch.

"How could you?"

Thump, thump.

"Do that to my girl?"

Thump. Thump.

"You dirty piece of filth."

Thump, thump.

Chester dragged Rockport away. At first he wouldn't let go of Osborne, which pulled the man onto the coffee table again. But finally, he let go and Chester pulled him out of the apartment and back down to the car.

That was the last lead Rockport ever had on his daughter. The next time he saw her was in the morgue in Joliet.

Chapter 30

Sara knocked and Angel grunted, so Sara opened the door and peeked in. “Can I come in?” Sara asked. Angel just waved, so Sara stepped through the door and closed it. “How are you feeling, hon?”

Angel sat up, rubbed her eyes, stretched and said, “So-so. Kind of nauseous.”

“You want something to eat?”

Angel shook her head.

Another knock and the door opened again. Emily walked in. The gown she’d arrived in had been replaced by loose jeans and an old St. Louis Rams T-shirt, one that was a bit large on the thin girl. She also wore Adidas running shoes. The entire ensemble had probably belonged to Carolyn, Rockport’s daughter.

“Have a seat, hon.”

The young girl eyed Sara suspiciously and gave Angel a brief smile.

Angel said, “Hey, baby girl. What’s up?”

“I’m better at checkers than the big black dude.”

“Awesome,” Angel said. She even smiled. Both girls looked at Sara, waiting. Angel asked, “What is this, group therapy?”

In answer Sara said, “Tell me about your families.”

Emily looked down and studied her hands. Angel watched the younger girl for a few seconds.

“Sure, I’ll start. Not that much to tell.” Angel studied the ceiling for a few seconds, then sighed. She swept her hair back and frowned. Emily’s gaze was glued to her. “My mother died when I was eleven. I never really knew my real dad 'cause he died when I was a baby. Seems cancer runs early in my family. Both my dad and mom died from it and my aunt even had it."

"You grew up with just you and your mother?" Sara asked.

Angel's jaw clenched and her hands did a washing motion. "Till I was seven. Then my mom remarried."

"Did you get along with your mother's new husband?"

"We tolerated each other until my mother died."

"Then what?" asked Sara.

Angel looked at Emily and said, "What about you, baby girl? Your turn."

"Do I have to?" Emily turned wide eyes to Sara.

"You're underage, hon. We need to know what to do with you."

"Just let me go."

"And where would you go? You're in a strange city. You don't know anyone."

Tears formed in the corners of Emily's eyes.

"Look, hon," Sara continued, "we have two choices. You can stay here for a while or we'll have to call child services, who will probably take you back to Houston and turn you over to child services there. And they'll notify your parents."

"Parent. Just my dad." Several tears ran down her cheeks. She dipped her head and shook it slowly. Sara envied her gorgeous red hair. "We used to be so close. Then...then he...he." Emily started crying, covering her face with her hands. Before Sara could react, Angel jumped up and hugged the twelve-year-old. She didn't say anything, just held her. Emily's crying subsided.

Sara softly asked, "Did he start abusing you?"

Emily shook her head and uncovered her face. Without looking up, she said, "But he started scaring me. He was drinking so much. One time...one time he swung at me because I did something to make him mad. He blamed me for my mom's death."

"Did your mother die when you were born?"

"Huh?" Emily looked up. She clung to Angel, who gently rocked her. "No, she died last year. In a car wreck."

"Why did your dad blame you?"

More tears welled up in her eyes. "We were arguing." She dipped her head again and started sobbing. Through the sobs, Emily said, "I distracted her. My dad, he never forgave me."

Sara said nothing. There really wasn't anything to say.

Angel filled the silence. "Stay here, baby girl. Stay with me. I'll take care of you. I'll be your big sister."

Softly, Emily answered, "I'd like that. I never had a sister."

"Me neither."

Sara let the two hug and rock for a few minutes. When it seemed Emily was over the worst of it, she said, "Emily, hon, I need to talk with Angel for a bit."

Emily raised her head. "Okay. Can I play checkers again with that nice black man?"

Sara smiled and texted Chester. For the five minutes it took Chester to arrive, Sara silently watched the two girls chat, watched Angel comfort Emily, and realized how right Rockport had been. Emily was exactly what Angel needed. Not that she would admit it to him.

Chester walked in. "You ready for some more beating down at the checkerboard?" He grinned broadly.

"Yeah, right. You know I won all those games." Emily passed Chester and walked into the hallway. Chester winked at Sara. "And I'm going to destroy you again!"

"We'll see about that, little one." They left and Chester closed the door behind him.

Sara asked Angel, "Do you think your stepdad is looking for you?"

Angel's face contorted. She clenched her fists. She yelled, "Don't you dare tell my stepdad I'm here. Don't you fricking dare!"

Sara moved next to Angel, who flinched and pressed herself into the corner of the wall as far as she could go. Sara touched the frightened girl's knee. "We won't do that if you don't want us to, hon."

"Then why do you care if he's looking for me? I'm an adult, you can't turn me over to him."

Sara waited, trying to maintain a comforting expression. Angel breathed heavy and glared at her. Slowly, the anger and fear subsided, but didn't vacate.

"Someone hired a private detective to find you. We're only trying to determine who."

Dripping with contempt, Angel spit out, "He wouldn't spend a freaking dime on me."

"You mentioned an aunt who had cancer. Did she die?"

"My aunt Eileen? No, she's alive, she's..." Angel failed to fight back tears. "I...I didn't even say goodbye to her when I left. It was my..." She lowered her head, covered her face and wept. Sara let her cry herself out. After a few minutes, Angel snuffled, wiped her eyes with her fists. "I ran away on my birthday."

"Could your aunt be looking for you?"

"She could be. She works for the cops. The Iowa Highway Patrol, I think."

"Should we contact her? Let her know you're safe?"

"Sure, but I don't know what she can do. She's barely supporting herself. She...she lost a leg to cancer. Now has a pros, proth, pro—"

"Prosthetic leg?"

"Yeah. I wouldn't want to bother her with my problems." Tears clung to the corners of her eyes waiting to be pushed down her cheek. She wiped both hands across her eyes. "But I would like to talk to her. Can I see her?"

"What's her relationship with your stepdad?"

Fire returned to Angel's eyes. "Hates him."

"Come here." Sara opened her arms. Angel hesitated, but finally unfolded her legs, scooted close to Sara and wrapped her arms around her. Once she did, she buried her head in Sara's shoulder and cried some more. "We'll see what we can do, hon. In the meantime, let's get you whole again."

Angel just nodded and clung tighter to Sara.

Fifteen minutes later, Sara knocked on Rockport's office door.

"Come in."

She slipped in and immediately noticed how defeated Rockport looked. "What's up? You don't look so good."

"Just a stroll down memory lane."

"Your daughter?"

Rockport nodded and looked out the window. Several of the magnolia flowers were already starting to brown, though more buds were starting to open as well. She knew Rockport viewed that tree as a symbol of hope. Always green through searing summers and frigid winters, with pure, white flowers in the spring.

"What did you find out from Angel and Emily?"

Sara told Rockport first about Emily.

He asked, "Do you think that relationship between father and daughter can be salvaged?"

"Let's talk with her some more. I certainly want to hope so. She's not cut out for being placed in the system. Maybe we can talk with some other family members. If she'll open up a bit."

"Good thinking. And Angel?"

She told him about Angel's fear and hatred of her stepdad and what Angel had said about her aunt.

Rockport said, "I have a PI looking into Stiltson. And the aunt's in town. Maybe it's time we met Mr. George Bruder."

"Sounds like a plan." Sara smiled. "It's lunchtime. You're here, today. Come eat with the girls. Let them spend some time with their benefactor."

He glanced again out the window at his tree, probably thinking of his daughter. But he had to move on. Had to see the good he was doing, the plan God had for him, to help all these others in trouble.

He sighed, stood, and said, "You win. I'll join you."

After lunch Sara left the dining room and headed for the library downstairs. As she walked through the foyer, she felt a slight breeze of hot air. She stopped and stared at the front door. It was slightly ajar. She opened the door and stepped out onto the front porch. Across the street, a dusty green pickup with a trailer attached was parked in their neighbor's driveway. A tanned man in grungy white painter pants and no shirt stood on a self-propelled professional mower. Sara smelled the cut grass. She glanced left then right. No one else in sight. She heard nothing other than the mower.

She stepped back in the house, closed the door, and latched the dead bolt. Were any of the girls scheduled to go anywhere that afternoon? She didn't think so. She walked through the kitchen, down the stairs, and as she reached the library door, a hunch hit her.

She deviated and returned to the other side of the basement, where the new girls stayed. Angel's door was closed. Sara tried it. Unlocked. She opened the door. Empty. She tried to recall if Angel had still been in the dining room when she'd left but couldn't. Back up the stairs and to the dining room. Only Marsha and Rockport, sitting at a far table talking.

Sara searched the house. First, she went bedroom to bedroom upstairs. None of the girls had seen Angel since lunch. On the main floor she checked every room. Again, no one had seen Angel. Sara also realized she'd not seen Emily during her search. She went back down into the basement and checked all the rooms. Two doors were locked, which she unlocked and peeked in. The three girls that should have been in the two rooms were, all asleep. Emily and Angel were nowhere to be found.

Sara calmed herself with a deep breath then headed back upstairs. She glanced in the dining room. No one. So, she headed to Rockport's office, dreading having to tell him that both Angel and Emily were gone.

Chapter 31

"Well?" Lieutenant Pratt asked. "Is it her?"

Lefty shivered. Not sure if it was from the frigid air in the county morgue or from the young, blonde woman lying on the slab, her lips blue, eyes wide open staring at nothing. Probably both. He willed her to blink so things would be okay. His stomach bubbled. Again, he wasn't sure if that was because of who might be dead before him or the mixed smells of formaldehyde, disinfectant, and death. "I don't know. Could be her. What happened? Where did you find her?"

"Cause of death has not yet been ascertained," said Riley Morris, the county coroner. He was tall, medium build, had wisps of salt-and-pepper hair on a pointed head. Black-framed glasses rested on the end of a pointed nose. He wore a lab coat over a maroon dress shirt and black dress pants, sharply creased.

"Can you give me an educated guess?" Lefty asked.

Morris lifted the young woman's left arm and showed them the tracks running down it. "Heroin overdose, would be my educated guess."

"She was found in an alley close to the library on Lindbergh," Pratt said. "Some guy saw a homeless man rifling through her pockets and yelled. When he went to help the girl, she didn't respond. He dialed 911."

"Huh," Lefty grunted. "Someone actually got involved."

"Yeah, surprised me as well," Pratt said.

"Any identification?" Lefty asked.

"Nope. If there was, the homeless man must have stolen it."

The three men stared at the girl for half a minute.

Morris said, "Can I get to work?"

"Let me call someone first." Lefty's stomach stopped boiling and twisted into a knot. As he stepped into the outer lobby, he pulled his cell phone from his jeans pocket. His thumb hovered over the recent call entry for Eileen Seager. He closed his eyes, took a deep breath, opened his eyes and pressed.

After three rings, Eileen answered, "Hello. George, I hope you have good news."

Well, wasn't that a great opening line. Now what was he supposed to say? "I'm hoping it's nothing, but I need you to come to the county morgue."

Silence for nearly a minute, then Eileen whispered, "She's dead?"

"Someone is. I don't know if it's Angel or not. No ID on the girl. And all I've seen is a single picture, so I can't say it's her or not."

"How...how did she die?"

"Overdose."

"Oh, Lord. Please, God, I pray it's not Angel."

Lefty heard some sounds. Thinking she'd set the phone down. "Eileen, you there?"

"Yes, I'm here. On my way." She hung up.

He sat in a metal frame chair with sparse padding and waited. It was the longest fifteen minutes of his life.

A young morgue attendant led Eileen into the outer lobby. She was expressionless, but her eyes flitted back and forth, refusing to lock onto his. She wrapped her arms around herself and shivered. Her Hawkeyes T-shirt and jean shorts didn't offer much warmth in the cold building. He approached her, put his hand on her back, and gently led her into the autopsy room, where Pratt and Morris chatted. They stopped talking as soon as Lefty and Eileen walked in.

"Ms. Seager?" asked Pratt. "We've met, briefly. I'm Lieutenant Pratt. Thank you for coming down."

Eileen nodded and stared at the girl on the slab. Tears started rolling down her eyes. She fell to her knees, bowed her head and started muttering something. Lefty knelt and put his arm around her shoulder. "I'm so sorry, Eileen, that I couldn't get to her in time."

She raised her head and despite tears streaming down her cheeks, she smiled. "It's not her, George. It's not her. Praise the Lord, it's not her." Her expression changed. She frowned and shook her head. "But it's someone's little girl. That poor thing." She stood and brushed the back of her hand across the dead girl's cheek. "This poor thing. I pray she knew you, Lord." Addressing Pratt she said, "I'm sorry, Lieutenant, I can't help you identify her."

"I'm glad it's not your niece, Ms. Seager." He shook her hand. "And if anyone can find your niece, George can."

Eileen smiled at Pratt then looked at Lefty. "Now what?"

He led her out of the room because the smell was nauseating him. "I'm going to follow up on a lead. I'll call you tonight with an update."

"You better."

She hugged him. He hesitated putting his arm around her, but when she didn't release him right away, he did. They stayed that way a bit, then Eileen pushed away and left the morgue. Lefty waited a minute or so then headed out himself, on his way to Big Eddie's.

Lefty slowly walked up the sidewalk leading to the front stoop of Big Eddie's massive home. He didn't like the expression of the man stationed at the door, a mixture of disgust, surprise, and feral delight. Lefty felt like a mouse who had just rounded a corner to find himself face to face with a cat. The man's expression remained unchanged and he didn't say anything until Lefty had climbed the six steps.

"Arms up and turn around," the guard said. Lefty stared at him. "Okay, arm up, man. Hurry up." Lefty raised his arm and the man patted him down. Nothing to find—he never carried a piece anymore. "Wait here." The man disappeared into the house then returned less than a minute later. He grinned, even more feral than before. "Go on in."

As soon as Lefty entered the one hundred-year-old, three-story mansion, two more goons grabbed him. Well, one grabbed his arm, and the other made an attempt to grab him, but with no arm there whiffed then grabbed ahold of Lefty's shirt sleeve.

"What's the deal, guys?" Lefty asked.

Big Eddie appeared from the hallway. "In the kitchen. Tie him to a chair."

The two dragged Lefty down the hall, under a sparkling chandelier, past modern-era paintings, and into a large kitchen with a brick oven, island counter, and broad bay window looking out onto a deck and pool. And of course, white walls. Even white pots and pans, hanging from hooks over the island. Outside, several bikinied women lay on loungers or strutted their stuff from a bar to their chairs.

One of the cookie-cutter goons pulled a chair from a white ceramic tile table and shoved it under Lefty. The other shoved him down onto it. The first produced a short length of rope from a drawer in the island counter. Must do this frequently.

The two goons stared at him for a few seconds. Then the one with the rope turned to Big Eddie. "Now what, Boss?"

"Tie him up."

"How? He only got one arm."

Big Eddie lowered his head and shook it. "Can I assume you patted him down?"

Goon number one repeated the routine of the goon at the door. "Clean, boss."

Big Eddie shooed away the two men, who took up positions by the island counter. "I'm surprised you'd show your face here, little man."

"Why?"

"Why?" Big Eddie crouched and put his bear paws on Lefty's knees. "You ask why? Where were you last night?"

Lefty smiled. "I think you know. I was where you sent me."

"And what did you do there?"

"Watched something that made me sick to my stomach."

"Anything else?"

"Yeah. Watched some dude that had sold a bunch of girls get ripped off."

Big Eddie squeezed both of Lefty's knees, hard. Lefty resisted the urge to belt his large face that was now only inches away.

"And I suppose you knew nothing about that?"

"You think I was involved with that?" Lefty gritted his teeth, hoping Big Eddie wouldn't crush his kneecaps.

"Seems a bit of a coincidence."

"I'm going to kick you in the groin, if you don't let go," Lefty said.

Big Eddie smiled, but released the pressure. "And what do you think would happen after that?"

"Probably something painful."

Big Eddie stood. "What do you know about last night?"

Lefty started to reach into his back pocket. One of the goons grabbed his arm and twisted it hard. Lefty grimaced but refused to cry out.

Big Eddie shouted, "What are you doing?"

"He might be going for a piece."

Big Eddie looked down and shook his head. "Didn't you just pat him down? Let him go." The goon released Lefty's arm and backed away. Addressing Lefty, Big Eddie said, "You should come work for me, little man. I could use someone with some brains."

"Thanks for the offer, but after what I saw last night, no thanks." He pulled his cell phone from his pocket and found the video from the night before. After hitting play he handed it to Big Eddie. "Watch this."

Big Eddie took the phone and watched the video. He asked, "You know who those two are?" Big Eddie handed the phone back to Lefty.

"Not yet."

"And when you find out, you're going to tell me, right?"

Lefty stared at Big Eddie. Yeah, right. But he said, "Maybe."

"What do you mean, maybe?" He stepped closer to Lefty, towering over him, glowering down at him. Beads of sweat clung to his forehead. Lefty hoped one wouldn't drop onto him. He had enough of his own.

"Depends on who they are. I don't want you messing up my chance to find Angel."

"Email me that video."

"Not yet."

Big Eddie knelt again and again squeezed Lefty's knees. "Little man, you ain't in no bargaining position."

Trying hard not to wince, Lefty asked, "You know where I was before I came here?"

"No, I didn't have no one following you."

"The county morgue. With Lieutenant Pratt, who doesn't like you nearly as much as I do. Guess what I told him when I left?"

"I'm on pins and needles."

"I told him where I was going next." A lie, but he hoped the bluff would buy him some time.

Big Eddie released Lefty's knees and stood. "Why are you here?"

"I was hoping you could give me some names. The two that ripped off the buyer."

"Like I said, I don't know who they are. You two, come here." The two goons flanked Big Eddie. "Show them the video," Big Eddie commanded Lefty. He did. When the video finished, Big Eddie looked at his two goons. "Well?"

Goon number one, a man about three inches shorter than Big Eddie, but not as round, answered. "Ain't ever seen the white dude, but I think the brother did some time when I was in. Don't know his name, though."

Big Eddie muttered, "That's something, anyway." He then said to Lefty, "I could take that phone from you."

"Probably, but it would hurt."

Big Eddie smiled. "You or me?"

Lefty smiled back. "Probably both of us. And maybe one or two of them."

Big Eddie nodded. The smile disappeared. "I think it wise you give up looking for Angel. You don't want to get caught in the crossfire."

"One more question."

"What?" Big Eddie frowned, fists on his hips.

"Who's the dude that got ripped off?"

Big Eddie stared at Lefty, shaking his head slightly, blinking slowly. "You got balls, little man. That I have to admit." He shook his head some more, then sighed deeply. "Why not? His name is Jackson McCormitt. He's from Houston. And little man, you don't want to mess with this dude." Lefty raised his eyebrows. "I don't want to mess with this man. You dig?"

Lefty nodded then stood. No one made a move to stop him. "Thanks for the warning, but as far as I could see, he didn't buy Angel, so shouldn't be anything to cross him on."

"Why don't you let us find Angel?" Big Eddie asked.

"And when you do, you'll turn her over to her aunt, right?" Big Eddie just grinned. "Didn't think so." Lefty glanced at the two goons then brushed past Big Eddie, heading for the front door. He took several steps relieved he had not been yanked back. Over his shoulder he said, "And stop following me, Big Eddie."

"I already told you I don't have anyone following you."

"Then tell Keyshawn to stop."

Big Eddie chuckled.

When Lefty walked out the door, back into the heavy humidity, and down the sidewalk, he glanced left and saw a black Mustang about two blocks away parked on the street. They must have got another set of keys made, and someone in Big Eddie's house must have tipped them off, because they weren't there when he'd gone in.

Oh well, he'd just have to lose them again.

Chapter 32

Sara came up the basement stairs and walked swiftly toward the front of the house. At the spiral staircase to the second level, she turned right. One step toward Rockport's office and she stopped. The front door rattled. Then she heard a key being inserted into the deadbolt. She turned and watched the door. It opened and Chester walked in, followed by Angel and Emily.

"Where the—where were you three?" Sara asked, an edge in her voice.

"Went for a walk, mother," Chester replied.

Sara frowned. "Who authorized that?"

"Excuse me?"

"I mean..." She waved to Chester to follow her.

Angel and Emily left the foyer, heading for their room in the basement.

Chester followed Sara to Rockport's office. She knocked and Rockport shouted something, so Sara opened the door, and she and Chester walked in.

Rockport put down a sheet of paper he'd been reading and looked up at them.

"What's the matter?" Rockport asked.

Sara was at a loss for words. She started to ask if Rockport had authorized a walk for Angel and Emily, but that didn't sound right to her. Then she started to tell Rockport that they had been out. But in her head she sounded like a junior high student telling on someone.

Finally, Chester said, "Tell her we talked about Angel and Emily going for a walk and you was fine with it." He left the office.

Rockport said, "Yes, that's right. At lunch the two girls asked if they could go for a walk. They wanted to get out for a bit." He paused. Sara said nothing. "Chester said he'd go with them."

"And what if they'd run?" Sara finally managed to ask.

"First, they promised not to. Second, Angel is an adult. Technically, and legally, I might add, she can leave anytime she wants. And third, Chester is a lot faster than he looks."

"But not Emily. We've assumed responsibility for her until we can find somewhere for her to go."

"Emily doesn't know the city. She's not going to bolt. Besides, the way she and Angel have become attached at the hip, I think they'll both stick around a while." He stared at her.

She said nothing. What he'd said made sense. So why was she so mad?

"Sara, we're starting to get stretched here. And if we're going to grow, add more girls, you can't be in on every little thing that goes on. You've got to let others make decisions."

Was that it? Did she have a desire to control everything? No, not necessarily. "You're right. Not every small thing."

"But?"

"But next time you decide to grab or buy four girls at once, please talk to me about it first."

Rockport scratched his chin then ran his fingers over his goatee. He nodded and said, "Fair enough."

"Thanks."

Sara left the office, maybe still a little angry, but at least satisfied she got her point across. She went looking for Chester to apologize. That wasn't going to be easy.

Chapter 33

The GPS app on Lefty's phone told him Stick Sullivan's house was fifteen minutes from Big Eddie's mansion. Forty-five minutes later, Lefty rolled up in front of the small brick-and-stone cottage in south St. Louis city. It had taken him longer than he thought to shake the Mustang. He'd finally lost them in a maze of streets in Saint Louis County and had been able to get on Interstate 55 without the tail.

The late afternoon sun bleached the surrounding neighborhood. The car's air conditioner blew directly into Lefty's face, drying out his eyes and barely cooling him off. He needed more Freon, but had heard it could no longer be purchased. Several cars drove by. One pulled into a driveway about three houses down. Many of the people in this neighborhood probably worked hourly jobs, seven to three-thirty, and they were starting to filter home. Many, he assumed, worked at the brewery just a couple miles east.

Sullivan's house, like all of them in the neighborhood, was brick. Brown brick on the bottom three feet, edged by a white trim line. Red brick above for most of the rest, with a gray stone façade near the top of the one-story house. The typical St. Louis red brick used to be made in the city and dominated most of the older buildings all through town. When they demolished buildings with this brick, they'd comb through the rubble and salvage as much of the good bricks that they could and reuse them.

Sullivan's house had two thin front windows with white trim. Curtains drawn over both. Cement steps led up to an arched doorway and a white door with a small semi-circular window at the top. Weeds and grass grew in the cracks of the sidewalk. The lawn seemed thirsty with only occasional patches of green.

These row houses were deeper than they were wide, often with garages in the back accessed by an alley. Lefty had driven down the alley first and there had been no car parked out back and there was no car parked directly in front of the house either.

Lefty opened his door and waded through the blast of July heat, instantly feeling drenched from the high humidity. The strip of lawn between street and sidewalk crackled as he walked to the cement steps, which he ascended. A row of desiccated daisies drooped along the front of the house. A round evergreen bush, struggling to remain ever green, occupied the right corner. Lefty peered through the small window on the door. The interior was dark. He knocked anyway. Waited, then tried the doorbell. He heard a chime. Waited some more. No one came.

He walked around the side to the left, as the right had overgrown bushes blocking any access. No one in the backyard. No dog, or evidence of one. Just a couple mature elm trees and a screened-in porch.

Lefty returned to the front and climbed back in his car and waited. An hour later, he was about ready to give up when he noticed a black Cadillac Escalade in his rearview mirror coming toward him. When the SUV drew parallel to him, it slowed. Eyes stared at him through a heavily tinted window. It inched by on low-profile tires mounted on gleaming chrome wheels. When the tailgate drew even with the front of his car, it sped off and turned right at the next block. Lefty waited another fifteen minutes, but Sullivan never returned home, and the SUV did not reappear. He drove home.

A couple hours later, while preparing a late dinner of spaghetti with sauce from a jar, along with a can of corn and a loaf of frozen garlic bread, his cell phone came alive, playing "Bad Day" by Daniel Powter. He figured it was Eileen, since he'd not called her yet to check in. He intended to after he'd eaten. However, when he pulled the phone out, he recognized the number as the St. Louis

County Police main exchange. Maybe a break? Hopefully not another blond stiff. Lefty answered.

"George, it's Lieutenant Pratt. I need you to come to my office."

"Can it wait until tomorrow?" Lefty asked.

"Nope. Sorry."

"Can you tell me what it's about?"

"When you get here."

Lefty sighed. "Be there in twenty." He hadn't liked the tone Pratt had used: Too formal. Something was up. He ended the call, shut down the stove, and drove to Clayton.

A sergeant he didn't know manned the front desk. Lefty asked for Lieutenant Pratt, but before the sergeant could buzz him, the tall, lanky lieutenant rounded the corner. Pratt's expression betrayed nothing, his mouth a straight line, his eyes fixed on Lefty. Flanking him were two of his detectives: Frank Morris, a hefty, shorter white guy who was smarter and faster than he looked, and Ellis Johnson, a thin, black man with a shaved head and quick tongue. Pratt extended his hand. Lefty shook it.

"Let's go to my office, George." He turned and walked briskly away.

Both detectives waited until Lefty followed then they fell into rank, saying nothing. Lefty didn't like what all this implied. He felt confident if he deviated from following Pratt he'd be grabbed and brought back in line.

Pratt walked through his already open door. Three chairs were lined in front of his desk, the third a desk chair on wheels, apparently borrowed from someone else's office. "Have a seat, George," Pratt said. "You guys, too. Sit."

Everyone sat, Lefty in the middle chair, flanked by Morris on his left and Johnson on his right. Pratt sat behind his desk.

The lieutenant looked through a couple papers and, Lefty noticed, a couple eight by ten photos. He couldn't see what they depicted, though. Pratt sighed and put the stack down.

"Did you go see Russell Sullivan, also known as 'Stick'?

Lefty glanced left, then right. Both detectives eagerly awaited his answer. Pratt sat statue still. He blinked a couple times.

"I went to his house. He wasn't there. I waited about ninety minutes, but he never showed."

"Anyone else show?" Asked Morris.

"No one stopped. A black Escalade strolled by some time around five. They checked me out as they passed but didn't stop. I waited twenty minutes, but they never returned."

"Did you get a license?" asked Johnson.

"I was a detective, Johnson, so yeah, I noted the license."

He recited it. Pratt wrote it down.

"What's this about, anyway?"

Pratt handed him the stack of photos. Lefty scanned them, seeing several angles of a dead Stick Sullivan, on his back, arms spread, blood pooling around him.

Pratt said, "A neighbor called, said she heard shots. First officers on the scene saw him lying on the floor through the door. No one else was around."

"You sure he wasn't home when you got there?" Morris leaned close to Lefty. "Maybe he was there but wasn't as cooperative as you wanted him to be."

Lefty caught and held Morris' stare.

"Or maybe it was self-defense," Johnson added.

Lefty continued to lock stares with Morris.

"Maybe he pulled that piece on you, and you had no choice. But you should have reported it, Lefty."

Lefty finally broke off the staring contest and looked at Pratt. "You think I did this?"

"Your prints were on the door. It was broken in. Neighbor described a car close to yours."

"I told you I was there."

"Did you go in his house?" Morris asked. "Break in. Check the place out. Maybe he came home, found you there."

"What time did the neighbor call?" Lefty asked.

"Six twenty-three," Pratt answered.

Lefty looked at the photos again. "He was shot in the chest, from someone standing between him and the door." He tossed the photos on the desk. "He wasn't there when I was. I looked through the window on the door. No one was lying on the floor."

"Morris, run this plate." Pratt handed Morris a piece of paper. "George, it's time you desisted in looking for Angel Atkins."

"You know I can't do that."

Pratt sighed again. "Yeah, I figured as much. But this is your only warning. More dead bodies show up and we place you at the scene, we'll detain you until we clear things up. Got it?"

"Yes, sir." Lefty retrieved his cell phone. "Let me make a call. I may be able shed some light on this."

Pratt shrugged. Lefty found Big Eddie's cell number, dialed, and put in on speaker.

"Stumpy, I ain't got time for you or any questions about your lost whore."

Johnson broke out in a big grin. Pratt remained stoic.

"Hello to you too, Big Eddie." Lefty glanced at Pratt and smiled. "You having a bad night?"

"I hope, for your sake little man, you had nothing to do with Stick's death."

"Nope, but you just answered my first question. I assume you didn't either."

"Why would I kill him?"

"He screwed up?"

"I need that video, little man. Send it to me, or I'll come and take it from you."

"You think it was those guys?"

"Just send me the video. And like I said before, don't get in the crossfire." Big Eddie disconnected.

Lefty slipped his phone back into a pants pocket. "As you heard, it wasn't Big Eddie. He was pretty upset."

"Any theories?" Pratt asked.

"Sure, two. Either the two that did the snatch and grab at the buy Sunday night. No real motive, though. Or the guy that got ripped off, trying to find the two that did the grabbing or just wanting some vindication. Seems the more likely scenario."

"Did you leave us a copy of that video you took?" Pratt asked.

"Nope."

"We'll need one. Email it to me."

"Okay."

Pratt stared at Lefty. Both men said nothing for a while. Pratt said, "Well?"

"Well what?"

"Are you going to send it to me?"

"Sure. When I get home. It's too big to send without WiFi. I have a limited data plan. And I don't know the password here, anymore."

Pratt frowned. Lefty thought he'd give him the password to use County's WiFi, but he only nodded. "Don't forget."

Morris returned and placed a sheet of paper on Pratt's desk, then sat in the open chair. Pratt scanned the page and frowned again.

This time, Lefty asked, "Well?"

"Well, what?" asked Pratt.

"Who did the SUV belong to?"

"Rented under a bogus name."

"Can I have the name and the rental company?"

Morris said, "I think we're done here, don't you Lieutenant?"

Pratt looked at Morris, then at Johnson. "Thank you, detectives. Go home to your wives. Stick Sullivan isn't worth putting in more overtime for."

Both detectives hesitated, but Pratt waved them out, so they left, both with parting scowls for Lefty. Once they'd vacated Pratt's office, the lieutenant handed the page to Lefty. "Last warning, George. Bring us in if you find anything before someone else ends up dead."

"Thanks, Lieutenant." Lefty stood and started to leave.

"Don't forget to send me that video."

"Yes, sir."

Before Lefty climbed in his car, he scanned the street. No black Mustang. No black SUV. No other occupied vehicle

Chapter 34

Rockport's cell phone buzzed. He glanced at the time before he answered. Just after eight. Then he glanced at his cell phone. "Detective Warren, pretty late to be calling. You're not still working, are you?"

"Just getting ready to leave. A couple high-profile cases. This is a sick world, Calvin."

"Until the Lord Jesus returns, yes, it is."

"You might want to ask Jesus to speed things up."

Rockport chuckled then asked, "Have I ever told you about Jesus?"

"I know who he is, Calvin."

"That's great. But more important than knowing who he is—is knowing him." He swiveled in his chair, said a silent prayer for wisdom on what to say, and stared at the magnolia. The setting sun tinged the edge of the leaves with flame. The flowers glowed orangish pink.

"Okay, fine, we'll talk sometime, but it's late, I want to go home, and I wanted to tell you that you're a popular guy today."

He frowned. She had a knack for deflecting the conversation. Personally, he didn't see how any cop could not be a Christian, with all they saw and were involved in. How could anyone in that line of business think people are basically good, as she'd told him before. And that if God loved everyone, then why wouldn't everyone go to heaven.

"How am I so popular?"

"Two pictures of you came over the wire."

"What's that mean?"

"It means two separate people put your picture in the system asking other agencies if they know who you are."

He swiveled back toward his desk and straightened. "Can you tell who is looking for me?"

"Yup. The first was Lieutenant Pratt, my boss. More than likely that one was prompted by George Bruder, since Pratt was also his boss when he was a cop. And that picture is pretty grainy. Looks like it was lifted off a cell phone video. Shows you in a small booth with a dim overhead light above you. Only came through about an hour ago."

"Uh, huh. And the second?"

"That one is crystal clear. Taken about three feet from you, I'd guess. You're wearing the same suit, so my guess is it's the same place. Where were you, Calvin?"

"Who sent that request?"

"A city detective in the narcotics division. You want to explain what you did?"

"Not really. But I do wonder why a narcotics detective would have a picture."

"Tell me where you were and maybe I can help."

Rockport sighed. This relationship was based on trust. He had to be transparent or she'd start to shut him out. "The pictures were probably taken last night at an auction."

"Were you buying furniture or something?"

"Not that kind of auction. A girl auction."

"Oh. Did they get raided?"

"No."

"Bruder must have followed you there. But why the other one? And like you said, why is a narcotics cop looking for you? A little outside his purview."

He thought a moment, went through the activities of last night. Bruder made sense. They'd seen his car. And more than likely there were at least two others looking for him. The guy they'd ripped off and whoever ran the auction. "Well, it's complicated."

"Look, Calvin, I can't help you, or run interference for you, if you don't level with me. What happened at the auction?"

"I bought four girls."

"Four? You got that much room there?"

"Not really, but we're getting by."

"What else happened?"

He chewed his lip, then stroked his goatee. "Well...I saw an opportunity and I took it."

"What exactly did you take?"

"A seller's money."

"Oh, Calvin. Are you serious? You ripped off a seller?"

"Uh huh."

"Are you freaking nuts?"

"It was a way to hurt them, Lisa."

"Yeah, and a way to possibly lose everything, including your life. The seller or the organizer must have someone working for city in their pocket. I'll dig a little into this narcotics detective, but it's going way out of bounds for me. You might want to consider moving."

"This house isn't in my name."

"Then lay low for a while. Sounds like you're full up anyway. Just stay inside."

"Been there and done that when we were quarantined."

"Well, looks like you need to do it again."

"Yes, ma'am. And be careful, Lisa. I don't want you in trouble for something I did."

"Should have thought about that before you ripped off a sex trafficker. How did you rip this guy off? You're not exactly the physical type."

He described how they pulled it off. She listened without interrupting.

"That reminds me, I've been meaning to talk to you about Chester Henderson. You do know he's an ex-con, was in prison for murder?"

"Yes, Lisa, I'm well aware of Chester's background. Do you know who he killed and why?"

"No, only that he was pardoned by the governor."

"Chester killed the guy who kidnapped his daughter and sold her into sexual slavery. Like my daughter, his daughter overdosed on heroin."

Detective Warren said nothing for a bit then asked, "Why was he pardoned?"

"Calvin, so good to see you, what can I do for you?"

Rockport walked through the fifteen-foot ornate wood-and-glass doors of the Missouri governor's mansion.

"Harold, come take Mr. Rockport's coat."

"No need, William. I won't take much of your time."

"Okay." He waved Harold back. "Is there something I can do for you?"

Rockport had always admired William Stockman's servant attitude. In every situation, Stockman looked for how he could help, what he could do for others. Rockport hoped this time would be no different.

"Come," Governor Stockman said, "Let's go sit in the library."

The first floor of the historic mansion, built in 1871, featured a great hall with a seventeen-foot high ceiling, patterned oak floors and canary yellow walls. A dark mahogany wood fireplace decorated the right wall, though currently nothing was burning in it.

As they went left toward the library, Rockport noticed an American flag and a state of Missouri flag in the corner, in plain stands and poles no more than six feet high. Rather bland trappings for the ornate house.

They entered the library. Governor Stockman must have already been there before Rockport arrived. A fire burned in the white marble fireplace. A novel laid open, face down on a nineteenth century table with a travertine top. On either side of the table were what appeared to be more modern dining room chairs with deep green cushions. The Stockman family mainly lived on the second and third floors, with the ground floor reserved for tours and preservation of the original décor and furniture. Rockport assumed the dining chairs would be gone in the morning, before tourists started arriving.

Governor Stockman sat in one of the out-of-place chairs and motioned Rockport to sit in the other.

"I realize you're preserving the original trappings," Rockport said, "but really, bright yellow in the great hall and this almost lime green here?"

"Believe it or not, Marcella loves this color and this room. She was sitting with me earlier just staring at the walls and the bronze statues. Smiling the entire time. It's just something I have to go along with."

Rockport chuckled, then frowned, yearning for another chance to sit quietly and read with his wife sitting nearby. He sighed. "Anyway, there's a man in prison named Chester Henderson. I don't know if you've heard of his case."

"Can't say I have, Calvin. Tell me about him." Governor Stockman crossed his legs and interlocked his hands in his lap, giving Rockport full attention.

"He killed a man."

"Okay. Is he on death row? And how does this involve you?"

"Not on death row. There were extenuating circumstances, so the judge gave him twenty."

"Uh huh."

Harold appeared at the door with a tray and some glasses along with a crystal decanter of water. "Would you like something to drink, Governor?"

The governor waved him in. When Harold offered a glass to Rockport, he shook his head. The butler placed a three-quarters full glass on the table for the governor and left the room.

Rockport said, "I'd like Mr. Henderson out so he can come work for me. To help me find Carolyn. I need someone with his—let's say—skills and background."

Stockman stared at Rockport for a full fifteen seconds. "You want him granted clemency?"

Rockport nodded.

"On what grounds?"

Rockport's mouth felt dry. He now wished he'd accepted the water. He licked his lips. "That if he'd been white and did what he'd done, you'd be pinning a medal on him rather than allowing him to rot in prison for twenty years."

"You want me to admit our criminal justice system is racially prejudiced?"

"No. I want Chester Henderson released from prison. He's served three years. More than enough for what he did. Like I said, William, had you or I killed the man he killed, we'd get a community service award."

Again, a full fifteen seconds of silence. Stockman scratched his chin, took a quick drink of water, and looked past Rockport, who held back his ace in the hole. He hoped he would not have to play it, as he considered William Stockman a good friend and never wanted to use money as leverage against friends.

"Tell me more about Mr. Henderson."

Rockport sucked in a deep breath. He sat straighter in the chair, not wanting to look too comfortable. "He killed the man who kidnapped his daughter and sold her into prostitution."

"There's indisputable proof of this?"

Rockport nodded.

"And what is that proof?"

"The man admitted it and told Chester where to find his daughter, and who he'd sold her to."

"Did anyone other than Henderson hear this confession?"

Rockport shook his head.

"And did Mr. Henderson get his daughter back? Did she confirm who had kidnapped her?"

"No." Rockport paused for dramatic effect. "By the time he found her, she had died of a heroin overdose."

Rockport let that sink in. Stockman was aware that Rockport's daughter had run away and the latest suspicion held that she was going down the same road.

Stockman sighed and rubbed his chin, a habit he still had, though several years ago, before running for governor, he'd shaved his goatee. "All we have is Henderson's word?"

"William, he admitted to killing the guy. There was no trial, only sentencing, but I had a PI do a little digging."

"And?"

"A girl that worked with his daughter was grabbed by the same guy. She confirmed Chester's story."

Stockman waved a hand in the air. "Fine." He sighed again. "We'll assume the circumstances are what Mr. Henderson said. But what are you planning, Calvin? I can understand wanting Mr. Henderson out of prison, but what do you want with him?"

"I'm in my fifties, William. Not in the greatest shape. I don't know the streets or the type of people Carolyn may have become involved with. Chester Henderson went through all this. He found his daughter. I need his help."

Another lengthy pause. Rockport could see the wheels turning in Stockman's head, probably thinking how he could do this, but do it quietly with no media attention. Finally, Stockman sighed.

"Calvin, I appreciate you simply appealing to my sensibilities, my sense of justice and not pulling the contribution card, which you could easily do."

Another reason Rockport liked Stockman so much: the man was smart and didn't play games.

"I'll see what I can do. No guarantees," Stockman said.

"That's all I can ask, William. I appreciate your help."

They both stood and walked toward the door back into the foyer. At the front door, Rockport shook Stockman's hand, turned, opened the door and was about to leave.

"Calvin?"

Rockport paused and said, "Yes, William."

"Don't do anything where I'd have to grant you clemency."

Rockport smiled and walked out the door, saying over his shoulder, "I'll try my best, but no guarantees."

Rockport said to Lisa Warren, "Chester Henderson was released from prison one week later and came to work with me. He's been with me for years. He's a good man who took things into his own hands." Rockport paused. "Sometimes, we need to take things into our own hands."

Warren sighed. "Unofficially, I agree with you. But if you ever quote me, I'll disavow any knowledge of you whatsoever, understand?"

"Absolutely. Now go home, Detective Warren."

"I think I will. Goodnight, Calvin."

"Goodnight, Lisa. And don't forget, you owe me a conversation about Jesus."

"Sure, Calvin." She disconnected.

He laid his cell phone on the desk and said another silent prayer for Lisa Warren's salvation. Another glance at the clock. Eight-thirty-four. He felt a little guilty for keeping her so long. Although, he also knew she had no one to go home to, anyway. Her husband had walked out on her six months ago, claiming she was married to her work, which she was. Good for him—but not so good for her marriage or social life.

He sighed, scooped his cell phone off the desk, and headed out of his office. Speaking of being married to work...

He turned off the light to the office and headed downstairs to the library for a little contemplation before retiring.

Chapter 35

In his dream, Lefty slammed the car door, then stood perplexed, staring at the 2014 Corvette wondering why the slam had sounded like splintering wood. He also wondered why the car alarm was going off. This thought lasted only a second before he flung off his covers and swung his legs over the side of the bed.

It wasn't a car alarm in his dream going off, it was his house alarm blaring in real life. The slam had been splintering wood. His front door. Someone had kicked it in.

Lefty grabbed the nunchucks he kept on the nightstand. He heard muffled voices, footsteps. A dark shadow appeared outside his bedroom door. He flattened himself against the wall on the other side of his nightstand.

Someone entered his bedroom. He swung the nunchucks and felt the dragon stick connect. He heard a twank then a grunt. He swung again, but the man had lifted his arm and the dragon stick connected with forearm. The man shuffled out of reach.

Another person came through the bedroom door. Lefty bolted for the other side of the room. When he reached the closet door, he turned saw the second man's arm extended toward him. He expected a shot, so dodged left, colliding with his dresser.

Someone in the hall yelled, "The boss wants him alive."

The man lowered his arm. Simultaneously, Lefty saw the flash and heard the deafening explosion. Had to be a forty-five. A cannon. Wood splintered between his legs.

Lefty jumped forward and swung the nunchucks. The sound of wood on metal. The gun clattered to the floor. He swung again.

Heard another twank. Shoulder.

The man backed up. Lefty felt the air shift behind him. He whirled and swung the nunchuck head height without aim. The chain wrapped around the first man's neck. The dragon stick came around and caught the guy's nose.

Lefty kicked out and connected with soft flesh. The man grunted and fell back against the closet. Lefty spun again, swung without thinking. This time full on the side of the second man's skull.

He kicked out again. The second man bent forward as Lefty caught his groin. He did a roundhouse kick, caught the side of the attacker's head. The man stumbled sideways and collided with the far wall.

A third man came through the door. Lefty whirled and ran to his closet, flung open the door. His light came on. He bent into the closet.

"Get out here," someone shouted. Presumably the third guy. "I will shoot you."

Lefty reached into the corner of his closet and gripped the pistol-handled shotgun, hoping he had a shell chambered. He stayed in his crouch but whirled. He lost his balance, but while falling over, was able to bring the shotgun up.

He fired.

The third guy fired his handgun. A bullet went into the drywall. Chalk sprayed into Lefty's face. The man, wearing a ski mask and black long-sleeved T-shirt, stumbled back a couple steps. He looked down at his chest. Dark spots had formed.

Lefty fired his semi-automatic shotgun again. The size four buckshot pushed the man into the hall hard against the wall.

The two men on the floor both stood. Lefty aimed at the closest, the first who had come in, but didn't fire, as both men retreated through the bedroom door. They hooked their comrade under the armpits and dragged him.

Lefty scrambled to his feet. By the time he got into the living room, the three men were already outside.

They dragged the injured man to a black SUV. Someone inside opened the back door. They threw the man in. One of the others climbed in after. The other entered the front passenger side. Before he even closed his door, the SUV took off. No license plate on this one.

Lefty tried to close his front door, but the latch was shattered. He returned to his bedroom. A Glock nine-millimeter semi-automatic handgun lay in the middle of his floor. Blood spatters and holes littered his wall by the door and the hallway wall outside the door.

Lefty found his cell phone and called Lieutenant Pratt. First, he apologized for waking him, then he explained what had happened. Pratt brushed aside the apology and said he'd call it in. He told Lefty not to touch anything. Lefty sat on the side of his bed and waited.

Twenty minutes later two patrolmen walked through his front door calling his name. Lefty met them in the living room. The round, institutional looking clock on his living room wall read three-twenty-two.

***

Lefty got no more sleep that night and spent the first several hours of daylight in a county police sub-station giving his statement to detectives. Pratt joined him around seven and listened to the debriefing.

Afterwards, Pratt took Lefty to breakfast and convinced his former detective to move into his house for a few days. Lefty agreed, knowing his house would be a crime scene for at least the rest of that day, and then he had repairs to do.

Around nine-fifteen, Lefty fell asleep on Lieutenant Pratt's sofa. And around nine-fifty, his cell phone woke him up.

"Why didn't you call me last night?" Eileen asked, irritation in her voice.

"It was a busy night." Lefty explained what had happened.

"Oh my gosh, are you alright?"

"Yes, just tired and not that far along with finding your niece."

"What's next? Do you have any leads?"

"I do. I need to take a trip to Jefferson City and see if I can get lucky and get a name."

Eileen's voice became soft, no more irritation. "I really appreciate you doing this for me, Lefty. I'm so sorry about the situation."

"Not your fault. Hazards of the job."

"Do you want me to go with you, keep you company on the drive?"

Lefty's impulse was immediately to say no, but he curbed his impulse and thought about it.

"Well?" Eileen asked.

"Sure. I'll pick you up in thirty."

"Okay, George. I'll be ready."

They hung up. Lieutenant Pratt's house was empty and silent. The smell of cinnamon drifted throughout. The kids were off to school, Pratt's wife to her job, and Pratt to Clayton.

Lefty showered, made a couple pieces of toast, which he downed with orange juice, cleaned up after himself, and headed downtown to pick up Eileen for a trip to Jefferson City. While waiting outside her hotel, he called a buddy of his at the Jefferson City Correctional Center, who agreed to help him when he got there.

Chapter 36

On the way back from the prison, with Eileen driving, Lefty called Lieutenant Pratt, who, surprisingly, answered.

"Slow day, today, Lieutenant?"

"Not at all, George. Just happen to be grabbing a quick lunch at my desk. What can I do for you?"

Lefty realized he was hungry too. He'd suggest to Eileen they stop somewhere along Highway 44 for some lunch of their own. "Chester Henderson. He was one of the black guys in the video of the rip-off I showed you."

"Okay."

"Can you run him and get me an address?"

A pause, then Pratt asked, "And if you find him?"

"I just want to ask him some questions. He works for or with the guy who took Angel."

Pratt said nothing.

"Besides, you saw how big that guy is."

More silence, then some clicking keys. Eileen switched lanes, muttered something about incompetent drivers, then sped up. Lefty looked at her.

She apparently felt the stare, so glanced his way. "What?"

Lefty smiled and shook his head.

"The guy was driving fifty-five in a seventy zone. I mean, jeez, At least move over to the right lane."

"You there, George?" Pratt asked.

"Yup."

"No known address after he left prison. Full pardon from the governor several years ago. Different governor, obviously."

"Any known associates?"

"Nothing. He had no record. Went up for killing a man." A pause. "You know, now I remember that case. He claimed the man he killed kidnapped his daughter, who died of a heroin overdose."

"Why was he pardoned?"

"Other than the governor saying something about the circumstances, don't know."

"Thanks."

"Oh, and George, we ran that license plate on the picture you sent with the video."

Lefty had completely forgot he'd taken a picture of the limo's plate before watching the snatch and grab Sunday night.

"Came back registered to a Mrs. Estelle Garber. Who died two years ago at the age of eighty-seven."

"Great. Thanks for looking into it. Can you transfer me to Fischer?"

"Sure. Hold on."

The line went dead, then it rang.

"Detective Fischer, how can I help you?"

Maybe he should play the lottery today, thought Lefty. Got them both at their desks. "Good afternoon, Detective Fischer, this is Lefty Bruder."

"Mr. Bruder, what can I do for you?"

Was that a hint of irritation in his voice? "I got a name for you. It's the seller, the one ripped off."

"Okay." A pause. "I won't bother asking how or where you got it."

Lefty laughed. "Smart man. Anyway, Jackson McCormitt. Some badass from Houston who grabs girls and sells them. So bad, even our resident badass, Big Eddie, doesn't want to cross him."

Out of the corner of his eye, he saw movement and turned to look at Eileen. She was frowning at him.

"What?"

She only shook her head and returned her attention to the traffic. He figured it must have been his use of profanity.

"What, what?" Fischer asked.

"Huh? Oh, nothing. I'm in a car. Talking to the driver. Anyway, would you find out anything about him that you can?"

Hesitation. "Sure. I'll get back to you."

"Thanks."

The connection ended without Fischer saying anything more.

Lefty pocketed his cell phone. "Are you hungry?"

Ten minutes later they pulled off the interstate and into a Wendy's. Food in hand, they took a table by the window. Lefty had a spicy chicken, fries, soda, and large chocolate frosty. Eileen had a grilled chicken, no bun, no fries, and black coffee.

Before Lefty even took a bite, Eileen asked, "So, where are we?"

He stuffed a couple fries in his mouth and shook his head. "Not far enough." After swallowing, he summarized for Eileen what he knew. "Angel was grabbed from her pimp by a white guy and a black guy in a large limo. I saw the same limo at the auction both the day before and the night of. The rich dude bought four girls. After the auction, they ripped off one of the sellers." He paused.

Eileen chewed slowly.

He bit a big chunk of his spicy chicken and washed it down with soda. "The dude who ran the auction is dead. A bunch of guys broke into my house and tried to kill me. I'm guessing they work for the seller and killed Sullivan."

Eileen raised her brows.

"The auction organizer. While I was scoping that dude's house a black SUV drove by slowly. Another black SUV—different though, the first being a Cadillac the second a Lincoln—was the getaway vehicle at my house. Those guys didn't want to kill me, they wanted to grab me. I'm guessing the seller thinks I may know something."

Eileen nodded. A family with two loud, over-rambunctious kids swept by, making conversation impossible for a few seconds.

Lefty took another bite of sandwich, ate a couple fries and looked out at the interstate. He certainly didn't have much.

Eileen said, "Did you see any license plates on these vehicles?"

"Yup. The Cadillac was rented under a bogus name. And the limo is registered to an old lady that died a few years ago."

Eileen nibbled her grilled chicken and stared at him, nodding slowly. She swallowed. "Maybe the old lady is some relative of the man who's driving the limo."

It was his turn to stare at Eileen. She raised her brows again.

"Huh. Didn't think of that. Thanks, that gives me something to pursue."

Ninety minutes later, he and Eileen sat in front of his computer. He'd crossed the police tape. No one was there and he wanted to use his own computer. Besides, he didn't know the password for Pratt's.

A simple search found the obituary of Estelle Garber, mother of three: Carla, Carl, and Cassandra. Cassandra was married to one Robert Smithson, who currently resided in Memphis. Further search yielded the information that Carl Garber lived in Seattle. That left Carla Garber, who, according to the obituary, had been married to a Calvin Rockport.

When he dug further he found that Carla had died several years ago of cancer. He searched for Calvin Rockport. Very little recent information, but several news articles from seven to ten years ago. From what Lefty garnered, Rockport was wealthy. No address, though. So he looked again at Carla Garber and found a house in Huntleigh Woods still listed under her name. Clever, he thought. Keep the house in his wife's maiden name.

An image search of Calvin Rockport showed a couple pictures from the same old news stories, the most recent being seven years ago. The man in the picture was clean shaven. He stared at it and decided, yes, that could be the same man he'd seen at the auction. Not certain, but it was something to go on. He wrote the address in Huntleigh Woods down on a piece of paper and pocketed it.

Eileen leaned over his shoulder. "Well, have you got a lead?"

"I do. Time to pay Mr. Rockport a visit."

Chapter 37

"Well, hello, George." Jeannine Pratt greeted Lefty as he walked into his former lieutenant's house. All three of the Pratt children were gathered around their mother. Lefty had dropped Eileen off at her hotel then headed directly to Pratt's house in south St. Louis County. He'd decided he'd check out Rockport's house in the morning. He was too tired after the activity the night before and the drive to Jefferson City and back.

And now, he felt unbelievably short. Jeannine had been a volleyball player in college and, like her husband kept herself in shape. Their oldest daughter, Jamie, followed in her mother's footsteps and played volleyball for Oakville Senior High. Both mother and daughter stood about six foot two. But, the middle child, Cameron, exceeded even that height, standing what Lefty figured to be about six feet five inches. Last time he'd see him, he was barely over Lefty's five-eleven. And then there was their youngest, who Lefty figured was in seventh grade. Though looking at him, one would never have thought that, as he too towered over Lefty at probably about six foot three.

"Hello, Jeannine. How have you been?" He ignored the stares of all three teenagers, fixated on his stump.

"Stop staring, you three." Jeannine turned to Lefty. "We've been doing well. As you can see, the kids have grown since last time you visited."

"Just a bit."

"It's so good to see you again. But I'm really sorry about the circumstances."

"Dad said you really kicked some butt," Cameron said.

Lefty chuckled. "Got the better of them, anyway." He asked Jeannine, "You mind if I use the workout room downstairs? I'd like to go through a few routines then shower."

"Please. Make yourself at home, George. Our house is your house for as long as you need it."

"That's kind of you. Hopefully, I can get into my place tomorrow or Thursday."

"Karate routines?" asked William. Everyone called him Billy.

Lefty nodded.

Billy asked, "Can we watch?"

"Sure," Lefty answered.

The three giants followed him downstairs to the finished basement of the two-story house where he first ducked into the spare bedroom and changed into shorts and a T-shirt.

Lefty took about ten minutes to stretch. He cut the routine a couple minutes short as the audience grew restless. Instead, he decided to warm up with some katas. From his Sanshin instructor, he'd learned ten, so he started with number one, the most basic, but slightly modified by Lefty to accommodate having only one arm. Slide forward, block, punch, turn ninety degrees, slide forward, block, punch.

"Can you show me how to do that?" Billy asked.

"Shh," his sister chastised.

Lefty stopped. "No problem." He lined the three teenagers up in front of him. Cameron's head was only inches below the drop ceiling. "Let's start with a simple block. First, good stance. Almost like you're sitting on a horse, legs about shoulder length apart, squat."

Each teen took their stance. Lefty went to each and pushed on their shoulders. Jamie had a solid stance. He had to reach to push Cameron on his shoulders and the boy stumbled.

"Bend your knees more. Like this." Lefty took his stance. "Push me." Cameron did, hard, but Lefty only rocked a bit.

"Wow," said Cameron.

"Try it."

The skyscraper teen did and Lefty pushed again. This time he didn't budge the boy. Billy also had a good stance.

"Good. Now, hands up, close to your body." He demonstrated in front of Billy. "Hit me, Billy."

"Huh?"

"Go ahead. Try to punch me in the nose."

The youngest teen glanced at his siblings, who both had grins on their faces and both nodded.

"Go for it, dude," Cameron said.

Billy struck out. Quick, straight, not much power, though. Lefty easily blocked with his arm, then did a backwards karate chop to the boy's neck, stopping just as he made contact. He also stepped around, put the boy into a choke hold and brought his knee up into his tailbone, again, stopping just on contact.

"Fluid motion is the key. Practice and more practice, so the move is automatic. No thinking about it."

All the teens nodded, their eyes wide.

He released Billy and positioned himself to the boy's left. "Cameron, come over here and face your brother." Cameron did. "Billy, bring your hands up." The boy did. "Cameron, slow punch to his face. I want to teach you a move that you all can do since you have two arms. Stop about three quarters there."

Cameron did a slow-motion punch.

"Billy, use your right to block with your palm, just bring it up like this." He demonstrated and the boy repeated the move. "Good. Push a little, then bring your left up and finish the block with the back of your hand. Bring your right into your side ready to punch. Step forward, and while stepping, punch, putting your body into it."

Billy gave a good try, but punched from where he was, not stepping in.

"You need to step in while you punch. Does two things. First, gets you inside your opponent, where he won't have any power. Important because he's so much bigger."

Billy nodded.

"Second, gives you more power punching while stepping." Lefty worked with him a little to get the moves down. Then he had the other two try it and in ten minutes he had them punching at each other about half speed, while their partner blocked, stepped, and punched.

Next, he showed them a simple move for a midsection block, and quick pivot around it and a kidney punch. Another ten minutes of working and he heard footsteps coming down the stairs.

"Evening, George." Lieutenant Pratt laughed. "Teaching my kids to fight, huh? We teach them to avoid fighting."

Lefty stopped and faced him. "Sometimes, sir, a fight cannot be avoided."

"True. Dinner is served." He shook Lefty's hand, turned and marched up the stairs. Lefty followed, as did the teens.

Once they were all situated around a blonde oak table with a white tile top, Pratt asked his family if they had any prayer requests. Each had at least one and Billy had a couple. Two kids he knew from school had started using drugs and one of his teachers had lost his father the other day. Billy asked that they pray for comfort and peace for the teacher and for wisdom and God's intervention for the two teens into drugs.

After the family had finished offering up prayer requests, Pratt looked at Lefty. "What about you, George? Anything we can pray for in your life?"

"Another arm?"

Pratt smiled and nodded. "We can, but maybe God has you that way for a reason."

"I'd like to know what it is."

"You may not know this side of heaven. But hopefully, one day you can have the conversation with Jesus about that."

"Are you saved, Mr. Bruder?" Billy asked.

Lefty looked at the middle schooler. "Saved from what?"

"Uh, hell, of course."

"Not sure I believe in hell."

"It's real and not somewhere you ever want to go." Then, speaking quickly, Billy added, "And all you have to do is trust Jesus as your Lord and Savior and one day you'll be with all of us in heaven, and we'll have all the time we need to learn all those cool moves you have."

Lefty smiled. Pratt laughed. Jeannine patted her son on the shoulder. Cameron gave him a thumbs up.

Jamie said, "Well, Mr. Bruder, what do you say? Are you ready to trust Jesus?"

Lefty opened his mouth, closed it, then opened it again, but had nothing to say.

Pratt came to his rescue. "How about a small step, George. How about another prayer request? How can we pray for you?"

"That I find Angel and she's okay?"

"Perfect. Bow your heads, everyone."

Lefty did but kept his eyes open. Pratt prayed. Lefty stole a glance around the table. The other four all had their lips moving, their heads moving up and down, their eyes squeezed shut. That is until Billy also stole a glance.

He looked directly at Lefty and winked, then closed his eyes again.

The prayer ended and the food was passed. Though he'd tell anyone who asked that the food was delicious, he didn't really remember tasting any of it, too occupied was he with the thought of hell, Jesus, and Billy having such incredible faith. At one point, he wondered if Billy lost his arm like Lefty had, would he still have that same faith. He concluded that yes, Billy would probably retain that faith even in the face of such adversity. Then Lefty wondered if God—that is if there is a God—did He really have some reason why Lefty should lose his arm? He thought about Eileen. She hadn't seemed to lose her faith, though she lost her leg and her husband.

Dinner ended. The kids dispersed to do homework. Jeannine and Pratt cleared the table. Once it was cleared, Pratt joined Lefty back at the table.

"Billy gave you something to think about, didn't he?"

Lefty nodded.

"It always amazes me," Pratt said, "when I see the words of Jesus acted out. He said, 'whoever does not receive the kingdom of God like a child shall not enter it.' Billy has such simple faith, yet such strong faith. He's been that way since he was eight, when he accepted Christ as Lord and Savior."

"But isn't that because it's all he's heard?" Lefty asked.

"Maybe for the first few years. But Billy's a smart kid. He's been asking questions and he's been digging. Plus, many of his friends don't go to church, so he gets challenged by them. And his faith has stood strong."

Lefty studied his hand, which rested in his lap.

"Was it worth it?" Pratt asked.

"Was what worth it?"

"All the bitterness and anger you had after your injury. Did it help you to be that way, to shut everyone out? Are you a better person today than you were five years ago because of that?"

Lefty looked at Pratt. Studied his face to see if he was joking. "No. Why do you ask that?"

"Stupid question, wasn't it?"

"Yeah."

"And yet, you continue to wallow in self-pity. You continue to question if God exists and if He does, how could He do that to you." Pratt pointed at Lefty's right shoulder.

Lefty shrugged.

"Calvin Rockport."

"Huh?" Though he recognized the name, Lefty couldn't figure out how it fit in with their conversation.

"That's the guy who took Angel, ripped off the seller from Houston. The man in your video."

"Yeah, I figured that out. How did you know?"

"The picture. Matched it to a news article on the Internet."

"What are you going to do about it?" Lefty asked.

"Absolutely nothing."

"What?"

"What should we do, George? The seller hasn't pressed charges and I'm not really worried about him getting ripped off, considering what he does. And Keyshawn hasn't come forward. Angel is an adult. No foul play reported yet."

Lefty glared at Pratt. "What about Rockport buying four girls? Is that legal?"

"How do you know he didn't let them go?"

"Why would he do that?"

"I did some digging, George. Calvin Rockport's daughter died of a heroin overdose. She worked the streets for a few years. Maybe Rockport is trying to rescue these girls."

Lefty relaxed a little. Pratt was right, of course. At least about not being able to officially do anything. Not yet, anyway. He wasn't convinced Rockport was innocent, but he could find that out. "I guess we'll see, won't we?"

"Exactly," Pratt said. "You'll see. You'll go where we can't. You'll ask the questions, find the answers, and probably help get Angel back to a place where she's safe and can live a decent life."

"Thanks for your confidence," Lefty said.

"You don't see it, do you George?"

"See what?"

"Not yet. Let's talk again in a few days." Pratt pushed away from the table and joined his wife in the kitchen.

Lefty remained at the table for about twenty minutes listening to the sounds of clinking dishes, the occasional footsteps from upstairs, then the television in the living room being turned on. He'd never known Pratt to be so cryptic. Usually, the man just came out and said what was on his mind.

He pondered what he'd said about Rockport. A rich dude grabbing one girl, buying four others. Ripping off a sex trafficker. Could he be a good guy? And how did all that tie into their conversation about God? He shook his head, stood, and went downstairs. Tomorrow, he'd pay Calvin Rockport a visit and hopefully get some, if not all, of the answers.

Chapter 38

Lefty dreamed about teaching Pratt's kids karate, only in the dream he had both his arms. While helping Billy with a reverse kick, his phone rang in the dream. He answered it. Eileen wailed into the phone that Angel was dead and why hadn't he helped her.

He started to protest that he had been helping her, when he noticed instead of wearing his sweats and T-shirt, he had on his dress blues. At the bottom of the stairs, Pratt appeared and asked him why he wasn't back on his beat. Why wasn't he at work.

Eileen continued to scream at him. Pratt also started yelling at him, telling him there's nothing they can do, Angel is an adult, and they have real cases to work. His dress blues disappeared. Now he was wearing a suit, like he used to wear as a detective.

His cell phone rang again. Then again. And again, even though, in his dream, he was holding it and talking into it. It kept ringing.

Lefty woke up and realized his phone was ringing. He answered it.

"Mr. Bruder, it's Detective Fischer."

"Uh, yeah. Hey, good morning."

"Sorry to call so early, but it's the only chance I'll have to get with you. Busy day ahead."

"No problem. I appreciate it. What's up?"

"Pratt already told you we identified Calvin Rockport. Also, from your video, we were able to confirm the identity of the sex trafficker he ripped off. Jackson McCormitt."

"Uh huh." Lefty glanced at the clock on the nightstand. Blurry red digits showed it was eight thirty-two. He must have been tired.

"McCormitt is from Houston. Very connected. Takes girls all over the country and sells them. I talked to a cop in Houston. This guy's dangerous and quite a piece of work. He transports girls in a semi-truck, just throws them in the back."

"Nice." Lefty didn't bother to tell Fischer he knew most of this from Big Eddie. "Do you know if he's still in town?"

"No, we don't know. Nothing we could find under his name, but that's not surprising."

Lefty swung his legs around and stood up out of bed.

Fischer continued, "The guy with him is Manuel Rodriquez. He's McCormitt's bodyguard. Ex-ranger. Suspected for several hits, but nothing has stuck. Again, nothing registering under his name locally."

That was new information. Lefty padded into the adjoining bathroom, decided against trying to cradle his cell phone between cheek and shoulder and just stood there, moving from leg to leg, as he had to pee something terrible.

He thought a moment about when the men hit his house. Didn't recall seeing anyone Hispanic. A couple had been black, the other white. In the few words he heard, he didn't think there'd been a Texas twang. He assumed they had not belonged to Rockport. Keyshawn? Too bold, too many. Big Eddie? Why? Didn't make any sense.

"You still there, Mr. Bruder?"

"Yeah. Does McCormitt usually bring a bunch of muscle with him?"

"Not according to my contact. Hires local muscle if he needs any help with anything."

That would explain it. At first, he'd thought a rental vehicle because they were from out of town. But even if local, harder to trace if a rental was used. "Anything else?"

"That's about it." A pause. "Mr. Bruder?"

"Yeah."

"If you happen to run into this guy, please give us a call. Don't take action yourself."

"Will do, detective. Thanks for the intel."

"No problem. Goodbye."

The connection ended. Lefty put his cell phone on a shelf above the toilet and relieved himself.

Lefty drove into Huntleigh Woods. The road looked more like a wide walking trail than a street. No summer potholes here. He knew one of the houses in the area belonged to someone in the Busch family, but wasn't sure which.

He followed the winding road with no painted lines for about a mile, traveling what he thought was west. Twenty-foot pine trees, blue spruces, majestic maples, and oak trees rippled his car in shadow.

As soon as he'd entered the town, borough, village, he didn't know what to call it, the temperature of the air dropped at least fifteen degrees, cool enough on a July mid-morning to allow him to open his windows. The smell of pine perfumed the air. The engine of his car drowned out the songbirds. No one out and about.

He drove past stately mansions of brick, arched doorways, colonnades, winding driveways and multi-car garages. Multiples of greater than two.

He approached the address he'd written down for Rockport. One of the stately mansions. This one was a two-story with reddish brown brick and a black roof. Four black, square columns that rested on brick bases supported a widow's walk with a black iron railing over the entryway. The decorative widow's walk was not accessible, as only a small round window adorned the wall behind it. At the top center of the roof was a white cupola with six vertical windows and a black dome. Lefty figured it also to be only decorative. Lots of decoration going on with the outside of this house.

The house had a pull-through driveway and two perpendicular wings off the center part of the house, one on each side. He drove by slowly. Just past the house, on the other side of the road he passed a parked, gray SUV. At least it wasn't black. At least one person occupied it. He kept driving, the road curving to the left past one more monstrous mansion. He pulled into the driveway of the second house after Rockport's, a long ranch. He could still see both the SUV and the front door of Rockport's house.

He wondered, though, how long he'd be able to sit in this neighborhood with his slightly less than fancy car. The gray SUV was an Escalade, so it did not look out of place. His ten-year old Nissan, though, with the dent in the passenger side door and one taillight lens missing, replaced by translucent red tape? Servant's car?

Maybe if he stayed in the driveway of the neighbor's house he'd not arouse too much attention. Seemed the occupants were out for the day. No lights were on in any of the windows. He thought about trying to sneak up on the person in the SUV, but he decided without knowing how many were inside that could turn out bad. Instead he waited and watched.

Chapter 39

Rockport heard a knock on his office door. "Come in."

The door opened slightly and Chester poked his massive head through, followed by his arm. He motioned for Rockport to follow him. "Got something to show you, boss."

Rockport pushed back from his desk and followed Chester out of the office, across the hall, past the ornate, wooden throne chairs complete with footstools, to one of the bedrooms. Amanda, the girl who stayed in the room, was not there.

Chester walked past the double bed to one of two windows, this one on the left side of a black dresser. He then motioned Rockport to go to the other window.

When Rockport reached the window, Chester pointed outside.

"That gray Escalade has been there for at least thirty minutes. The driver is still in it. No plates. I've been watching it since I noticed it."

Rockport watched the SUV a minute or so. No one ever parked there, or anywhere on the street, unless someone was throwing a party. All the houses had massive driveways, as his did, so no reason to park in the street.

"Cops or confrontation?" Rockport asked.

"Windows are tinted in back, so I can't tell if it's just the driver. Not sure I want to go out there alone if there could be several armed men."

"Doesn't seem to be our private eye buddy."

"Nope. He's up the street parked in the Pederson's driveway. Saw him drive by about fifteen minutes ago."

"Hmm. Since it's an Escalade, I doubt it's cops. But I'll give Detective Warren a call and see what she knows and how she wants to handle it." He pulled his cell phone out of the belt case. "Who do you think that is?"

"I'm afraid it may be someone working for the dude we ripped off."

Rockport found Detective Warren's number in his contact list and punched the call icon. He said to Chester, "I know you two tell each other everything, but let's not tell Sara about this yet, okay?"

Chester nodded then continued watching out the window.

"What's up, Calvin?" Lisa Warren asked.

"There appears to be someone watching our house. Gray Escalade. No plates. Driver has been in the car for at least half an hour."

Silence for several seconds.

"How do you want to handle it?"

Rockport smiled at her question. "I was hoping you'd have a suggestion."

"You're in Huntleigh Woods, right?"

"Correct."

"Okay, I'll get a couple patrol cars to drive by. If the SUV stays there, they'll stop and talk to them. Best I can do right now."

"That's perfect. Thanks again, Lisa."

"Sure." More silence. Just as Rockport was about to say goodbye, Warren said, "Probably not George Bruder, huh?"

"Not unless he bought a new car."

"Unlikely. I don't have a comfortable feeling about this, Calvin. I haven't felt good since I saw your picture go across the wire."

"Did you find anything out about the narcotics detective that sent one of the pictures?"

The other picture had come from Lieutenant Pratt, George Bruder's former lieutenant, so Rockport and Detective Warren figured that one was to help Bruder locate Angel.

"Not a lot. But the word on the street is he's corrupt. Couldn't get anything solid, though. Just rumors and feelings."

"Okay. Thanks, Lisa. I'll let you know what goes down when the patrols arrive."

"Be careful, Calvin. Maybe it's time for a vacation."

"Maybe." He disconnected, wondering how he'd take eight—or was it nine, now, he'd lost track—ex-prostitutes on a vacation.

He joined Chester watching the SUV, the outline of the driver barely visible through the partially tinted driver-side window.

Chapter 40

"Oh, crap," Lefty muttered.

Coming around the corner just before Rockport's house was a white and red St. Louis County patrol car. And just behind the first one, a second one.

He ducked but stayed high enough to watch. The taillights of the Escalade lit up. It started moving forward slowly.

"Dang it." He sat up and started his car.

The Escalade drove by the patrol cars. Neither cop car stopped. Lefty backed out, wondering if someone had called him in. He drove toward the patrol cars, waiting for one of them to block the road, but neither did. As he passed them, he got two long looks, but both patrol cars kept going. The Escalade accelerated and disappeared around a curve. No mystery where it would go, though, as there was only the one road in and out of Huntleigh Woods.

Lefty let the patrol cars round a curve, then he accelerated to try and catch the Escalade. Fortunately, traffic on Lindbergh Boulevard was heavy, delaying the Escalade long enough for Lefty to catch it.

The SUV turned right and Lefty followed, dropping back enough to avoid detection in the lunch time traffic. The SUV turned right on Manchester Road and stayed there a couple miles into Des Peres where it turned south on Lindeman Road. They passed about five side streets before the SUV turned left.

Lefty slowed, allowing the Escalade to get a little farther ahead, then also turned. As he rounded the corner, the gray SUV was pulling into a driveway on the left side of the street. Lefty parked on the wrong side of the street about a block back.

He waited. Seconds later, a tall, thin, African American climbed out of the Escalade and walked through the front door of the house. No one else got out.

He waited another fifteen minutes, then climbed out of his car and crossed the street. He walked toward the house, on the far side of the street, being no sidewalks. When he drew parallel to the large blue spruce just before the white ranch house, he pulled out his cell phone and dictated the address into a note.

As he passed the house, he glanced at the three side-by-side front windows. Two heads turned. The two black men watched him walk by. Fortunately, his left side was to them, so he hoped they would not notice he was one-armed. Other than that feature, he'd always thought of himself as nondescript.

He kept going, past three more houses on each side of the street, a mixture of ranches and split levels, some with brick, others all siding, all with large trees of various kinds: Pines, maples, oaks. This was an older neighborhood, probably built in the sixties or seventies.

By the time he reached the corner, his soaked shirt clung to his back. Not the ideal day for a stroll. At the corner he turned left, then walked past two more houses on his left and a park with a couple empty tennis courts on his right. At the next street, he turned left again, wanting to check out the back of the house where he felt certain Jackson McCormitt camped out.

After passing three houses, he stopped and examined the layout. He could not see much of the ranch's backyard, as the house directly behind it had a privacy fence. Fortunately, the house next to that one had no fence, thus he could approach McCormitt's back yard unseen until he reached the back corner.

Out of the corner of his eye he spotted movement, so he glanced left, where he'd come from. A black man stood at the corner, staring at him. He couldn't tell if it was one of the men he'd seen through the window. Different build than the one that had been driving the SUV. Much bigger.

Lefty kept his left side toward the man, but he couldn't stay that way indefinitely, not unless he wanted to appear really odd, side-stepping his way up the street. The man stayed at the corner, hands behind his back, legs shoulder width, waiting. No choice. Lefty pivoted right and walked away from the man

At the next corner he started to turn left, then stopped. Ahead one block, another black man stood. Same stance. Almost same build. About Lefty's height, he guessed. Tight brown T-shirt, jeans, heavily muscled. Lefty crossed the street and continued his previous direction. While walking he glanced back and saw the first man still guarding his corner. At least he wasn't following.

He reached the next cross street and glanced left. No one. A dog barked. Big golden retriever, sticking his nose through wooden slats, tail wagging. The street dead ended, so he turned left. No one in view. Now eerily silent. In the afternoon heat, even the birds remained mute. Sweat dripped down both cheeks.

He drew even with a mail truck that had pulled to the curb. An older man sorted through mail, stuffed a pile into a mailbox, and drove to the next house.

A woman, small child in tow, walked out of a two-story, light brown brick house. They glanced at Lefty. The child pointed and said something which Lefty could not hear but could guess about the subject. The woman opened the door of a Buick SUV and quickly ushered the child in.

As Lefty passed the SUV, he heard the woman say, "Hush."

An idea occurred to him. He quickened his pace passed the mail truck, the mailman still sorting mail for the last house before the corner. Lefty stepped off the street onto the grass and waited under a large maple tree, hoping none of the neighbors would report a one-armed dude loitering.

The mail truck engine whined as the truck pulled forward and started to pass Lefty. He jogged alongside it, getting a funny look from the mailman, especially when the truck stopped at the corner and Lefty did as well, then resumed jogging when the truck crossed the street. Lefty had not been able to see enough through the truck to know if the black man he was trying to avoid was still guarding the corner a block away. Didn't matter.

Once Lefty got across the street, he assumed unseen, he crossed in front of the mail truck when it stopped at the next house. He jogged across the street. The corner house had no fence, giving him a straight, concealed path to the next block where his car patiently waited.

He walked through the yard behind the green ranch house, again hoping no one was watching to alert the police.

When he reached the end of the house, he could see his Nissan to his right across the street. He walked that way between the green ranch and a white bungalow, which had a matching white shed close to the street by their driveway. Extending from the shed was a wooden slat privacy fence and beyond that two small evergreen trees, giving Lefty enough cover to get nearly all the way to the curb, only a street-width from his car.

At the fence, he glanced up the street. One of the men was leaning against a tree positioned between his car and the corner. Lefty waited, rubbed his hand through his hair. It came away wet. He wiped it on his jeans.

The sun beat down. Heat shimmered off the blacktop. Heaving a deep sigh, he started toward the back of his car. The other man immediately saw him. He scowled at Lefty, and quickly approached the Nissan, positioning himself near the passenger door.

Lefty said nothing as he closed the gap. The large man slid slowly toward the back of the Nissan. The good news, both the man's hands were empty and in view, at his sides. His T-shirt was untucked, no doubt hiding a gun stuffed into his waistband.

"How's it going, neighbor?" Lefty asked. "Hot day for a walk, but it helps sweat out the poison, know what I mean?"

The man said nothing. Lefty noticed an ear bud in the guy's right ear.

The man tilted his head and spoke to his shoulder. "He's here. Block and a half up the street. Crappy Nissan."

"Hey, it runs, dude. Gets great gas mileage." Now only a couple feet away. He veered a little left to go around the back of the car.

The other man moved with him, blocking his way.

Lefty said, "I really don't have time to chat, neighbor. So, if you could move aside, I have an appointment."

The man said nothing. He flexed and unflexed his fingers, arms still hanging at his sides.

Now only a foot away, Lefty smiled and reached his left hand out as if to shake.

The man glanced at the PI's outstretched hand. Lefty kicked out with his right leg, caught the man in the groin. The big goon grunted and bent over.

Lefty moved in close, cupped his left hand over the man's neck and brought a knee up into his face. The crunch of the man's nose sounded like someone stepped on a dry tree branch. Red dripped onto the blacktop.

There was a bulge in the man's back. Lefty grabbed the gun, a black semi-automatic. He flipped the gun, rotating it, grabbing the barrel and brought the handle down hard on the back of the guy's head. The man crumpled to the street.

"Hey!"

To Lefty's right, the other bodyguard sprinted toward him, still over a block away. Lefty flipped the gun again, caught it by the handle and pointed. He pulled the trigger. The explosion ripped through the silent neighborhood. A whine as the bullet bounced off the street, well to the right of the charging man. He had purposely missed, but the shot did its job as the man stopped, did a beeline toward the closest parked car, a small red Ford SUV, and ducked behind it.

Lefty hit the cartridge release and the cartridge, minus one shell, fell to the ground. He then tossed the gun behind him, ducked down, and fumbled in his pocket for his keys. He peered over the top of his car. The other guy ventured a look as well.

Lefty opened his car door. Another man sprinted up the street from the house of interest, gun out, pointed at Lefty. The man on the concrete by his car groaned, tried to turn over. Lefty climbed in the car, keeping his head down below the dash.

He heard a shot. His windshield shattered. Bits of glass rained onto the back of his neck. He got the key into the ignition. Quick prayer to the God he wasn't sure he believed in. Turned the key.

The car started. He shoved the transmission into drive, slammed the accelerator to the floor.

Another shot. This one hit his car, not sure where. The car rocketed down the street. He whipped the steering wheel hard left at the first corner. Tires squealed. Another shot. A house window past his car shattered. Not a nice way to treat your neighbors now, is it?

He sped away down the side street. He kept going as long as the street went, two lousy blocks, then turned a hard left, drove one block, then a hard right. He floored it again until he reached Manchester road, where he slowed, merged on, and drove east for a while.

He gripped the steering wheel, his knuckles white, to keep from trembling. After a couple miles, he pulled off onto Geyer road, then into a tire store parking lot. He let out a huge breath and just sat for several minutes, violently shaking.

As soon as the trembling eased, he decided he'd had enough excitement for one afternoon. He headed back to Lieutenant Pratt's house.

He'd get the windshield fixed later.

Chapter 41

Rockport and Chester watched the gray SUV roll away and the two squad cars drive by it, slow down, then move past. Seconds later, the little Nissan that had been parked in his neighbor's driveway followed the SUV.

"That, I assume," said Rockport, "is George Bruder."

Chester grunted.

"I think, my friend, it's time to give him a call. I'll have Sara confirm with Angel she's ready for the outside world to know she's here."

"I ain't worried about the private dick."

"The SUV?"

"Umm hmm."

"Yeah, that worries me a bit as well. Detective Warren told me a couple days ago that my picture went out over the wire. Twice."

Chester glanced at Rockport and raised his eyebrows. "Twice?"

"One was the lieutenant Mr. Bruder used to work for. That makes sense."

"And the other?"

"Some other detective. Today, Lisa said word on the street is the guy's dirty."

"The seller?"

"That's my fear. If he has connections."

Chester said, "I'll get Leroy over here for a few days."

"Good idea. And see if he has any other friends that he, and more importantly, you trust."

"I guess I should tell them they'll be sleeping on the floor?" Chester turned away from the window. "Sara?"

"What's going on?" Sara looked first at Chester, then at Rockport as he turned to face her.

"She's all yours boss man," Chester muttered, moving toward her to leave the room.

Sara continued to glare at Rockport as Chester brushed by her. His footsteps faded down the hall. She said, "Why would we need Leroy and some of his friends here?"

"A party?" Rockport shrugged and gave a half smile.

Sara placed both hands on her hips and stared even harder. "Calvin?"

Rockport heaved a huge sigh. "We had a couple people watching the house this afternoon."

Sara asked, "And do we know who they were?"

"One of them. George Bruder." Sara started to say something else, but Rockport added, "So I think it's time to ask Angel if she's ready to contact the outside world. I'd like to call Mr. Bruder and let him know Angel is safe."

Sara nodded. "Nice try, bub. Who else was watching us?"

Rockport turned back to the window. No cars parked on the street within view. The squad cars were long gone. He turned back to Sara, who had not budged. "We don't know."

"The guy you ripped off?"

"Could be." He waited for her to tear into him.

Instead, Sara dropped her hands to her side and sighed. "I'll have the girls ready to move quickly, if we need to. I'll call that guy we've used before for group events, the one that has a couple fifteen passenger vans. I'll have him drop one off and park it in back." She pirouetted and walked away.

"Hmm." Rockport turned once again to watch out the window, not expecting to see anything, but unsure what else to do right then. He muttered, "Not sure I'll ever figure her out."

Chapter 42

Manuel Rodriquez sat in the matching armchair watching his boss, not daring to say a word. When he'd heard the first shot, he'd cringed. With the second shot, he'd collapsed into the armchair and shook his head, dreading what was about to happen.

His longtime boss, Jackson McCormitt, sat on the edge of the cream brushed-fabric sofa, staring at his nine millimeter Glock, turning it over, raising it up, aiming it at the door, back down, rotated. Staring. One leg pumped up and down. The fingers of the hand not holding the gun strummed on the arm of the sofa.

The front door opened. Their three hired hands sauntered in. "What's you doing, boss?" said the tall, thin man, "cleaning your gun?"

McCormitt raised his head and smiled at the three of them. Then he raised the gun and pointed it at the thin guy first, then at the two muscled thugs.

"Hey," said the thin one. "What's the deal?"

"I'm trying to decide which of you I shoot first."

Rodriquez had his forty-five out, resting on his knee, just in case his boss actually did pull the trigger. If so, he'd take out the other two. With a seven-inch barrel, he was unlikely to need more than two shots from fifteen feet. Heck, he'd be able to drop them from a hundred feet, if needed. All three men shot glances at Rodriquez. He kept his expression neutral, but locked stares with each one in turn.

"Tell me this, did you at least get him?" McCormitt asked.

The three men shifted their attention to McCormitt. "Um," was the thin guy's only reply.

Muscled thug number one—Winston, Rodriquez thought his name was—said, "No, boss. He got away."

McCormitt nodded very slowly. He lowered the gun. "Get in here, you morons." He stood and in a considerably higher volume shouted, "What were you thinking? Firing your weapon in this neighborhood? There will be cops crawling around here soon." He sucked in several deep breaths as the three men moved into the living room, smart enough not to answer McCormitt. "Manuel, find another house, would you? Something closer to Rockport's."

Rodriquez nodded, slid his weapon into his shoulder holster, comfortable he could draw it and shoot the three idiots before anyone of them got a bead on him or his boss. He pulled his cell phone out of his pocket.

"And when the cops do show up, you three better be hiding in the basement."

"Why don't we move on that dude now?" said thin man, whose name Rodriquez just could not remember.

Rodriquez shook his head as he stabbed the browser icon on his phone, expecting his boss to shoot the thin hombre. He'd seen McCormitt do just that, even when an intelligent question had been asked.

Instead, McCormitt, in a surprisingly calm voice, said, "Not yet. We need more information about this guy, like why he bought these girls."

"Why else would he, other than he's a pimp?" thin guy asked again.

Rodriquez couldn't stand it anymore. He glanced up from his phone, where he'd been scrolling through a list of rental properties. "What is your name again?"

"Man, we been working together three days and you still don't know my name?" The thin black man asked.

McCormitt sat back on the sofa, a smirk on his mouth, watching his bodyguard. Rodriquez sighed, slipped his forty-five out of the holster. "Look, dude, I hate killing someone I don't know. What's your name?"

To the thin man's credit, he held Rodriquez's gaze a few seconds. "Rodney. Rodney Johnson."

Rodriquez smiled, holstered his gun. To McCormitt he said, "Sorry for the interruption, boss."

McCormitt smiled, shook his head. "No problem, Manuel. Find anything yet?"

"There's one that looks promising in a town called Frontenac. It's close to Huntleigh Woods, where Rockport's house is. A lot bigger. Pricier, obviously."

"That's fine. Now, Rodney, tell me why a billionaire would be a common pimp?" McCormitt still held his weapon. He laid it on his knee, pointing at Rodney.

"I don't know. Maybe that's how he made his money."

"High-end brothel, maybe?" McCormitt asked, more to himself than Rodney, though.

The other two men had the sense to stand quietly and study their shoes.

"Or maybe he's rescuing these girls. He could be working with one of those organizations that take girls off the street and try to rehabilitate them. According to our source in Houston, he's a retired CEO. His money came from there."

"What's the difference what the dude does? Let's take him out and be done with it."

Rodriquez decided that Rodney was not the brightest bulb in the Christmas tree. He glanced at McCormitt. Yup, this was it. Good thing he didn't bother taking anything out of his duffel bag except what he needed that day.

McCormitt raised his nine millimeter and pointed it at Rodney. The other two kept their heads down, but they edged away from Rodney.

"I'm going to have to talk with Big Eddie about the quality of help he supplied." He shook his head.

Rodney watched him, slowly stepping back toward the door.

Rodriquez almost laughed out loud. The idiot actually thought he could run away.

"Rodney, we appreciate your service, but your tenure is completed."

Rodriquez braced himself for the shot, but instead his boss's cell phone rang, the ring tone like an old-fashioned telephone.

"Hmm. Looks like it's your lucky day, Rodney." McCormitt laid his weapon on the glass-topped end table. "Maybe we'll keep you around a little longer." He picked up his phone from the table. He stabbed at it a few times then laid it back down. "What have you got, Rory?"

Through the speakerphone, Rory Anderson, McCormitt's errand boy in Houston, the one who'd supplied information on Rockport, said, "Identified the other two in the photo. Deepens the mystery, though, boss."

"Do tell, Rory. Do tell."

"The biggest dude is Chester Henderson. Spent some time in state prison for killing a man. Supposedly, this man raped his daughter or something like that. The governor pardoned him. Reason never disclosed."

"Really? Interesting. And now he works for Mr. Rockport. And the other?"

"Real bad dude, boss. Lewis Wilson."

Rodriquez noted that both muscled thugs, Winston and, what was that guy's name. Dang, he had to work on remembering names. Anyway, he noticed they both glanced up when Rory mentioned Lewis Wilson.

"What's so bad about him?" McCormitt asked.

"As a teenager, he was the leader of one of the biggest gangs in St. Louis. Police suspect him for over ten murders. Apparently had a close brush with death, got shot up. After that, came to Jesus or something. Walked away from the gang."

"Good information."

"Boss, if Rockport has these two with him, he may have others. Wilson's sure to have friends."

"Rory, I appreciate your concern. Anything more on Rockport?"

"Oh yeah, one thing. His daughter died of a heroin overdose. Apparently, she'd left home young, somehow got on hooch then started hooking to support her habit."

"That answers that question. Thanks Rory." He punched the cell phone. "Rescue operation, not brothel." He looked at Rodriquez.

"Well, Manuel, what do you think?"

Rodriquez wasn't really paid to think, but he knew his boss respected his tactical skills that he'd learned in the military. So, he gave it some thought, knowing McCormitt would be patient and wait for his wheels to slowly grind.

The other three men each shifted from leg to leg.

McCormitt waved and shouted, "Would you three sit somewhere? You're making me nervous."

The three men scattered, Winston to the opposite end from McCormitt in an armchair identical to the one Rodriquez occupied. The other muscled dude headed straight toward Rodriquez and sat in the kitchen behind him. And Rodney was stuck on the other end of the couch with McCormitt. He tentatively sat on the edge of the cushion, eyes darting between his boss and the nine millimeter on the end table.

Finally, Rodriquez asked Rodney, "Why'd you come back here? I didn't tell you to leave your post."

McCormitt looked first at Rodriquez then at Rodney, who shifted nervously, then back at Rodriquez. "Good question, Manuel. Good question." He turned back to Rodney and said, "Yes, Rodney, why are you here?"

"Uh, two cop cars came into the neighborhood. They slowed as they approached me. So I left."

"Two cop cars, together?" Rodriquez asked.

"Uh-huh."

Rodriquez shook his head. "You were made." He looked at McCormitt. "We should pack up and be ready to move should we get company. I'll look into this house I found. Tomorrow, Winston can do some more surveillance of Rockport."McCormitt nodded. Rodriquez continued, "Let's see what his reaction is to being watched." He then swiveled a bit to face Winston. "Tell me about Lewis Wilson."

Winston looked at the other muscled dude behind Rodriquez then back at Rodriquez.

"The man on the phone had it right. Bad mother. Could have an army if he wanted."

"Even though he left the gang," McCormitt said.

"Yeah. The brother was loaded, you know. Had all of the North Side. Then found Jesus. Walked away from the gang, but not the community. Started giving his money away, helping his gangstas' families, especially when a brother bought a bullet. They love him."

McCormitt sighed. "I think you're right, Manuel. We'll watch Rockport's place again tomorrow. Let's see if any of this army arrives." He glanced at Rodney. "What am I supposed to do with you, Rodney?"

Rodriquez drew his forty-five but McCormitt waved him off. "No, Manuel, let's try to keep things quiet." He stood. "Rodney, I want you to pay a visit to Big Eddie, let him know we'd like a couple other men."

Rodney stood, nodding vigorously, probably ecstatic at being allowed to live.

McCormitt added, "And tell Big Eddie, I want more like Winston and not like you, got it?" Rodney kept nodding. After a few seconds, McCormitt asked, "Are you waiting for something?" Rodney shook his head. "Then go." Rodney started to leave. "And try to avoid the cops." Rodney only nodded, then left the house.

McCormitt sighed again. "Friday. We need to get this done Friday."

Chapter 43

Sara did all she could to keep the panic out of her voice. In the kitchen, standing in a line facing her, were Marsha, Serena, Britany, Amanda, Angel, Emily, and the other three that Rockport had brought home Sunday night. The other four girls staying at the house were already upstairs packing, having been briefed by Sara earlier. She'd wanted Marsha, Amanda, Serena and Britany for stability while addressing the newest girls.

Chester hovered by the door just in case one of the newer girls decided to try and leave. He held his cell phone in his hand, waiting for Leroy to call back.

"Girls, thanks for meeting with me. We have a potential situation that we need to be ready for." She stopped, not sure how much she wanted to say.

Before Sara could continue, Angel said, "It's my pimp, isn't it? He's found us."

"Um, something like that, hon, but no, not your pimp."

This was not the first drill for Marsha, Serena, Britany and Amanda. A little over a year ago, an overzealous pimp had followed Amanda home when she'd gone out shopping. That time, the four girls and Sara had hidden in the basement inside the extra rooms, all of which had reinforced doors.

The pimp had only managed to get as far as the foyer before Chester had taken control of the situation. The pimp spent a few days in the hospital and never bothered them again.

This time, though, Sara feared it could be much worse.

"We need you all to have some things ready to take with you if we need to leave. One bag, girls. We have a fifteen-passenger van coming tomorrow morning. We'll leave it parked out back. But there are fourteen of us, so whatever you take sits in your lap for the drive."

"Where will we go?" Emily's eyes were wide. She clung to Angel, one arm under Angel's arm, with her other hand she held onto Angel's arm so tightly her fingers were white. Angel patted Emily's hand.

"We have another house we can use. It's down in Jefferson County, about a thirty-minute drive. A little smaller, but if we need to go there, hopefully it will only be for a few days."

"But who's coming here?" Emily asked.

"If anyone does, it's someone looking for something Mr. Rockport took from them. Don't worry, hon. We'll keep you safe." Sara heard the vibration of Chester's phone. She glanced at him. He lifted the phone to his ear. "Okay, girls," Sara said, "Go get some stuff together. For you new girls, we've put a duffle bag outside each of your rooms, one for each of you."

The girls filed out of the kitchen, some heading upstairs, the new ones downstairs.

"That's all," Chester said. "Uh huh. I guess it'll have to do." A pause. "Yeah, today. As soon as you can get here." Another pause. "They'll have to sleep on the floor or a couch or something." Chester listened some more.

Sara crept closer, but she couldn't hear what Leroy was saying.

"Yeah, see you soon. And park around back." Chester pocketed it.

"How many men?" Sara asked.

"Two plus Leroy. We'll have four guns, five if Mr. Rockport uses one."

Sara stared at Chester, breathing deeply. "Do you think we'll need guns?"

"Hope not." Chester pivoted and left the kitchen, leaving Sara standing alone.

She heard distant female voices. The front door opened then closed, Chester going out no doubt. The trembling started in her hands and spread rapidly throughout her midsection. She wrapped her arms around herself, suddenly chilled.

For several minutes she remained standing in the kitchen, shaking, teeth chattering, her mind imagining every bad scenario possible. An hour later, Sara was still in the kitchen, though now sitting at the table, holding tears back, sipping a cup of coffee, trying to get warm. The back door opened and three large black men walked in, Leroy in the lead.

He greeted her with only, "Sara." His serious expression, one that rarely darkened his face, increased her worry.

She nodded, tried a half smile.

"This is Derrick and Shawn." Leroy turned to the two men, both probably late teens or early twenties. "This is Sara. Do what she says."

He continued through the kitchen, the two others in tow, both nodding at her when they passed. Sara watched them walk out. Tucked in the waistbands of all three were large handguns. She heard the front door open.

Leroy, from the foyer said, "And you all know Chester. I don't need to tell you to do what he says."

"Library," Sara heard Chester say.

She listened to the footsteps going downstairs, then the banging closed of the library door. Her trembling overtook her with the force of a tornado.

Chapter 44

Lefty pulled into the parking lot of the downtown Hilton at the Ballpark, the late afternoon sun still high and brutal, the heat inside his Nissan oppressive. He stopped as soon as his backend cleared the street and swiveled to watch traffic. No black Mustang drove by. He stared hard at a black Pontiac 600 with tinted windows but could not see the driver. After a few minutes still no Mustang, so he pulled into an empty spot then waded through the humidity to the hotel lobby.

Eileen was already waiting for him sitting on a high-back, brown vinyl chair with a black frame, leaning her elbows on the round, black lacquered table. The desk clerk shouted a greeting. Lefty waved him off then joined Eileen. The lobby smelled like cinnamon. Several people dressed in Cardinals T-shirts milled about. No home game that evening, so they must be in for the weekend series. Two men in suits walked through the doors he'd just entered and headed toward the elevators.

"Well," Eileen said, "how was your day? I've been bored out of my mind. Too hot to walk around much outside."

Lefty sucked in a deep breath of cold, dry air. "I know where Angel is, well at least I'm pretty sure she's there and who has her."

"Great." Eileen slid off the chair, staring hard at Lefty. "Let's go get her."

"We can't yet. I just don't know what we'll be getting into." He hesitated, wondering if he should tell her about the other vehicle that had been staking out Rockport's house and who he found in

Des Peres. He decided transparency was the better route. "And there's a complication."

"What complication?"

"There's someone else watching the place as well. Remember I told you about the auction and the rip-off?" Eileen nodded. "The dude that got ripped off is still in town, and he knows where the guy is who took his money. The same guy I'm pretty sure has Angel."

"Oh."

"I want to do some more digging tomorrow, go out to the house and watch some more. Find out more about the seller that got ripped off, if I can."

"But why not just call the cops?"

"And say what? Angel is an adult. We have no evidence she's there against her will. And I'm not sure this guy is a bad guy. Besides, even with my connections, I don't think I could convince Lieutenant Pratt to send in officers to check out a private citizen. Especially a rich one."

"What about the theft and assault at the auction? Isn't that probable cause?"

Lefty shook his head. "He ripped off a known human trafficker at an illegal auction. The cops won't go after a wealthy, prominent citizen for that."

Eileen settled back into the chair and stared toward the hotel doors. She scratched her chin. One leg bounced up and down. She sighed. "I guess you're right. Can I go with you tomorrow?"

Lefty's first impulse was to say no, but he hesitated. His second thought was to say no. Still, he hesitated. Finally, he said, "Not a good idea. I may go to Des Peres where our mystery seller is. Already got shot at today, so don't want to risk having you around."

"Shot at?" Eileen again stood. "You didn't say anything about that. What happened?"

Lefty waved Eileen down and she sat. He then told her about his adventure in Des Peres. "So, no, you can't go with me tomorrow. You'll just have to fight boredom another day."

"Fine."

"How about dinner? I'm a little hungry after all my ducking bullets."

"Sure. And it's on me."

"No argument here. Especially after the several hundred I had to dish out for a new windshield."

Chapter 45

Lefty reached Rockport's by ten after nine the next morning. And even at that early hour and amongst the trees of Huntleigh Wood, heat draped over him like a woolen blanket. His shirt clung to him as he drove through the quiet neighborhood.

At first he didn't spot the gray SUV. They'd learned. Not as obvious as yesterday, but there it was a couple blocks down, still with a view of Rockport's front door. Lefty drove by and decided to keep going. He wound all the way back to the entrance to the exclusive township and headed toward Des Peres. He'd not been able to tell if the person inside the SUV had been the same as yesterday, but at least it meant one less person at the sex trafficker's house.

Twenty minutes later, Lefty passed first a house with yellow police tape and a boarded-up window, then McCormitt's house. He turned left at the next block then left again, pulling to the curb parallel to McCormitts house one street over. He waited a few minutes, watching the gray two-story house facing him to see if anyone was home. It had a Prudential Reality for sale sign, so he hoped they'd moved out. He didn't want to cut through someone's yard if they were there and might call the cops or yell, drawing attention to him.

A cop car was parked at the corner on the other side of the street. He didn't see the officer or anyone else around, though. The entire neighborhood looked deserted and after about fifteen minutes, he decided to chance it.

Waves of heat reflected off the blacktop. A robin sang in an oak tree in the front yard as he walked along the side of the house, several times glancing down the street to see if there were any police officers. He saw none.

The yard to his left had a white vinyl privacy fence. Not conducive to climbing even if he had two arms. He could do it if he had a running start, but no reason to do so right now as the house next door, diagonal to his target, had no fence. Also, the house next door to McCormitt's had no fence.

He walked along the privacy fence to the corner and peeked around the fence. No one in McCormitt's backyard. Nothing in the backyard at all. No signs that anyone lived there except the three heads he saw through a large, three-paned window that opened into the kitchen.

Movement came from a little further in the house. Two more men. One of the men sitting was the sex trafficker, the other a man with thick black hair, could have been Hispanic. Neither had been outside yesterday. The other three men he thought were black and he'd encountered three men yesterday. Add the one at Rockport's, the man from Houston had added at least one to his small army.

Lefty ducked back behind the fence and contemplated his next action. Just because he saw five in the kitchen did not mean there were no more in the front of the house, and he had even less cover in the front.

He surveyed the white split-level house next door to McCormitt's. No fences. Kids' toys, including two bicycles, a red tricycle, a little red wagon, and a multicolored children's play set with a slide. Also a basketball pole and hoop in the driveway. No movement inside the house.

He didn't want to return to the front of the house, were his car was, in case a cop was there, so he moved to about halfway back down the vinyl fence, then set out across the adjacent yard until he reached the end of that yard, turned left and trotted to the house next to McCormitt's.

He leaned against the garage door. The house had an L-shaped driveway off the side street with the garage entrance in the back.

The only sounds were a distant lawn mower and a couple birds singing. He moved slowly along the house. At the kitchen window he peered in, ready to run should someone see him. The inside was dark. He saw no one so kept on moving.

When he reached the far corner, he peeked around the corner to the front of the house. No one. He moved across the yard between the two houses.

At the corner of McCormitt's house, he ducked and moved along the back. When he got close to the kitchen window, he paused and listened. He could hear voices inside, muffled and unintelligible.

He waited. His thighs started to burn. Finally, someone raised their voice. "Not yet. We can't just barge in and start shooting."

The voices became muffled again. He shifted to ease the pain in his thighs, lost his balance, and fell against the wall with a thump. The voices inside stopped. Lefty held his breath and waited, not even daring to push off from the wall.

He heard the back-door latch.

"Crap."

Lefty stood and bolted across the yard. Someone came out the back door and yelled at him to stop. Lefty zigzagged and waited for a shot. None came. He glanced over his shoulder and saw two black men, one large, one skinny, come running after him. He recognized both from yesterday. He had a good seventy feet on them. He made the next yard and ran close to the privacy fence, then across the street to his car.

Down the block someone yelled, "Hey, you."

Lefty opened his car door and glanced down the street. A uniformed officer and another man in a suit were watching him. He climbed in the car. The officer started jogging toward him.

The two men chasing Lefty reached the corner of the house across the street. The officer glanced to his right, saw them, and veered toward them. The two black men reversed their direction and tore off toward McCormitt's, the officer following.

Lefty started his car. The plainclothes detective now trotted toward him. Lefty cranked his steering wheel hard left and accelerated, thankful he had a small car as he completed the U-turn, just missing the other curb.

He floored the accelerator and sped down the street. In his rearview mirror he saw the detective stop and watch him.

Lefty felt sure he'd get a phone call from Lieutenant Pratt sometime today, asking why he'd fled from county cops. He turned right at the first corner and when he passed the street McCormitt's house was on, he slowed and looked out his passenger window.

The two black guys had crossed the street still running, smart enough not to go into McCormitt's. They split about halfway across the street, one running up the street away from Lefty, the other toward him.

Lefty decided not to hang around to watch. He accelerated just as the cop appeared from between McCormitt's and the house next door. Lefty drove back to Huntleigh Woods to watch Rockport's some more and to ponder what his next move should be.

Chapter 46

Chester and Rockport were at their same vantage point as the day before. The difference was the three men downstairs, all heavily armed, watching out other windows around the first floor. All the men had ear buds in, using a wireless communication system Rockport had purchased the previous afternoon. Rockport monitored the sparse chatter. The only time any of the men spoke was when they saw movement outside.

Earlier that morning, one of the men, Shannon Carter, had said a gray SUV drove by. Rockport figured it was the same one from before. He'd asked Shannon to step outside and see where it went. A few minutes later, Shannon had reported the SUV had pulled along the side about four houses up and was just sitting there. No one got out.

He and Chester watched from the second-floor window saying nothing. He could hear girls walking around the second floor, the occasional chatter, but overall, the mood was quiet, nervous. He knew Sara was in the basement, also with an ear bud, monitoring the chatter and waiting for word to move the girls to the van parked out back. They could reach it through the basement, which had a door leading up a narrow set of stone steps in back.

A beat-up Nissan drove by.

Chester said, "Our favorite PI is back."

Rockport nodded. "I think it's time we met our favorite PI."

Chapter 47

This time, Miguel Rodriquez thought for sure his boss was going to shoot someone, even with cops lurking around the neighborhood. McCormitt aimed his gleaming, silver forty-five at the head of the skinny black dude, what was his name? Oh, yeah, Rodney.

McCormitt pointed it at Winston. No, wait, Winston was watching Rockport's house. What was this other dude's name? Rodriquez gave up and watched the gun go from pointing at Rodney's head to pointing at the other dude's chest, back and forth.

If he was a betting man—and he was actually, loved going to the casinos—he'd bet Rodney's brain was soon to be splattered on the light tan wall of the living room. Which would complicate things much more than he wished. He disliked gunfights with cops. And that's what this would lead to, should his boss pull the trigger.

McCormitt's face was bright red. He didn't say anything. His hand shook. Rodriquez had his own gun resting on his lap, ready should one of these bozos decide to get cute.

After several minutes of indecisiveness, McCormitt let out a loud, "Ahhhh" and lowered his gun. He looked at Rodriquez. "Well, Manuel, which one should I shoot?"

"Neither, boss. There's cops on the block over."

It appeared to Rodriquez that his boss was not too keen on that answer, but Rodriquez knew he was in McCormitt's employ because he kept a cool head and was a good tactician. Drawing the cops' attention now would do them no good. They were already scouring the streets a couple blocks down where, undoubtedly by now, they'd found their unconscious uniformed cop. At least that was Rodney's story, how the two of them had split, then circled, catching the uniformed officer on both sides and knocking him out.

McCormitt holstered his gun with a loud sigh. He extracted his cell phone from his jacket pocket. McCormitt always wore a sports coat, if not a full suit. Today, with the heat, only a dark blue sports coat, tan pants, and powder blue shirt, collar open. He punched in some numbers, waited.

"Winston, get back here and pick us up. I want to see what we're getting into." After hanging up, he looked at each man in the room. "Tomorrow, we move. Be ready. Anyone screws up, you deal with Mr. Rodriquez. And believe me, you don't want to deal with Manuel." He turned away from the impassive men and walked toward the kitchen. "Isn't that right, Manuel?"

Rodriquez smiled, nodded and said, "That's right, boss." To himself he muttered, "Finally."

Chapter 48

Lefty put his cell phone on his dash. He expected a call any minute from Lieutenant Pratt. In Huntleigh Woods once again. The SUV was gone, which worried him. Lefty had circled past the driveway he'd used the day before for surveillance. There was an AT&T truck parked there. The residence must be getting service, which also meant someone was probably home. He'd driven past, circled around, passed where the SUV had been, then parked in a driveway a couple houses before Rockport's.

The cell phone buzzed.

"That was fast," Lefty said to the empty car. He glanced at the screen, but it was an unknown number. "Hello."

"Mr. George Bruder?" asked a deep voice.

"That's me. Who is this?"

"My name is Calvin Rockport. I think it's time we met. What do you think, Mr. Bruder?"

Lefty thought about asking how Rockport knew his phone number but decided it didn't really matter. Instead he said, "Sounds like a plan. Give me your address and I'll be there in about twenty."

Rockport chuckled. "Really, Mr. Bruder, is the charade necessary? It will hardly take you twenty minutes to walk over two houses. I look forward to our chat." Rockport hung up.

"Touché," Lefty said.

Instead of walking two houses down, he backed out of the driveway he was in and drove to Rockport's, pulling into his driveway. He climbed out of his Nissan and headed to the front door. Before he reached it, a large black man in tan cargo shorts and a tight black T-shirt opened the door. Lefty entered the large house and stared at the large gun in the shoulder holster of the large man.

"First doorway to the right," said the large man.

"Nice piece," Lefty said.

The man said nothing. Instead he glanced outside, looking both left then right. The guy closed the door and locked it. "First doorway to the right."

"Gotcha."

Lefty walked to the first doorway to the right and entered the—what was it, living room, sitting room? He wasn't sure.

A man he recognized from a photo and a video, and his surveillance, Calvin Rockport, sat in a white fabric love seat on the far left side of the room, reading a book. When Lefty entered, he set the book aside and smiled.

Rockport stood and met Lefty in the middle of the room. "Nice to meet you, Mr. Bruder. I'm Calvin Rockport."

"George Bruder, though most people call me Lefty."

Rockport simply smiled and gestured for Lefty to sit, so he chose the other white fabric love seat perpendicular to the one Rockport had been in. The older man resumed his seat. The big black man entered the library.

"Give us fifteen, Chester," Rockport said, "then bring Angel in."

Chester nodded and left the room.

"Don't look so surprised, Mr. Bruder. Yes, Angel Atkins is here. She has been for several days. I assume that's why you're here."

"That's one of the reasons"

"Is she here against her will?"

"That gets into a real gray area," Rockport replied. "Probably she would have agreed with that when we first brought her here."

"And now?"

"Why don't you ask her when she comes in. Now, what was the second reason you're here?"

"Why don't you just give me Angel and I'll be on my way?"

"Because, Mr. Bruder, that would be the worst thing that could happen to her. She's not ready to leave, and there's no way we'll send her home. Why do you think she ran away in the first place?"

"Point taken. But her aunt's going to want to take her back with her."

"When she's ready, if that's what she wants to do. She's eighteen, Mr. Bruder. An adult. Capable of making her own decisions."

"Yeah, she's made some good ones up to this point."

Rockport frowned. "Why don't you reserve judgment until after you've talked with her? And now what is the second reason you're here?"

Lefty studied Rockport for a bit. Distinguished streaks of grey in his otherwise tawny goatee and slicked back hair. Tailored gray suit, probably with an Italian name attached to it. Black wingtips, recently polished. Lefty wondered if the big black dude did the polishing. Probably not. More a bodyguard than a butler.

"You're going to have company, soon, I believe. And they are not nice men."

"Jackson McCormitt, you mean? And his collection of Big Eddie's thugs?"

"So you know who McCormitt is?"

"I know of him, yes."

"You didn't exactly make friends with him when you ripped him off."

Rockport's bushy brows arched. "No, I suspect not. He had someone parked a couple houses down, watching us. They left about fifteen minutes before you arrived."

"Yup," Lefty said. "And I've stirred the hornet's nest twice, so he may be ready to move."

More brow arching. "Really, please do tell."

Lefty told him about his run-ins with McCormitt and his men over the past two days. Rockport allowed Lefty to tell his tale, then started to say something, but someone knocked on the door frame.

"Come in." Rockport never took his eyes off Lefty, his expression neutral.

Two stunning women walked through the doorway. The taller one, her arm around the shorter one, was probably in her late twenties. She had long blond hair, thin, glossy lips, high cheekbones, and sparkling green eyes. Her build was athletic, her gait confident. The other girl had to be Angel. While also extremely pretty, also with long blond hair, she had puffy lips and dark circles under her dark brown eyes, which darted to and fro, eventually landing on Lefty and unabashedly staring at the stump of his right shoulder.

"Who are you?" Angel's upper lip curled slightly.

"Angel," Rockport said, "This is Mr. George Bruder. Known to his friends as Lefty."

Angel laughed. "Figures. What do you want? You're obviously not a cop."

Lefty smiled. "Actually, I used to be a cop. Now, I'm working for your aunt. She hired me to find you."

"Aunt Elly? You know her? How is she?" Angel slipped out from under the other woman's arm and sat on the other side of the sofa from Lefty. She wore loose-fitting blue jeans, a bright yellow short-sleeved shirt, and slip-on sneakers, no socks.

"She's here in town and very concerned about you."

"I tried...I tried to call her, but no one answered. Oh, my Lord, I thought Jim had got to her. She's okay?" Her eyes grew wide. She clasped her hands together, almost prayer-like.

"Yes, she's okay. How about you? Are you okay? Having been kidnapped and all." Lefty glanced at Rockport, who only smiled.

The tall blond, however, grimaced and was about to speak when Rockport held up his hand, a slight, subtle gesture, but both the blond and Lefty caught it.

"Kidnapped? Is that what Aunt Elly thinks?"

"She doesn't know what to think." He looked at Rockport. The tall blonde moved to the side of Rockport's love seat, staring hard at Lefty. "This dirty old man hasn't hurt you, has he?" Lefty asked. "Or done other things?"

Again, Rockport held up a hand, this time not so subtly. The tall blond snapped off a reply that Lefty knew would not be flattering. "First of all," Rockport said, "I don't consider fifty-eight to be old. And second, my sexual tastes are quite normal. I assure you I've never slept with any of these young women, or even touched them in any manner remotely inappropriate."

Angel nodded. "That's right. Everyone here has been real nice to me, even when I wasn't so nice."

Lefty again glanced at Rockport and the tall blonde. The woman smiled. Lefty saw true affection in her alluring green eyes. "There are other women here, too?"

Angel nodded.

Rockport said, "Yes, Mr. Bruder. We are not what you think we are. This place is a rescue shelter for girls who stray, like Angel."

"Rescue shelter," Lefty repeated.

Rockport nodded.

"Okay, I'll bite," Lefty said. "Tell me your story, Mr. Rockport."

Angel said, "Yeah, I'd like to hear it, too. I've heard Sara's story, but not yours."

Lefty figured the tall blond was Sara.

"Very well. Sara, you might want to sit. Not sure about Mr. Bruder, but you're making me nervous."

Lefty nodded affirmation.

Sara moved to the other side of the room and sat in a black leather zebra-striped chair, though she perched on the edge, as if ready to launch herself at Lefty should she need to.

Rockport started by telling his captive audience about how his wife died when his daughter was ten. "I tried to raise her using nannies, maids, butlers. You have to understand, I was too busy making money." He paused, swallowed heavily and studied his hands, which were clasped together in his lap. "My daughter ran away when she was eighteen. She never made it to nineteen." He paused, looked at Sara, who smiled, looked at Angel, who stared at him, and finally settled his gaze on Lefty. "But that's not the story you want to hear." He took a deep breath. "Mr. Bruder, have you ever had God tell you to do something that you didn't want to do, but knew you had no choice?"

Lefty shook his head.

"About eight months after my daughter died of an overdose, I was walking down Washington Avenue. At that time, my office was downtown. I had to get out, get some air. I had strayed pretty far north, been walking about thirty minutes." Again, he paused, looked at each other person in the room, then back to Lefty. "It was hot that day, early September, and a tall, scantily clad young woman approached me. She was pretty, but looked worn, if you know what I mean. She looked beaten, not physically, but mentally beaten down."

"Hey, big daddy, looking for some action?" the young woman said.

Rockport glanced into her glazed eyes, which seemed to look right through him. He waved her off and continued past her. After four steps he stopped cold. He tried to take another step but could not. As he strained to make that step, sweat dripped down both temples.

"Change your mind, sugar?" the girl asked.

Rockport swiveled, not wanting to look at the young, blond girl, not wanting to be reminded of what had happened to Carolyn, but unable to stop himself, as if someone else controlled his body. Finally, his legs worked, but not moving him away from the thin girl, but toward her. She gave a forced, tired smile.

When he came within an arm's length, she said, "What's your pleasure, daddy?"

"I...I want to ask you something." The words came out without his even thinking them. He didn't know what he wanted to ask her.

The girl frowned. "Fifty bucks, old man. I got things to do, so if you're going to take my time, pay up."

He reached into his pocket and took out his wallet. His fingers fumbled through his cash extracting five one hundred-dollar bills. He handed her the money. "Will this do?"

The girl's eyes widened. She looked at the money then looked both ways up and down the street. She said, "You must really want to get it on, huh big fella."

"No. I said I only want to ask you something."

She stuffed the cash inside the small, black purse she had over her shoulder. "Ask away, sugar."

When he realized what he was supposed to ask, he hesitated. The words froze on his lips. The girl patiently waited, smiling her wan, forced smile the entire time, looking through him, over him, around him, just not at him.

"I…I want to know, um, do you, um…"

She stroked his shoulder. "It's okay, sir. Take your time. Maybe we should step inside where it's cooler."

He pulled away. "No, right here is fine." He sucked in a deep breath of hot, wet air. A car sorely in need of a muffler rumbled by, leaving a strong odor of exhaust. He blurted out, "Do you know Jesus Christ as your Lord and Savior?"

"What? You some kind of religious nut?"

"Not religion, a relationship."

"I don't understand."

Rockport said, "Do you know Jesus Christ?"

"I know who he was, yeah."

"Is," Rockport said. "He's alive and he loves you. And he wants to save you."

"First of all, no one loves me, okay. And I don't need no saving."

For the next twenty minutes, Rockport spoke words that were not from him.

The girl—Roxanne, he later learned—listened with rapt attention, actually looking at him, as he explained how Jesus had been born, lived a perfect life, and died, taking on all the sin of the world just so someone like Roxanne could give their dirty, soiled, seemingly worthless life to Him. And no matter what she endured on this earth she'd go into glory with God forever.

Rockport paused in his narration. Lefty glanced around the room. Both women gave him complete attention.

"And?" Lefty asked.

"Roxanne gave her life to Christ right there, on that hot, noisy street."

"I'm happy for her, but I'm not connecting this"—he waved his arms indicating the house, the women, everything—"to your story."

"Patience, Mr. Bruder. I'm not done." He smiled at Lefty, who frowned back. Then Rockport continued. "After leading Roxanne to Christ, I gave her a hug and started back toward the office."

"Hey, where you going?"

Rockport stopped and asked, "What do you mean?"

Roxanne put her hands on her hips and glared at him. "This salvation stuff is all great and everything, but now what? I can't stay here on the street. I...I can't keep doing what I've been doing. You just gonna leave me here? Ain't you got some kind of responsibility or something?"

Her words hit Rockport as hard as if a piano had been dropped from the third story window of the building he stood by. But he hesitated, unsure what to do. He took her hand, said, "Come with me," and led her away.

Rockport drove Roxanne to his home. His housekeeper met them at the door, as she was sweeping the foyer.

"Margie, we're going to have a guest for a little while," Rockport told her.

She gave him a look suggesting she thought him a dirty old man.

"Please put her up in Carolyn's old room."

His housekeeper nodded and asked, "Where are your things?"

Roxanne answered, "I ain't got nothing."

Margie said, "Mr. Rockport, she's about Carolyn's size, a little younger, but the clothes should fit. Can I give her some?"

"Younger?" Rockport said. "Carolyn was only eighteen."

Roxanne said, "That's my age, too."

Margie glared at the young girl. "Young lady, if you're going to stay in this house, you will not tell lies. How old are you really?"

"Margie!" Rockport said.

"Mr. Rockport, this here girl is no eighteen. Ain't right honey?"

"I'll be seventeen soon. In February."

"You're only sixteen?" Rockport asked. Roxanne nodded. Rockport wanted to cry. "Margie, she can have any clothes of Carolyn's she wants."

"Very well, sir." To Roxanne she said, "Please follow me." Margie led Roxanne upstairs to Carolyn's room.

"Roxanne stayed with me for eighteen months and was able to kick her heroin habit."

"She still here?" asked Lefty.

"No," Rockport answered. "I asked her if I could take her back to her parents. But she said her father abused her and her mother was a drunk. Therefore, I allowed her to stay with me for the rest of that year and into the next year." He paused, reached for a glass on one of the three square glass tables in the middle of the room and took a sip of what looked like water. He continued. "One day a few weeks after her eighteenth birthday, she told me she needed to make a life of her own."

"What is it you want to do?" Rockport asked Roxanne.

"Well, I'm pretty good at talkin'."

"That you are. And?"

They stood in the foyer. She'd already packed a small gym bag Margie had found for her and put in the clothes she'd accumulated over the past eighteen months along with her toiletries. She wore a yellow, short-sleeved, flowery dress that hung just below her knees, one of Carolyn's that she'd especially liked. One white sandaled foot did circles on the tile. She could not meet his gaze. Chester stood at the railing of the second floor watching them.

"What's wrong, Roxanne?"

She looked up.

"Wrong? Nothin's wrong. I just thought, well...I don't know, I mean—"

"Go ahead, spit it out."

"I was wonderin' if maybe you had a position for me at your company."

Rockport scratched his chin. "Hmm. Let me think." He pulled his cell phone from his pocket and flipped it open. "Hold on a minute." He punched in the numbers to his personnel manager. After a few rings she answered. "Good morning, Ginny."

"Good morning, sir."

"Say, do we still have that receptionist job open in our downtown office?"

"We do."

"Great. I'm sending a girl to you. Her name is Roxanne Bentley. Please help her with the paperwork and give her the job."

"Okay. Do we need anyone to interview her?"

"That won't be necessary. She's a great talker, quite friendly and outgoing." He smiled at Roxanne, who blushed. "I think she'll do well."

"Okay, sir."

Rockport hung up, pocketed his phone, took a small notepad and pen from his inside suit jacket pocket. He scrawled the address of his main office in Clayton and the downtown office on a page, tore it off and gave it to Roxanne. "Oh, wait. That's not all." He took the paper back and wrote down another address. He handed her the page again. "The first address is where you go to get hired. Ask for Ginny at the front desk. The second one is the office downtown where you'll be our new receptionist. And the third address is an apartment you can use until you get enough money to get your own."

For the first time since he'd met her, words failed Roxanne. She opened and closed her mouth several times and hugged him. She whispered in his ear, "Thank you so much, Mr. Rockport."

When she separated from him, he said, "Don't thank me, thank God. He made this all possible."

Roxanne nodded, picked up her bag and started to leave. She stopped, rotated and said, "But what about the others?"

"What others?" Rockport answered.

"The others just like me. All them young girls on the street. There are so many others just like me. Can we help them somehow?"

He stared at her for quite a while, not knowing what to say. "You know, you may have something there. I have what, five bedrooms, and lots of room on other floors. I could open up a boarding house, ask the girls to come stay here and work with them like I did with you."

Roxanne chuckled and said, "You're so cute when you're naïve."

"What do you mean?"

"Ask the girls? You think they'd come here on their own? You think they'd just walk away from their pimps?"

"You did."

"Jesus did that for me. You think everyone you talk to will accept Christ like I did?"

"Maybe?"

She chuckled again. "No, sir, you gonna have to grab them and bring them here, then make them stay here. I seen this special on television about these interventions, where these groups do that with the girls. Only way to get them clean is to force them."

He stared at her again. "You mean kidnap them?"

"Yup. But I don't know if it's kidnapping, since it's for their good."

Rockport looked at Lefty. "Well, I didn't believe her, so I tried the same thing I did with her. For several months I tried evangelizing and inviting the girls to come live in my house, to leave their life behind and start new."

"And?" Lefty asked.

"I got spit on, slapped, chased away by pimps, laughed at. Not one other girl gave her life to Christ or took me up on my offer. Then I convinced Chester, my driver, the big guy you met coming in here, to help me try it Roxanne's way."

"And how did that work out for you?"

Rockport pointed at Sara. "Ask her. She was the first one I grabbed."

Lefty stared at Sara. He opened his mouth to say something, but Angel cut him off.

"Great story, Mr. R. But when do I get to see my aunt?'

Lefty answered, "I'll take you right now."

Sara gripped the sides of her chair, her knuckles going white.

Angel shook her head. "No, but can you bring her here? I'm not sure I'm ready to leave just yet."

Sara smiled. Her hands relaxed but her lips quivered. Crying, she stood and hurriedly left the room.

Angel looked at Rockport with a confused look on her face. "What did I say to upset Sara?"

"You didn't upset her, you made her very happy."

Still with the confused look, Angel said, "Okay, but she was crying and ran out of the room."

"Tears of joy, dear. Because of what you said. It's a long story. I'll tell you about Mandy sometime."

Lefty interjected, "Then what should I tell your aunt?"

Angel turned her attention to Lefty. Her bright blue eyes glittered. She smiled her full lips, showing white teeth. She was an incredibly beautiful girl. He studied her facial features and decided he did see a little of Eileen in her, the high cheek bones, simple, small nose, thin brows.

"Tell her I'm fine. These people—Sara, Mr. Rockport, Chester—they're helping me. I…I'm clean for the first time in a long time. I don't have to, you know, do that stuff I had to do before. Not anymore." Tears collected in the corners of her eyes. "Tell her I'm so sorry I left without saying goodbye." She buried her face in her hands and cried. After a few moments of sobbing, she also left the room.

Both Rockport and Lefty allowed the silence to linger for a few moments.

Rockport finally said, "Your job is done, Mr. Bruder. You've found the girl you were looking for, and she's fine."

"Guess so. Her aunt will be happy she's doing okay."

"And eventually Angel will be ready to leave. The fact she recognizes she's not ready is a big deal, Mr. Bruder. Therefore we don't want to rush her out."

"Gotcha."

He started to stand, but Rockport held up his hand. "If you'd allow me," Rockport said, "I'd like to extend your employment."

Lefty collapsed back into the chair. "Oh, how's that?"

"I'd like you to continue to keep an eye on McCormitt and warn me should he make a move against us."

Lefty sighed. He wasn't completely sold that everything here was as kosher as Rockport made it sound, but what the heck, he had nothing else to do right now and he so enjoyed hanging around McCormitt and his friendly thugs.

"Sure. I can do that."

"Excellent."

Rockport stood, so Lefty did as well. The older man extended a hand, his left one, and Lefty shook it.

"I look forward to working with you, Mr. Bruder. You've proved yourself quite resourceful."

"Whatever."

Lefty turned away from Rockport and left the large house. On his way to the car, Lefty spotted the gray SUV which had returned. But now right behind it was a dark blue SUV, another Escalade. And then, Lefty spotted one more car, this one a little farther down from the pair of Cadillacs. A black mustang.

Chapter 49

Lefty thought it was a little far to walk from the downtown Hilton to Laclede's Landing, but Eileen insisted they walk and not drive, and she wanted to be farther away from Ballpark Village, which was overcrowded due to a Cardinals game that night. So they walked the ten or so blocks in the opposite direction of Ballpark Village. It was a pleasant walk since the hot humid weather decided to take a break for a day, or at least an evening.

They spoke little, which had been hard because he wanted to share the news. Earlier, when he'd called her, he'd simply said he had made significant progress. He feared telling her what that progress was for two reasons. First, she'd want to dash over to Rockport's immediately, but he'd agreed with Rockport that he'd bring her around tomorrow afternoon, provided things were safe.

Second, once aunt and niece were reunited, he was afraid that would be it, the last time he'd see Eileen Seager. Okay, so he had to admit, there was really only the one reason he guarded the good news. The first reason was his lame excuse to not put it all on his selfishness.

Now they sat in air-conditioned bliss, along with thousands of others, or so it seemed. He also hadn't been overly thrilled with sushi, but again, that's what Eileen wanted. The Drunken Fish buzzed with a mix of young upwardly mobile businesspeople in suits and red-clad baseball fans.

The young brunette waitress took their drink orders. Iced tea for both of them. What was happening to him? Iced tea?

Eileen leaned forward over the small square table. "Okay, time to tell me what progress you made."

Lefty also leaned forward. He opened his mouth and started to tell her he'd found Angel but hesitated and instead asked her a question. "What happens when you find your niece?"

Eileen scrunched her brows. "What do you mean?"

"Just what I said. What are you going to do when you find Angel?"

"Well, assuming she's okay, take her home, I guess. Why?"

"What if she doesn't want to go home?"

Eileen frowned. "Why wouldn't she?"

"For the same reason she left in the first place."

She leaned back and stared at him.

Lefty asked, "Are you going to ask her to come live with you?"

"Absolutely."

"And you're prepared to deal with a heroin addict?"

"What are you talking about? How do you know she's an addict?"

Brilliant interrogation techniques, Bruder. No place to go but forward. As he started to speak, the waitress appeared and deposited their ice teas on the table. Lefty wished he had ordered a Long Island iced tea instead, given the intense glare Eileen was giving him.

"What will it be?" the waitress asked.

Lefty jumped right in. "I'll take the teriyaki chicken." So much for chivalry, but he didn't want Eileen asking for a few more minutes.

Eileen sighed and gave the waitress the sheet with the rolls that she'd checked without even looking at her.

"I'll get this right in." The waitress left them to an uncomfortable silence.

About fifteen seconds into that silence, Eileen said, "You found her, didn't you?"

Lefty looked around. A young couple next to them held hands across the table and gazed lovingly at each other. He willed some of that good feeling to his table, but when he looked back at Eileen she still glared, her arms crossed, her head craned forward.

"Well?"

"Okay, before I answer, here's the ground rules."

"What are you talking about? Did you find Angel or not?"

Lefty sucked in a deep breath. "Yes, I found her. She's fine."

Eileen's hands went to the table, bracing herself as if to rise.

Lefty quickly said, "We can't go see her tonight. Not until tomorrow afternoon, and only if it's safe."

"Safe? What are you talking about?"

"Your niece is a hooker addicted to heroin, living in a kind of halfway house where this dude helps girls like her get out of the life."

Eileen stared at him, her mouth open, her eyes large. "Um..." She closed her mouth and scrunched her brows. "I...but...she's okay?"

Lefty reached across the table and took one of Eileen's hands. She allowed him to hold it, even squeezed a little. "She's getting there. I don't know if she's ready to go anywhere yet."

"Tell me about her situation."

And he did. He talked nonstop for fifteen minutes. The waitress came and deposited their food. Eileen had two rolls, one that looked like a caterpillar and the other that had raw fish draped over the top of each piece. Neither one touched their meals until Lefty finished telling Eileen all about Calvin Rockport and his house of formerly ill repute.

And when he'd finished, all Eileen said was, "Wow."

"Yeah, wow. I was a little skeptical at first as well. I mean this older man and all these young, beautiful women. But I was able to talk to Angel, and—"

"You talked to Angel?"

"Yes. And she seemed to be okay with where she was. I didn't sense any distress or coercion."

"And we can go see her?"

"Tomorrow."

"When?"

"Afternoon."

"What time?"

"One?"

"Great. Pick me up at twelve-thirty." She picked up her chopsticks and deftly grabbed one of the rolls with the raw fish on top and plopped it in her mouth, chewing slowly, looking at him, a half smile on her tanned face. She'd had a lot of pool time during the past week.

Lefty looked around the table but could not find a fork. He spied a waitress, not theirs, this one a shorter, dark-haired cutie that could not have been older than twelve. Okay, she had to be at least twenty-one, as she was carrying drinks to a table near them, but she sure looked younger. The waitress nodded at him when he hailed her. After serving the drinks she came by.

"How can I help?" she asked in a high, squeaky voice. Not unpleasant, just surprising.

"Can I get a fork, please?"

She nodded and left. In the meantime, Eileen had finished the first roll and was starting in on the other one, beginning at the tail of the caterpillar. The waitress returned with the fork, and Lefty picked at his chicken, occasionally taking a bite, wishing intensely he had a burger. During the rest of dinner, their conversation was small talk, Eileen seeming a little distracted. She never did answer his question about what she'd do after tomorrow.

They left the restaurant. It was still light out, and even cooler. They crossed the street under the I-55 overpass. Lefty again asked, "So what happens after you see Angel tomorrow?"

Eileen kept walking. "What do you mean?" She kept a good pace, despite the prosthetic, only a slight limp.

Even in the dryer, cooler air, Lefty felt sweat forming on the back of his neck, not sure if it was from keeping up with her or the conversation he was trying to have. "We see Angel tomorrow. She'll either want to come with you or not. Then what?"

"If she'll come with me, we'll go home. If not, I don't know. I'll probably still need to go home, but then I can come back when she's ready."

He said nothing, just walked alongside her, watching her swinging hand, wrestling with himself as to whether he should take it. Then he realized she was on his right side and he had nothing to take it with, anyway. Oh well, he thought, probably for the better. Shouldn't complicate business with a relationship. Besides, after tomorrow she'd be gone, possibly for good.

He realized she was talking to him.

"What did you say? Sorry, was distracted."

"I said, Why, did you have something else in mind?"

This was his chance. He certainly did have something else in mind. Problem was, he couldn't figure out how to put it. Then it came to him. He blurted out, "You can stay with me and wait for Angel."

She smiled, blushed, continued walking and said nothing for several steps. In a mock Southern accent, she said, "That's awful sweet of you, Mr. Bruder."

He smiled. She smiled. They continued walking and nothing else was said about that subject. He wasn't really sure what to make of that, so decided to see what tomorrow would bring.

They neared the hotel. The crowd at the ballpark roared and fireworks went off. One of the Cardinals had hit a homerun. Lefty didn't really follow baseball, but knew they were having a good season. He surveyed the street and the adjacent parking lot before they entered the lobby. No black mustang.

Eileen walked through the glass doors and a blast of cold air washed over him. Eileen shivered and hugged herself and kept going. Lefty hesitated, still watching the street. A black Pontiac 600 with tinted windows rolled slowly by on Broadway. He watched it go by. It kept going down Broadway toward the ballpark. A bus pulled in behind the car and he lost sight of it. Had that been the same car he'd seen a couple days ago?

The sliding doors opened again. Lefty felt another blast of cold air and then a tug on his sleeve. "Are you coming in?" Eileen asked.

One last glance down the street, but he could not find the Pontiac. He followed Eileen into the lobby. They reconfirmed their plan for him to pick her up at twelve-thirty the next day.

Before leaving he added, "Don't go anywhere else tonight, or tomorrow before I get here. Just wait in your room. Don't open the door for anyone."

"Why? What's going on?"

"The people Angel worked for are not all that thrilled she's no longer working for them. Just to be safe."

She hesitated but did not argue. She took his hand, shook it once. "Thank you so much for finding her. See you tomorrow." She walked away, toward the elevators.

He waited until the elevator doors closed on her, then he walked out of the hotel and back to his car. No sign of the Pontiac.

Chapter 50

Keyshawn Williams watched the one-armed PI drive away. Then he pulled his Pontiac 600 into the parking lot of the Hilton Ballpark Hotel. He strode to the hotel, sat in an armchair in the lobby, and made a call on his cell phone. "Get over to the Hilton Ballpark Hotel immediately."

"Sure, boss."

"Don't bring the mustang. Use my Lincoln. And bring Rufus." Keyshawn hung up and waited, sitting in the lobby of the hotel, watching the elevators, hoping the woman he'd seen Lefty with would come down to the lobby for something. If not, they'd have to find out what room she was in and do an extraction.

Twenty minutes later, two things happened simultaneously. Charlie and Rufus walked through the lobby doors, and the woman that had been with Lefty Bruder walked out of an elevator and headed toward the front desk.

Keyshawn pushed out of the cream-colored vinyl armchair and walked quickly to a spot between the desk and the elevator. He reached his spot just as the woman reached the desk. She had a slight limp when she walked, her right leg stiffer than usual. A knee brace? Just sore from something? Keyshawn waved to his men, gesturing for them to fan out, one to his right, one to his left, but not too close. He waited.

The woman turned from the desk, clutching something in her hand. Keyshawn could not make out what. He waited as she walked directly toward him. Just as she passed him, he grabbed her arm and whispered in her ear, "I have a gun and will use it if you don't come quietly with me."

She tried to pull away.

Again, he whispered, "The two men standing over there are my men. There's nowhere to go but with me." Keyshawn watched her closely. She opened her mouth. A little louder he said, "And if you scream, other people could get hurt."

He nodded to his men and both pulled guns out from under their shirts and cradled them against their bodies, pointing down, mostly hidden, but not so hidden the woman could not see them.

"Now come with us. And if your boyfriend cooperates, no one will get hurt. I promise."

"Boyfriend?"

"Yeah, that one-armed freak I saw you with earlier. Now come on."

They walked through the lobby. Halfway to the doors, Keyshawn's two men joined them, flanking the woman.

Outside, he stuffed the woman into the back seat of the Lincoln. "Take her to my other club. The one in Sauget. Got it?"

"Sure, boss." Rufus got in back with the woman and Charlie drove away.

A minute later, inside his Pontiac, Keyshawn dialed another number on his cell phone, then headed to his club in Sauget.

Chapter 51

"This isn't going to end well for you, Keyshawn, you do realize that don't you?" Lefty asked.

"How's that, little man?"

"Even if you pull off the exchange, I know where you work and where you live. Sometime, very soon, I will find you and beat you to an unrecognizable pulp." Lefty paused. "Or I just might put you out of your pathetic misery."

Keyshawn chuckled. "Sure, little man. Two hours. In the Walmart parking lot off 1-57. You got it? And bring the girl. One minute late or no girl, then no girlfriend. You got it, you one-armed freak?"

"Hmm. Start counting your days, punk. You don't have many of them left." Lefty hung up, waited a few minutes then dialed another number.

Some grunt answered, "Yeah, what do you want?"

"I want to talk to Big Eddie."

"Too bad. He don't want to talk to you right now. He's busy."

"Tell him to get un-busy or the next call I make is to the cops. I know enough to cause him trouble. Maybe pin a murder or two on him."

Silence for what seemed ten minutes.

"What do you want, Bruder?" Big Eddie asked. "I got things going on."

"I'm sure you do, but your man Keyshawn has branched out. He's not just running girls and skimming from you, now he's into kidnapping. And I want back the woman he kidnapped."

"Why should I care?" A pause. "Did you say skimming?"

"Hmm."

"How do you know?" Big Eddie asked.

"Uh-uh. This conversation is over until I get what I need."

"And that is?"

"Keshawn isn't the smartest guy around, but he's not stupid enough to take a kidnapped woman to his club. So where would he take her?"

"Hold on." Silence again. This time the wait was close to eight minutes. "He's at his club in Sauget."

"I didn't know he had another club."

"Probably why he's there. Anyway, he says he'll be there for another hour or so, then has some business. I told him I was sending someone out to collect today's receipts. Now tell me about the skimming."

"Promise me one thing?"

"Now what? My patience is running thin with you."

"Don't send anyone out until tomorrow."

"Yeah, okay. Now what do you know?"

Lefty told Big Eddie what he'd seen at the one club in East St. Louis several days ago. Big Eddie listened.

When Lefty was done, Big Eddie said, "You promise me one thing, too."

"What?"

"Don't kill Keyshawn tonight."

Before Lefty could respond, Big Eddie hung up. Not even a goodbye or thank you. No big deal, Lefty had work to do, anyway.

Like the club in East St. Louis, Keyshawn's club in Sauget, just off Highway 3, had no windows on the front, just a paneled door with a small square window in the center about head height. A blue neon sign crackled the name Jake's and underneath in smaller green letters, Girls blinked on and off at an irregular intervals. The parking lot was half full.

Lefty backed his Nissan into a spot at the far back corner of the lot and waited a few minutes, watching the door. When no one came out, he quietly opened the car door, grabbed the nunchucks he'd brought along, and slipped out. He hunched down behind the dark SUV he'd parked next to, eased his door shut just enough to put out the interior light, then moved to the front of the SUV.

Walking in the front door didn't strike him as the best option. He walked quickly along a fence line at the edge of the parking lot. There was another parking lot on the other side of the fence and another nightclub. Once he thought he was out of sight of the front door window, he sprinted to the south end of the building. No windows on that side either.

At the back corner he glanced around. Two cars parked out back. A black Lincoln MKZ with tinted windows and a Pontiac 600, also with tinted windows. The one he'd seen at the hotel, and yes, the one he'd seen the night before.

Dumb, dumb, dumb. He should not have left Eileen alone.

Lefty moved along the back wall. Again, no windows in sight. The back door was solid and metal. Trying to pick the lock would be too noisy. Couldn't break it in. Knocking would be suspicious.

But wait, didn't Big Eddie say he was sending someone over? Would that person come around back or walk in the front? That was one option. Knock and hope someone opened the door.

A single naked bulb sprinkled sparse light into the back lot and field behind it. Lots of dead brush from an old hedge that had been cut down and never disposed of. Lefty ventured toward the field. He found crumbled cement pieces, some about the size of softballs. He felt in his pocket. Yup, it was there. An idea formed in his head. Maybe not the best idea, but it gave him a better chance than just knocking or charging in the front door.

He gathered an arm load of the dead brush and piled it right behind the back door. Several more armloads and he had a pile that reached nearly to the top of the door.

He pulled the lighter from his pocket, knelt and flicked it on. After several seconds, some of the smaller pieces of brush ignited.

Lefty stepped back about fifteen feet, bent over and picked up a chunk of cement. He waited until the fire had traveled halfway up the brush pile. He could feel the heat where he stood. Good enough.

He heaved the cement chunk at the wall just left of the door. It made a hollow thud. He picked up another and threw it. Another hollow thud. Then he threw another, and again, a hollow thud. The back door opened. A man swore loudly and slammed the door shut. Lefty sprinted back to the front of the building.

Men and scantily clad women, including some not wearing tops, filed out of the front door. An alarm shrieked. A bright light strobed inside. He waded through the stream of people to the side of the door and watched the patrons exit the building, nunchucks at the ready.

Apparently, the last patron had exited. No one else came out for a minute or so. The door swung shut, muting the shrieking alarm. About half a minute later, the door eased open again. Lefty knelt down along the wall so he wasn't immediately visible through the port hole on the door. Someone stepped out, let the door swing closed, then turned toward Lefty.

He jumped up. Swung the nunchucks and clubbed the beefy black dude on the head.

The man staggered, stumbled back, and collapsed to his knees. Wide, glassy eyes stared at Lefty. The man fell over sideways and slid down the steps. Lefty retreated behind the door.

Seconds later, the door smashed against the wall. Lefty felt the breeze.

Another man exited, arm outstretched, holding a gun. He glanced down and saw his partner. Then arm and gun rotated toward Lefty.

Nunchucks whistled through the air. Crack.

The man screamed and the gun fell from his hand. The nunchucks whistled again, smashing the skinny white dude's head. The man fell down the steps onto his side.

Lefty moved into the doorway. Smoke billowed out of the building. The siren shrieked.

With each strobe, Lefty caught a good look at Keyshawn's wide eyes and snarling mouth. He had one arm around Eileen's neck. He pointed a gun straight ahead with the other.

Lefty jumped to the side.

An explosion. The sound of splintering wood as the bullet hit the door.

Lefty jumped forward, rolled. When he came up, he swung the nunchucks. Wrist bone cracked. Keyshawn wailed. Eileen screamed. The gun hit the floor. Another explosion. Plaster rained down.

Lefty dropped his nunchucks and moved behind Keyshawn. He got his arm in behind Eileen's head and wrapped it around Keyshawn's face, pulling down hard. Both Eileen and Keyshawn fell backwards. Lefty yanked his arm out.

When they hit the floor, Eileen rolled away from the loosened grip.

Lefty drove a foot into Keyshawn's face. A crack as loud as a bullwhip. Blood spurted from Keyshawn's nose.

"Grab the gun!" Lefty yelled.

Eileen stared at him. He drove his other foot into Keyshawn's gut. Air whumfed out of the pimp.

"The gun. Get it in case his goons come back in."

Eileen crawled to the gun and grabbed it.

"Point it at the door." She did.

He picked up his nunchucks and waited for Keyshawn to get up. His breathing came hard. An acrid smell of burning plastic. His eyes watered. He blinked them clear. Keyshawn struggled to his knees. Lefty swung and connected with Keyshawn's skull. The pimp went back down. Lefty raised this nunchucks to strike again.

"No!"

Lefty paused.

Eileen said, "Don't kill him. Let's get out of here."

Some of the adrenaline drained out of his system. Good thing she had more sense than he did. After all, he'd made a deal with Big Eddie.

He sprinted for the front door and pushed it open. The two thugs were still on the ground. Some of the patrons huddled together at the far end of the lot. Sirens screamed in the background, sounding a couple miles away.

A thud. Lefty turned. Eileen had dropped the gun. The two of them sprinted to Lefty's car and got in. He fumbled in his pocket for his key, found it, inserted it, prayed for it to start. It did.

About half a mile away, just before reaching Old State Route 3, they passed a fire department emergency vehicle, then a fire truck.

Lefty drove to Lieutenant Pratt's house. One a.m., but that was the safest place he could think of to deposit Eileen until they could go to Rockport's the next afternoon. And he wanted to pay another visit to McCormitt immediately.

Chapter 52

Lieutenant Pratt and family did not exactly express joy when Lefty and Eileen woke them up. After they'd explained the situation, the Pratt family seemed a little more amenable and of course, took Eileen in. Lefty hadn't stuck around long enough to see what type of accommodations they offered, but knowing that family, he was pretty sure one of the kids gave up their bed for her.

Lefty departed quick enough to avoid the need to explain his next moves. He had said over his shoulder to Pratt to keep his phone handy. Pratt had shouted after him, but Lefty never slowed down.

He turned onto the street with McCormitt's house, doused his lights, and slowed his Nissan. He drove by. No lights were on. No vehicles in the driveway. Lefty shivered despite in the cool, humid morning. Two houses down he stopped the car and watched the house. Nothing. After ten minutes, he eased the door open, stepped out, and eased the door closed. Even so, the click of the door latch sounded like a shotgun blast echoing through the silent neighborhood. Not even the whisk, whisk, whisk of a sprinkler sounded. He ducked behind his car and scanned the area. No lights on, other than outside door or garage lights.

After waiting a few minutes, he sprinted across the street and through the lawns of the two houses before McCormitt's, stopping at the corner of the sex trafficker's house. He put his ear against the wall but heard nothing more than the hum of the air conditioner. Not surprising. Even bad guys slept, though he figured McCormitt would post at least one guard. Even that didn't really bother him.

But no cars in the driveway? That bothered him.

Heck with it. Only one way to find out. He navigated the two low cement steps to the front door and rang the doorbell. In the silence, it sounded like the pealing bells of St. Louis Cathedral.

He jumped off the stoop and plastered himself against the wall and waited. Nothing. Not a sound from inside. He reached up and rang the doorbell again. This time, they didn't sound quite so loud, probably because they were drowned out by his thumping heart. Again he waited. Again, no sound. No one came to the door.

"Crap."

He sprinted back to his car and hoped he wasn't too late.

As Lefty turned off Lindbergh Avenue into the exclusive neighborhood of Huntleigh Woods, he doused his lights. There were enough streetlights that he could see the road okay, but that also meant anyone watching could see him coming. He rounded the curve just before Rockport's and saw the SUVs parked opposite Rockport's house. His eyes burned. He blinked them hard and shook his head to clear the cobwebs. The second SUV parked just behind the first was darker color, probably black, but hard to tell in the early morning dimness. He assumed the same ones he'd seen...yesterday.

Seven doors opened simultaneously. Silently, eight men dressed in black climbed out of the two vehicles. They gathered between the two SUVs. Lefty pulled over, still about fifty yards away. He undid his seatbelt

The eight men spread out along the side of the SUVs closest to the house.

Lefty pulled his cell phone out of his pocket, found Calvin Rockport's number and dialed.

Chapter 53

"Mr. Bruder, what gets you up at this early hour?" Rockport stood on one side of the front bedroom window. Chester stood on the other, a silver plated, ivory-handled cannon in his right hand. His left pulled just enough curtain aside for them to watch the eight men below start to disperse. Two went right, two left toward the private eye's car, and four straight at the house.

"There are eight men coming toward your house. You have about a minute before they get there."

"Thank you, Mr. Bruder. We're well aware and were watching them."

He nodded to Chester, who quickly left the room to gather his small band of men to hold the fort, so to speak.

"I need to let you go, though, as I have a police detective on hold."

"Protect Angel, Rockport."

"We'll do our best, Mr. Bruder."

He clicked off that conversation and resumed his conversation with Detective Lisa Warren.

Chapter 54

Lefty quickly dialed Lieutenant Pratt. Two of McCormitt's men trotted between Rockport's house and the adjoining house farthest from him. One stayed by the corner. The other disappeared. The same happened between Rockport's house and the one closest to Lefty.

After seven rings, Lefty hung up. The other four men split into pairs, each to one side of the walkway leading to Rockport's front door.

Lefty searched through his contact list for Detective James Fischer's phone number. He hoped it was his cell. He dialed.

Two of McCormitt's men positioned themselves in front of Rockport's entry door.

"This is Detective Fischer," a groggy voice said into Lefty's ear.

"Thank God you're a light sleeper, Detective."

"Who is this?"

"Lefty Bruder."

"And why are you calling me at two-thirty in the morning?"

The last door on the lead SUV opened and a ninth man emerged. Jackson McCormitt, probably. He put a phone to his ear briefly then tucked it back in his pocket. At the same time, he started walking slowly toward Rockport's house.

One of the men at Rockport's entry kicked in the door.

"Get to Calvin Rockport's house right away. It's in Huntleigh Woods on the main road. Won't be hard to find, two large SUVs are parked outside, and you'll probably hear gunfire."

"What's going on?"

"No time to explain, just get men out here."

Lefty hung up and exited his car, He ran up the sidewalk, away from Rockport's house, for about twenty yards, then crossed the street as quietly as he could. Once he reached the house next to Rockport's he ran along it straight at the man posted on the nearest corner of Rockport's house.

The twig he stepped on sounded like a rifle crack. He was only ten feet from the man, who pivoted and raised his weapon.

Lefty ducked, pirouetted, and swept the man's legs out from underneath him. Lefty jumped up and came down hard, driving his foot into the man's face. Bone crunched.

The man shuddered. Laid still. Lefty continued toward the back of the house, noticing a wide-open gate.

Chapter 55

Sara counted again. She prayed to God she had the right number. Her brain was too numb to try and do a roster of the girls. "Hurry, to the back door."

The line of groggy, scared girls shuffled through the back hallway. Suddenly everyone stopped. Sara squeezed past three of the girls and finally got the front of the line.

Four successive gunshots exploded somewhere near the front of the house. Two more boomed, sounding like canon fire. She prayed that was Chester's gun, but also prayed no one got seriously hurt. Three more shots.

Sara opened the back door and peered out into the murky, muggy darkness. Nothing moved. She heard soft scuffling off to the right, the barest crunch of gravel. Only fifteen feet or so to the van.

"Shush, girls. Please."

They ceased their tittering.

Sara whispered, "Wait here until you see the van light go on and the side door open. Then run to the van as quietly as you can and get in."

Marsha nodded, then whispered to several girls behind her. The whispering went down the line of pajama-clad girls like a game of slumber party telephone.

Sara sprinted, expecting to hear a gunshot. She did and froze. But the shots came from inside the house. Another couple booms. Chester's gun. At least that meant he was still alive. Then the rat-a-tat of an automatic, and she shivered.

She reached the van and flipped the handle and pulled open the first door. The dome light turned on, nearly blinding her. She felt along the frame of the second door for the handle. Behind her she heard soft footsteps. The girls coming. She flung open the second door then froze.

A man dressed in black stood only a couple feet from her and pointed a large semi-automatic at her. He shook his head and motioned with the gun, indicating she should back away from the van. She hesitated. He stepped forward. Sara glanced at the line of girls. They had stopped and with wide eyes, the whites glowing in the semi-dark, watched the two of them.

Sara swallowed. "Please, mister, they are only young girls."

"Some of them are Mr. McCormitt's girls." Slight accent. Texas, maybe. A ski mask covered his face. That had to be hot and itchy.

She glanced at the girls, then at the van.

"Back away, miss. I don't wanna shoot you."

She let go of the van door and stepped back. A blur of movement behind the man. Crack. The man grunted. He collapsed to his knees. Another blur followed by a thud. The man fell on his face. Behind him another man stood. No ski mask. Familiar face. Did he have only one arm?

"Go!" He shouted, motioning she should get into the van.

She hesitated.

"Go!" He shouted again. "Get the girls out of here."

She nodded and climbed into the van.

"Where is Angel?" George Bruder asked.

Sara pointed at the line of girls, who had started toward the van. She climbed into the driver's seat. At least she hoped Angel was in that line. Had she seen her?

She tried several times, finally succeeding to put the key into the ignition. The van started immediately. The radio blasted and Sara jumped. She punched the nob to turn it off as the first girl climbed into the van.

Five or so had climbed in when the next stopped Angel. The man said something briefly to her, then took off toward the house. The last girl climbed in. At least she thought she'd counted right. "Close the doors!"

Someone pulled the wrong door shut first, then tried the second, but it bounced off the first.

"The other door first," Sara said.

The girl at the door, the blond Rockport had recently brought to the house, froze. Marsha reached around her and pushed open the one door, closed the other, then slammed the second door into place.

Sara backed out. The driveway was L-shaped and the outside lights were not on. She had difficulty seeing the wall. A scrape. A jolt. She found the wall. She shifted to drive, moved forward a bit, cranked the wheel hard, then back to reverse. The van cleared the wall. She pushed a little harder on the accelerator.

Something slammed the side of the van, near the back. A couple of the girls screamed.

One shouted, "He has a gun!"

Sara slammed on the brake and looked over her shoulder. She couldn't see anything or anyone.

"He's coming around!" someone shouted.

A shadow appeared in the back window. She prayed he wasn't one of Calvin's or Chester's men and punched the accelerator. She heard metal on metal and as the van passed, saw the man twirl around and fall to the ground. Not staying there long, he popped up and aimed his gun.

She ducked. "Get down!"

The bullet shattered the windshield. She did not let up on the accelerator. Another shot. More glass broke. The van bounced. She sat up and cranked the wheel to the left.

"Everyone okay? Anyone hit?" All she heard was whimpering. "Anyone hit?"

"I...I don't think so," someone said. She didn't know who.

With the van pointed forward on the street, she slammed the accelerator and headed for the safe house, about thirty minutes away. No more shots. No more shattered glass.

Chapter 56

After telling Angel that her aunt was okay and waiting for her, Lefty walked through the door all the girls had come out. Before he got halfway down the dark hall, he heard a loud scraping. The van must have caught a wall, or something. Gunshots rang out in front of him. Shouting. Rapid fire from an automatic. Two loud booms. Big gun.

Gunshots from behind. He stopped and thought about going out to check on the girls. But when he turned to head back, he heard a footstep behind him. He whirled around A man faced him. Arms at his side. Hard to see who it was in the dimness. About his height, his build. Lefty squared himself to this man.

"Ah, you're the man whose been causing me so much trouble. And here I am just trying to take back what's mine."

"Jackson McCormitt?"

"And your name is?"

"You can call me Lefty." He eased forward. Another couple feet and he'd be within range. More shots from behind. At least three different guns. The faint sound of sirens approaching.

"It's over, McCormitt. You lose."

"You think so? I'll find those girls."

One more step. McCormitt started to turn as the sirens sounded only blocks away. The gunfire had stopped.

"Until meet again, Lefty."

McCormitt swiveled ninety degrees. Lefty jumped straight up and kicked out. His foot caught McCormitt under the jaw. Bone crunched. Even in the dimness Lefty could see how violently the sex trafficker's head snapped sideways. It never really came back up. He fell against the hallway wall, crumpled, finally falling over, head at an odd angle.

Lefty stood over him, waiting for him to move. He didn't. Too dark to tell if McCormitt was still breathing. The rest of the house had turned eerily quiet. He heard the faint rumble of a far-off engine, hoping, praying, it was the girls driving away, safe. He leaned against the wall and breathed a heavy sigh.

A large black man appeared at the end of the hall, giant gun in his hand, pointing at the floor.

"You Lefty?"

"The one and only."

"Who's that?" He pointed his cannon at McCormitt.

"The ringleader."

"He dead?"

"Probably."

The large black man smiled then disappeared from the hall. Footsteps retreated toward the front of the house. Lefty sighed again and waited. Hard to tell how long, but Lefty figured about five minutes. He heard more engines outside, along with a few squeals. He figured the cops had arrived. About thirty seconds later he heard shouting, chaos, thumps, car doors slamming shut. He just waited there.

Maybe ten minutes elapsed. A man appeared at the end of the hall, backlit. Hard to tell who it was, but no doubt it was a detective as he saw the outline of a suit jacket. He stepped out into the middle of the hall.

The detective raised his gun and pointed it at Lefty. "Don't move. Put your hands up."

"Hand," said Lefty. He raised his left hand above his head.

"Mr. Bruder?"

"That's me."

The detective lowered his weapon and walked toward Lefty. He ran his hand along the wall as he walked and found a light switch, which he flipped up. Lefty squinted and shielded his eyes from the bright light.

Sex crimes detective James Fischer looked at the immobile body of Jackson McCormitt then looked up at Lefty. "Your handiwork?"

Lefty nodded and put his hand out.

"What are you doing?" Fisher asked.

"I killed him. Figure you're going to arrest me. He didn't have his gun out. Hard to claim self-defense."

"Really?" Fischer bent over and flipped open McCormitt's suit jacket with the barrel of his gun. A semi-automatic was holstered under his left armpit. "Not how I see it at all." With a plastic-gloved hand, Fischer extracted the semi-automatic and dropped it by McCormitt's right hand.

"Looks like self-defense to me." He straightened. "Besides, how am I supposed to cuff you with only one hand?"

Lefty dropped his arm. "Why are you doing this?"

Fischer smiled and nodded. "You haven't known me that long, Mr. Bruder. I could say something about brotherhood of cops and all that, but that's not why I'm doing this." He paused, looked down at McCormitt, and shook his head. He looked back at Lefty with an intense stare. "This man was an animal. All men like him are out of control animals. They deserve to be put down like rabid dogs. He probably would have never faced any jail time and he'd have gone on ruining young girls' lives." He pivoted and started back down the hall, away from Lefty. Over his shoulder Detective Fischer said, "You did the world a favor, Mr. Bruder." He stopped and looked back. "Now, if you could come down to my office tomorrow sometime, we'll get a statement. Think about what that statement is overnight. You get my meaning, Mr. Bruder?" He continued walking away.

"Yes, I get your meaning." Lefty also turned away and headed back outside, tarantulas crawling around in his gut.

Chapter 57

Lefty turned onto Rockport's street. Cop cars still lined the lush road.

Neighbors stood on their porches watching the scene at Rockport's. Not really much of a choice, as most of the driveways were blocked. Uniformed officers talked with small groups of neighbors.

In the semi-circular driveway at Rockport's house stood a cluster of young women, several large black men, and Rockport himself. The van the girls had escaped in was parked at one end of the driveway. It had been four hours since the raid on Rockport's. No more ambulances. All the dead and wounded must have been carted away.

"There she is!" Eileen pointed at the group of women. "There's Angel. Hurry up."

Lefty just shook his head and crept along, avoiding the cop cars on both sides of the road. A uniformed officer stopped him just before he got to Rockport's driveway. Lefty rolled down his window.

"This is a crime scene, sir," said the officer. "Please back away and go around."

"This woman is the aunt of one of those girls."

"Okay. Please back away and go around."

Lefty saw Detective Fisher come out of Rockport's house. He honked his horn.

"Sir, please back away," the officer said again.

Fischer looked toward them. Lefty honked again. The detective said something. The uniformed officer looked away and shouted, "A one-armed man and some woman."

Fischer gestured and the uniform stepped aside. "Detective Fisher wants to talk with you."

Lefty pulled forward until he was behind the van. Eileen had the door open before he'd completely stopped. And as soon as he did, she jumped out.

"Angel!" She sprinted toward the group of women.

Angel Atkins stepped away from Sara and ran toward her aunt.

As they embraced, Lefty climbed out of his Nissan and sauntered toward them. By the time he reached them. Rockport had also joined them.

"You must be Angel's aunt. My name is Calvin Rockport. Angel has been with us for a little while. She's a wonderful young woman."

Rockport and Eileen shook hands.

"Thank you so much for helping her out." Eileen put her arm over Angel's shoulders. "I was so worried I'd lost her." She asked Angel, "Are you ready to come home? You can live with me."

Chapter 58

When Angel heard Aunt Eileen call her name, she had simultaneously felt elated and torn. She'd been anxiously waiting to be reunited with the one person in this world that really loved her. Well, at least until recently. And that was why she was torn. She knew her aunt was going to try and take her home. And now she faced that question.

Aunt Eileen gazed at her intently, waiting for her answer.

"I'm not so sure, Aunt Eileen. I'm not sure that's the best thing for me right now."

Sara joined the little group. "Is this your aunt, Angel?"

Grateful for the distraction, Angel said, "Aunt Eileen, this is Sara Hanley. She's been taking care of me here. She's been so great."

Her aunt and Sara shook hands.

Sara said, "Angel's made remarkable progress. We're pretty sure she's off the heroin."

Tears formed in her aunt's eyes. One slowly dripped down her cheekbone and to the corner of her mouth. She squeezed Angel. "And now it's time for her to come home, right?"

Sara looked at Angel, at Rockport, then at Eileen. She sucked in a deep breath. "That's really up to her."

And now she'd have to give an answer.

Aunt Eileen separated from her, grabbed both of Angel's shoulders and turned her, staring hard at her. "Well? Can I take you home?"

Angel studied the concrete. Two recent conversations replayed through her mind. First, the talk with Sara, where the former prostitute told her why she had remained with Rockport these past several years. Jesus Christ paid a debt for me. He saved my rotten, filthy soul. I figure the least I can do is try to help other girls like you.

Angel didn't quite get the Jesus stuff, but that feeling of needing to give back convicted her. And then there was the story Rockport had told her of the first girl he had brought in, the prostitute who had challenged him. Ain't you got some kind of responsibility or something? Meaning he just couldn't leave her there and do nothing.

Rockport had stepped up and was doing his part to help with this problem, a problem Angel had found herself stuck in. And these people—Sara, Rockport, even this one-armed dude—had helped her. Could she just pack up and head home, forgetting all they had done for her?

And what about little Emily? Could she just leave her here, all alone and scared? Besides, she didn't want to return to her hometown anyway, not with her stepdad still there. With Sara's help and others', she was working on forgiving that monster, but she wasn't quite there. She also thought it would be foolish to put herself in more potential danger.

Finally, she raised her head and stared into her aunt's moist eyes. Angel hugged her tight. "I'm not ready to go home, yet, Aunt Eileen. I hope you understand."

She felt her aunt nod. They embraced for quite a while, then Angel pushed away and looked at Sara. "Can I stay here a while longer?"

Before Sara could answer, Rockport said, "Of course you can. You can stay as long as you want." He started walking away but stopped and smiled at her. "And I hope that's a long time."

Sara smiled at Angel, seemingly choking back tears, then turned and followed Rockport over to a man in a gray suit.

The man with only one arm said to her aunt, "I'll meet you in the car."

"Don't you have to talk to the police?" her aunt asked.

"Tomorrow." He walked away, leaving only Angel and her aunt.

"I need to talk to the police." Angel's throat closed and her eyes burned. "I…I just—"

Her aunt grabbed her and pulled her close. "Shh. You don't need to say anything. I'm so happy you're safe."

"Thank you so much for coming after me," Angel finally managed to whisper into her aunt's shoulder. After about a minute, they separated.

Her aunt gave out a big sigh. "You have my number. Call me once in a while and let me know how it's going."

Angel nodded then slowly walked past her aunt toward Rockport and Sara. She had to give a statement to the police detective.

"Love you," Aunt Eileen said, as she passed.

"Love you, too," Angel managed to choke out. She quickened her pace, not wanting to completely break down.

Chapter 59

"You really didn't have to send me off," Lefty and Eileen stood outside her Impala, parked in the hotel driveway.

"Nothing else to do, so I don't mind."

Eileen let out a short laugh. "You're such a romantic, George Bruder."

He shrugged.

Eileen said, "I hope we can keep in touch."

"Me, too." Lefty studied her face. Slight crows feet in the corners of her eyes. Tiny bit of mascara. No other makeup. Her hair hung straight to both sides, brushing her shoulders. She had told him with the humidity she gave up trying to curl it. Dressed in faded jeans and a short-sleeved, plain black nylon top

"Do you have Facebook? I'll friend you," she said

"No, no Facebook. Only use the computer for cases."

"Do you even have a computer?"

"Old one."

"Oh. There's an app for your phone."

"Okay. I'll look for it."

Several more minutes of silence. Eileen opened the car door. "There's always old-fashioned phone calls, right?"

"Yup."

"Thank you so much for your help, George. I'll never forget what you did for Angel."

They hugged. He thought about trying to kiss her but decided there wasn't really any point. They'd never see each other again, anyway. She wouldn't call. She'd get back to her ordinary life and forget all about him. He didn't really want to join the Facebook crowd.

She pulled away first. He let his arm drop to his side. She climbed into the car and started it. As she pulled away, he waved, figuring that was it. The last time he'd see her.

Epilogue

The first week after Eileen departed dragged for Lefty. Nothing to do. No new case. Trying not to drink as much and actually succeeding, which led to boredom and more television watching than he'd done in the past several years.

A break in the monotony came Monday, fourteen days after she'd left, but who's counting. His phone rang. It turned out to be a surveillance case for a divorce settlement. Boring stuff, but at least some cash coming in. And of course, hot, sweaty work.

Lefty watched the man, around his age, and a woman who was maybe half his age meet outside an apartment building downtown just off Washington Avenue. It was half hotel and half apartments separated by a glass barrier inside with a secure door.

His air conditioning still didn't work. Maybe after this job, he'd get it fixed. Or maybe not. July was nearly over. Only one more month of blistering heat and humidity. However, today, he couldn't really complain about the weather. Only in the low eighties and humidity manageable. But sunny, so the inside of his car was still hot.

Lefty took several photos of the man and excessively young woman entering the apartment half of the building. His cell phone rang. He considered ignoring it, but maybe it was another job. This one would end soon. And not well for the man.

He stared at it. E. Seager it read. Really? Eileen calling him? After the third ring he shook himself out of his stupor and answered. "Hello?"

"Hey there, one-armed man. How are you?

"Hot and sweaty, but other than that, not bad for a cripple. How about you? Still limping around the corn fields?"

"Yup. That's all we have here. Can't really avoid them. And don't feel bad, it's hot and humid here as well."

A long pause. Lefty asked, "What's up?"

"Um...what do you think about hot and dry instead of hot and humid?"

"Why?"

Another long pause. Lefty could hear Eileen breathing. "There's this girl from down the street. A friend of Angel's actually—"

"How's Angel doing?"

"Oh, she's doing real well. Still clean. Still at Rockport's. I understand she starts training for a cashier job at one of the local grocery stores, Schnuck's, I think."

"Uh-huh. Any problems with the stepdad?"

"Nope. I haven't been anywhere near him, so he doesn't know where Angel is. Just in case, though, I got a restraining order, you know, using my connections."

Lefty laughed. "Good idea. So who's this other girl?"

"She's a school friend of Angel's. They've sort of reconnected via social media. Anyway, Tuesday, she left town. Went to Phoenix, according to Angel. Then Friday, she called Angel. Sounded real distressed. Said she'd hooked up with some guy, but he'd turned out to be a sleazebag and hooked her on heroin. Angel said while Talia was talking to her, she heard a loud slap, then some noises like the phone had been dropped. And just before the call ended, Talia cried out to Angel to come help her get away from this guy."

Lefty said nothing for several seconds. "And you're telling me about this why?"

"Well, I was wondering if you want to meet me in Phoenix and look for Talia. I told Angel I'd go look and see what I could do."

Lefty wiped his brow. Sweat dripped into his lap, leaving spots on his khaki shorts. He looked at the apartment complex, sighed. "Sure, why not, hot and dry can't be as bad as this."

The End

Letter from the author

Dear Reader,

Thank you for journeying with Lefty as he battled the underbelly of St. Louis sex trafficking pursuing Angel. I hope you enjoyed the story. Whether you did or not, please leave a review on Amazon and/or BookReads. Here is the link where you can leave a review on Amazon of An Angel and a One-Armed Man: Write Review

I look forward to your comments and suggestions.

And I hope you're ready for more from Lefty and Eileen. They will be back soon in a story that moves to Phoenix, AZ. Coming in late 2022 or early 2023 look for A Coyote and a One-Armed Man. This book will dive into cross-border trafficking, a major issue in this country.

I'll also be publishing other crime fiction novels centered around justice, vengeance and redemption. In 2022 I should be releasing Killer Redemption. Can one of the most notorious assassins leave his profession, settle down with the girl of his dreams, and find redemption?

If you have comments or questions, you can submit them from my website at https://bdlawrence.com/contact/.

Or email me at bdlawrence@bdlawrence.com. I promise I'll read every email and respond where appropriate.

Again, thank you for reading this book. You are why I write these stories.

B.D. Lawrence.

Acknowledgments

A special thank you to Sgt. Kavanaugh of the St. Louis County Police Special Investigations Unit for his insight into human trafficking in the St. Louis metro area.

Thank you to Michael Kahn, Wayde Howell, Evan Smith, Christie Wesch and Barry Fluth for their reviews of this novel.

Thank you to Gary Val T. for his wonderful cover artwork on this book and other stories.

About Author

B.D. Lawrence has always loved reading fiction. Ironically, though, his worst subject in high school was English. One night, sitting in a master's level computer programming class, daydreaming about vigilantes, he decided to give writing a try. Out of that came his first novel, which went nowhere. That was many years ago. During his writing journey he's dabbled in several genres, including mysteries, suspense, science fiction, fantasy, and literary fiction. He currently is focusing on stories of justice, vengeance, and redemption.

Find out more about B.D. Lawrence by visiting his website at www.bdlawrence.com. If you sign up for his newsletter, you'll receive monthly updates on upcoming books, short stories, book reviews and other news.

The Lefty Bruder series focuses on a major worldwide problem that gets little press attention, human trafficking. In books to come, Lefty Bruder will continue his fight against this scourge. B.D. Lawrence hopes you come along on that journey with Lefty. Be on the look out for A Coyote and a One-Armed Man.

Also By B.D. Lawrence

A Vigilante and a Two-Armed Man: The Lefty Bruder Origin Story (novella)

The Finger Snatcher and a One-Armed Man (short story – Lefty Bruder's first P.I. case).

Questions and Answers (short story)

Life Debt (short story)

Footsteps in the Snow (short story)

Attics (short story)

Just a Brief Encounter (short story)